A FAMILY TO CHERISH

BOOK THREE OF THE CALDWELL SERIES

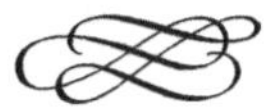

LAUREL WENSON

Cover design by Noel Sellon

Map created by Sarah Neville

*This book is dedicated to Bob, Beth, & Rebecca —
my very own family to cherish forever.*

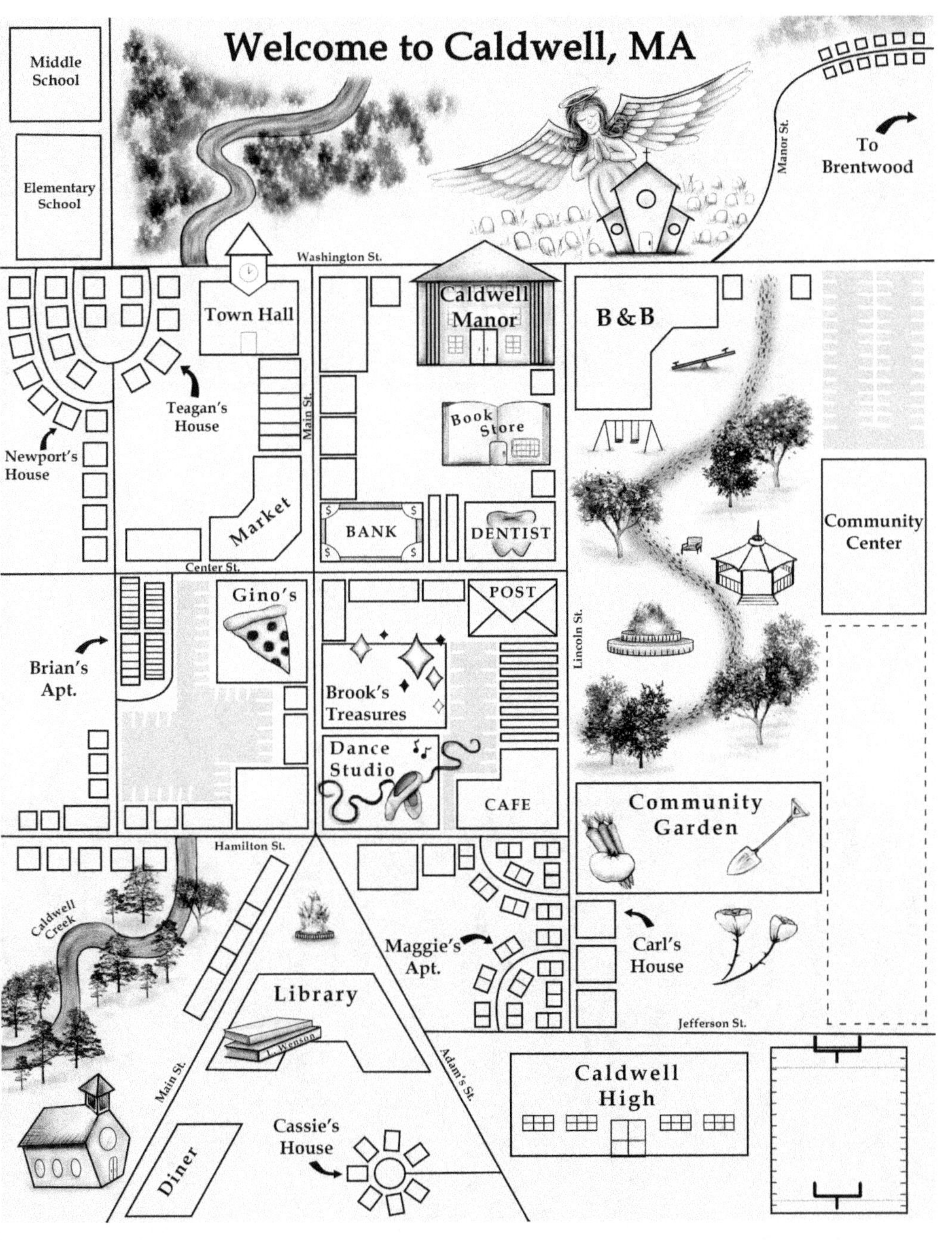

Welcome to Caldwell, MA
Middle School
Elementary School
Washington St.
Town Hall
Caldwell Manor
B & B
To Brentwood
Manor St.
Teagan's House
Newport's House
Main St.
Book Store
Market
BANK
DENTIST
Center St.
Community Center
Gino's
POST
Lincoln St.
Brian's Apt.
Brook's Treasures
Community Garden
Dance Studio
CAFE
Carl's House
Hamilton St.
Caldwell Creek
Maggie's Apt.
Jefferson St.
Library
L. Wenson
Main St.
Adam's St.
Caldwell High
Diner
Cassie's House

CHAPTER 1

Seventeen year old Cassie Durand arrived at Colleen Peterson's dance studio a few minutes before class started. Before the anorexia had taken hold, she had spent numerous hours in various dance classes, and it still hurt that she wasn't ready to start dancing again. The weekly yoga class was a welcomed substitute, allowing some movement that kept her centered. Colleen greeted her as she walked in.

"Morning, Cassie! Go on in – we're waiting for a couple more."

Cassie hung up her bag and kicked off her flip-flops, placing them in a shoe cubby along the wall. Laughter and hugs greeted her when she walked into the studio.

"Cassie!" squealed Kyleigh Sorrento, rushing over to give her a hug with Julia Jackson right behind her. "God, we miss you!"

"Thanks, guys. I'm glad I at least have yoga. Hey, Julia."

Julia smiled warmly. "Welcome back. Happy to be home?"

"Yeah – so far things are going okay."

Kyleigh spun out and stretched into a lunge. "Can you believe we start school in a few weeks? I'm *so* excited about senior year!" She turned sharply toward Cassie. "Wait. Are you gonna be able to come back to dance this year? It's senior showcase, girl."

Cassie cringed inside. Senior showcase was something she'd anticipated for years, and it was only a possibility at this point. "Not sure. I may have to choose between dance and the show – and I'm thinking the show might be a healthier choice for me."

"I can't wait to find out what we're doing! I hope Mr. C. tells us the first day we're back."

Julia rolled her eyes at her dramatic friend. She was the quieter of the two. "So Cassie, what classes are you taking this year?"

"Composition, Psychology, Consumer Math, and Art – and Theater, of course."

"We'll have psych together. That'll be nice."

Colleen headed in with Maggie Richmond and Brooke Martin in tow. Cassie smiled and waved as Maggie and Brooke came over for quick hugs.

"Morning, beautiful," Maggie said with a wink.

"Looking forward to seeing you at work later," Brooke whispered as she spread out her yoga mat.

Cassie joined the others as class began, and for the next hour she focused on the slow movements and stretches that allowed her body to move without trying to hijack her brain to excessively exercise. She was grateful for all the movement therapy she had gotten at the Phoenix Center; she had learned how important it was to find exercise that integrated the brain and the body without any competition. Yoga had been a perfect solution.

As the class ended, Colleen approached her. "I have to say, you're still as graceful as ever. I know it's difficult not being able to jump back in to dance, but be patient. Like any injury, you can't come back too early or you might do more damage."

"Thanks. I do miss it – a lot. But I don't want to go back to where I was."

"Damn straight you don't." Maggie Richmond joined the conversation. "But you're working hard on recovery and it shows. You ready to head up to see your grandmother?"

Cassie nodded, waving and saying goodbye to Julia and Kyleigh as they left. "You don't have to walk me up. I'm not gonna jog, I promise."

"We both know that, but I made an agreement with your mom and I'm not messing with that. Nor should you. Besides, it gives us a chance to catch up."

Outside, Maggie pointed in both directions. "Which way? Past Brooke's and the post office, or past the café and the park?"

"The latter. I'd like to stop in and pick up a cinnamon roll for Gram – she loves them."

They turned left and rounded the corner. "Gonna order one for yourself as well?" Maggie asked.

"I still find the icing super sweet," Cassie replied, "but I might buy a fresh chocolate croissant."

"Thatta girl. I might do the same, and bring an almond one home for Lucy."

"You're a thoughtful sister. So you're not heading over to Tim's from here?"

"Nope. Going for dinner tomorrow. He's headed up to Gloucester for the day. He wanted to show his mom and granddad his townhouse and the harbor."

"So what's the deal with that? Will you guys have a long distance relationship?"

Maggie shook her head as they stepped into the café. She took a long slow whiff of eggs, coffee, onions, and baked goods. "This isn't quite the diner, but their breakfast sandwiches are so damn tasty. I love having this place just a block from home." After giving their order, she answered Cassie's question. "Tim's moving in to Mr. Pritchard's – I mean Carl's – house."

"I guess you can't call him Mr. Pritchard now that you're dating his grandson. Or what's the other name? The old—"

"Curmudgeon. And I'm not sure that name even fits him anymore. He's so much happier now that his daughter has come back home – and he loves learning everything he can about his grandson."

"So will Tim sell the townhouse?"

"He's not sure yet. Right now he's moving a bunch of stuff down and he's doing weekly rentals through the middle of September – with a place a block from the beach it was easy to book. Gives him some time to figure out what he wants to do with it. I'm kind of hoping he manages to keep it awhile. The view is so beautiful up there."

As their orders were completed Cassie grabbed Maggie's hand as she went to pay. "This one is on *me*. It's the least I can do for all the support you've given these past months. I'm so grateful that you agreed to be my recovery coach – and besides, I'm making a little money now at Brooke's, and it's satisfying to be able to spend a bit on others."

Maggie tucked her money back into her pocket. "Well, thank you. I'll pay next time. And trust me, being your coach helps my own recovery when I watch you getting stronger each day."

They stepped back outside and walked past the park toward Caldwell Manor.

"So have you heard from any of your Phoenix friends?" Maggie asked. "Haven't you kept in touch with a few of them?"

"Yeah. Juanita had left before me and sent me a card when I got home. She's getting ready for college this year."

"What about the girl you roomed with?"

"That's Molly, who texts every few weeks; she went home a month ago and seems to be doing okay. The only one I connected with that's still there is Ellie - she's supposed to leave soon, but Molly said she's struggling."

"Recovery's never easy in the beginning," Maggie replied. "You could send Ellie a note offering some support – I think she'd appreciate that."

A couple of residents greeted Maggie as they passed by with baskets of produce they'd just picked from the community garden. Cassie smiled politely as she noted their zucchini and tomatoes as they continued on. "Do you know every person who has a garden plot?"

Maggie nodded. "Just about. Caldwell's a small town and everyone with a plot is there almost daily this time of year. Those two are often showing up as I'm leaving in the morning."

"Did you go early this morning before yoga?"

"Nope. I'll head over this afternoon with Tramp after we go for a walk. You should come with me sometime – you might enjoy it."

"Maybe next year. I think my plate is pretty full right now – no pun intended."

Maggie chuckled. "How are things going at home?"

Cassie sighed. "I wish things weren't so tense with my dad. This morning I had that automatic reaction in my head to stop eating and push my plate away. I don't like it when it happens – it's scary this early in recovery."

"So what triggered it?"

"He brought up college and the SATs again. Wants me to work on applications."

"That's a big step – I imagine it *is* somewhat scary."

"It's not that I don't want to go to college – I'm just not sure I'm ready yet."

"Did you tell him that?"

"Not yet. We had a ton of family therapy while I was at the Phoenix, but since I've been home, he's more like his old self."

"I'm sure familiar patterns of communication are hard to break."

"Exactly. And I tend to clam up more when he gets all domineering. And then my poor mom – she's stuck in the middle, trying to play referee and keep the lines open like they had been for awhile."

"Sounds like you need some therapy time with Natalie," Maggie said, referring to the counselor at the Phoenix Center who they both still went to see weekly. "In the meantime, you can go in for some grandma therapy, which is almost as good."

They had gotten to the parking lot of Caldwell Manor, and Maggie stopped. "You're not coming in?" Cassie asked.

Maggie laughed, holding up her bag from the café. "If I head inside I'll stop by my office - which means Lucy & I won't eat these for hours. Give her a big hug from me, okay?"

"I will, and thanks for the company." She started to head toward the building, but whirled around. "Wait, I forgot to ask you. Are we all set for having Teagan's surprise party this week?"

"Down to every detail. Ida will fill you in on the details, but

Wednesday at 3:00 is all set. I hope the residents don't give it away; I swear Kitty is ready to explode from excitement. I'll see you around – have a pleasant visit."

As Maggie left, Cassie gave thanks for the woman who convinced her to go to the Phoenix Center. *"I hope my own recovery is that strong someday,"* she thought as she turned toward the back door.

She found Melvin, one of the residents, sitting inside the door at his adopted post. He loved to greet visitors and staff alike as he had no family nearby. He smiled at Cassie and pointed down the hall. "She's in her room, and she's waiting for you."

"Thanks, Melvin. You have a great day, okay?"

He nodded as she passed, turning his attention back to his watch.

She found Ida sitting with a book, but at the sight of her grand-daughter she closed it quickly. "Cassandra – it makes my day every time you come to visit."

Cassie gave her a warm hug. "Me, too, Gram. And I brought you a cinnamon roll." She held the bag up in front of the older woman who took a long whiff.

"I think there's chocolate in there besides my cinnamon – I hope that means you brought yourself something to eat?"

"I did. I love the café's chocolate croissants – hey, I love almost anything on a croissant these days. They've become my favorite food. Should we eat in here, or go find a spot?"

"Let's head to the library. Then we can have a little peace and quiet."

Cassie offered to wheel her grandmother down, but the older woman shook her head. "I'm quite capable of wheeling myself – and it keeps my strength up." Once they were settled, Cassie opened the bag of baked goods and handed Ida a napkin.

"I brought extra. They do smell heavenly, don't they?"

Ida nodded, waiting for Cassie to take the first bite of her crois-sant. "I've told you before, but I'm so happy to sit and eat with you again. You had us all so worried this past year."

Cassie chewed slowly as Ida bit into her cinnamon roll. "I'm comfortable eating with you, Gram. I never feel anything but peace and acceptance from you."

Ida looked at her pensively. "I detect that's not true everywhere?"

Cassie sighed, loving that her grandmother picked up on the subtlest clues. "You know me so well. I'm under a little pressure at home right now; no big deal."

"Your father?"

"Isn't it obvious?"

Ida thought for a moment before answering. "He loves you more than life itself - but he is a bit stubborn and set in his ways. I think adapting to all the therapy and open communication these past months has been tough on him."

"Oh, he's trying, Gram. I only wish he'd lighten up a bit about the whole college thing right now."

"Ahhh, college." Ida put her cinnamon roll back down and wiped her fingers. "I take it he's still pushing you a bit to work on those applications?"

Cassie nodded, but noted that the subject didn't bring about the violent reaction toward her food that her father caused. "Maggie said I should talk to Natalie about setting up a counseling session with him to talk about it, but my appointment's not until this coming week, and he wants to sit down and work on it tonight. I'm not sure how to tell him that I may not be ready."

"Your mom said as much yesterday when she was here. I don't have any answers for you, except to trust what others are saying more than your own brain right now. I think your dad is one the biggest challenges you've got since coming home. Am I right?"

"Yeah. And he doesn't have a clue. I'll try to at least bring up my concerns tonight, and then hopefully we can all talk to Natalie this coming week. It doesn't help that he's so busy with his job."

Ida reached out and patted her hand before picking her cinnamon roll back up for another bite. "You'll be fine. He's tough, but he adores you. Now, changing the subject, are we all set for Teagan's party? Everything is set to go at this end."

Cassie took another small bite of her croissant, letting the chocolate and butter flavors swirl in her mouth before answering. "That's what Maggie told me. Said you'd have all the details. I think they should put you on the payroll here."

Ida laughed. "This is one party I was thrilled to help plan. Teagan is, after all, the one that brought you back from the brink of anorexia. And just look at the friendship that's blossomed since then."

"I hated her for awhile – but you're right. If she hadn't seen the signs and pushed a bit, I may not have gotten the help I needed. I'm so blessed to have her as a friend. So what are the details at this end?"

"Well, Maggie and I told the residents that we'll surprise her on Wednesday. She'll just think we're having a singalong, but we'll surprise her by starting off with 'Happy Birthday' instead. I'll let you wheel me down and say goodbye, and then you can wait in the hall with the others. Once we all start singing that's the cue for you and the others to bring in the cake and balloons."

"Sounds good. Brian's bringing the cake and he'll go and hide in Maggie's office until we're ready. He's so excited."

"And you have the tickets?"

Cassie nodded. "Mom went over to pick them up this week. I can't believe Fiddler on the Roof is coming to Brentwood Playhouse this fall – talk about the perfect gift for her."

"I still remember taking you the last time it played back in the 7th grade when you were up visiting from Houston. Hard to believe that Teagan and Brian were there the same night."

"And Joanne – it was her birthday present from them. I wish I could have known her. Teagan's always telling me how much we're alike – even beyond the eating disorder."

"Teagan's lucky to have you now. You've both fought some hard battles the past few years, Teagan with losing Joanne, and you almost following the same path."

"I try to remember that every day. I don't want to be another Joanne. Too many lose that battle every year, and I'm determined not to be one of them."

Cassie picked up her croissant and took another bite almost defiantly. "Besides, these are so yummy." She looked up as her mom, Eliana, walked into the library.

"There you are. I hope you've had a lovely visit. Hello, mother," she said, reaching down to kiss Ida on the cheek. "I see your buddy brought you a favorite treat."

Ida licked her fingers. "Only thing better than cinnamon rolls are Greek pastries – and the café doesn't make those. Luckily that young man Brian still brings me a treat on occasion – or makes them when he comes to bake with Teagan."

"He's bringing her cake, right? I picked up the tickets like you asked. I hope that someone is reimbursing me for the extras."

Ida nodded. "I have a check from Maggie in my room for the balance. I'm looking forward to having her and that old curmudgeon's family along. I so enjoyed getting to know Carl when he was here for his cardiac rehab. He's come up to visit a couple of times since going home."

"Well, let's wheel you back to your room and you can give it to me. I need to bring this one home to eat lunch before she heads to work later. I'll stop by sometime this week to catch up."

Ida wrapped the last bit of cinnamon roll in her napkin. "I'll take this back to nibble on later," she said to Cassie. "And I'll be thinking of you later on, my dear. Remember that you have the strength inside to face any obstacle that comes your way."

"Thanks, Gram," Cassie whispered as she leaned over to give her a hug. "You're one of the best reasons I have to keep getting better. Love you – and I'll be back on Wednesday."

On the way home, she tried to focus on the strength she'd need to deal with her father and the issue of college.

CHAPTER 2

Maggie was just getting out of bed when her phone rang. Tramp was still stretched out on her quilt and thumped a morning greeting with his tail.

"Good morning," she said as she settled back down into her pillows to chat. "How was your trip?" Tramp took this as a sign to snuggle up next to Maggie for a head scratch as she chatted.

"It went well – but being up there made me miss you like crazy. We should have had a family breakfast instead of family dinner today."

She could picture that dimple in his cheek as he spoke. "I bet your granddad liked your handiwork up there."

"He liked it, but still found a few things to complain about. Said the sliding door let too much sun in."

Maggie laughed. "That sounds like my old curmudgeon. How did your mom like it?"

"She loved it. She was so glad that I hadn't put it on the market. I suspect we'll be holding on to it, as she might be asking for some time up there, too."

"That makes sense. Having lived up in Portland I'm sure she'd miss the shore – and let's face it, even though she's thrilled to be home and making up for lost time with her dad, he can't *always* be easy to live with."

"So far, it hasn't been too difficult. By the way, I don't think I've told you that I love you yet today."

"Love you, too. And I don't think I'll ever get tired of hearing it."

"So when are you coming over? I have half a mind to walk the quarter mile just to kiss you."

"Considering I was just getting up when you called that might not be a good idea."

"Or maybe it makes the idea even *more* enticing," Tim teased.

Maggie sighed as the butterflies in her stomach started fluttering; she hadn't been intimate with Tim yet, and the idea still made her nervous. "How about I drag myself out of bed and start my day so I can be there sooner? I thought I might make the mac & cheese here and bring it over while still warm."

"Oh, hell, no," Tim replied. "I think you need to put all the ingredients in a bag and come over here to prepare it. We can share the kitchen together – that might be an important test for our relationship."

Maggie giggled. "I can't believe that your grandfather has let you take over his kitchen. I guess he's not as protective of his pots and pans as he is his rose bushes."

"I don't think he did much more than heat up canned soup and make sandwiches here. He's been thrilled to have the kitchen bustling again."

"Honey, he'd be happy if you only made canned soup. He's a different man since you came to town and your mom came home."

There was a pause at the other end and Maggie knew that Tim was enjoying the moment. "He truly is. He and my mom have spent so much time just sitting and talking. I think they both realize how much time was wasted over the years, and they're trying to erase all the hurts."

"Well, I'm honored to be invited over to be a part of that."

"Get used to it, Maggie. I want you to be a part of it for a long time to come."

"So what time do you want me to arrive?"

"Is 'a few hours ago' an appropriate answer?" Tim said kiddingly.

"I mean what time does dinner prep begin?" Maggie replied, her cheeks blushing at his suggestion.

"Why don't you shoot for noon – that way we can enjoy cooking together and have dinner ready around 2:00?"

"Sounds perfect. I'll be there soon, Mr. Collins."

"Not soon enough – but I'll settle for noon. Love you, Maggie."

"Love you, too." She hung up her phone and Tramp licked her hand. "Yeah, he wanted to kiss me, too, boy," she whispered. "How about we go and find some coffee and then I'll take you out?"

The beagle stretched and jumped off of her bed, leading the way to the kitchen. Maggie was still smiling when she got to the coffee pot. Her sister Lucy was making some avocado toast as she walked in.

"Someone's got a smile on her face this morning. Want some toast?"

Maggie nodded as she pulled up a stool. "I'd love some. And yeah, I got a certain phone call this morning from a handsome man around the corner."

Lucy grinned as she took a bite of her toast. "Love looks good on you, sis. You're heading over there today, aren't you?"

"Around noon. He even told me to bring my stuff and make the food there so we can practice sharing the kitchen."

"He just wants you over there sooner."

"Pretty much," Maggie said with a smile. "I'm so glad that Carl is happy again. He's been all alone in that house for years, and now both Sharon and Tim have moved in with him. He won't be the old curmudgeon anymore."

Lucy licked some avocado off of her finger. "I don't know. He might become his grouchy self once they all settle in. I wonder if he'll be hard to live with – or if he'll feel like they've invaded his space after awhile."

"I wonder about that as well. It will certainly be an adjustment for all of them. They've all lived alone. But they're also so happy to have reconnected. I think they'll make it work."

"I suspect Tim might be here more often. I can't imagine taking your romance to the next level with Tim's mom and grandfather in the house."

Maggie took in a deep breath and exhaled, reaching for her coffee. "Trust me, I've been wondering about that a lot. I just hope I'm ready for it when it happens."

Lucy finished her coffee and smiled. "Believe me, sis, you'll know when the time is right – and it will be wonderful. Tim's such a wonderful guy."

"He is, isn't he? Sometimes I can't believe that I'm the lucky one that got him."

"I think it's karma for being such a loyal friend to his grumpy grandfather all these years."

Maggie laughed. "Possibly. I do love his grandfather, though. And I guess I better take Tramp out for a quick walk and then grab a shower before thinking about what ingredients I need to pack. You home all day?"

Lucy nodded as she put her dish in the sink. "Liz is heading over for the afternoon with Watson. As long as the little sister is gonna be out we might as well make use of the privacy," she said with a wink. "We'll have to start making a schedule."

Maggie threw her napkin at her as she headed in to change her clothes. "You're so vulgar sometimes." At the door she paused and turned back. "And I love you tons."

* * *

SHE ARRIVED at Carl's house around noon to find the old man sitting out on his front porch. "Good afternoon, Mr. Pritchard – I mean, Carl."

"Glad you didn't bring that pesky dog with you," he replied. "Don't suppose you have any tomatoes in that bag."

Maggie smiled as she reached in and pulled out a giant beefsteak. "As a matter of fact, I picked some yesterday. Was gonna leave them on your doorstep but I knew you were out for the day. There are about half a dozen here for you."

Carl's face lit up. "You're okay, tomato girl. I'll have to hide them so I don't have to share 'em."

Maggie laughed. "There are still plenty over on the vine, so don't worry. I'll be begging you to take them by the time the cold weather gets here."

The front door opened and Tim's smile greeted her from behind the screen. "I thought I heard my favorite voice out here." He opened the door and reached for her bag. "Let me take that for you." He leaned over the bag and kissed her on the cheek, making her face blush.

"So what else is in the bag?" the old man asked. "I thought this guy was cooking today."

"I'm making some macaroni and cheese to go with the meatloaf. Tim insisted."

"Homemade, with the real cheese and breadcrumbs?"

"Is there any other kind?" Maggie teased.

The old man leaned back in his rocker and smiled. "Ruthie used to make that as soon as the weather started getting cooler. Haven't had any homemade since she's been gone – the stuff in the box is lousy. It better be extra cheesy, tomato girl."

Tim laughed. "How about we head to the kitchen to start putting it all together, okay?" He opened the door with his free hand and held it for Maggie to head in before him. As she stepped inside, she stopped to look around. Since Sharon had moved home, the place had a woman's touch showing up again in the small details. Fresh roses sat in a vase on a corner table in the living room, as well as the center of the dining room table.

"Smells heavenly in here," Maggie said. "Is your mom home?"

Tim shook his head. "Gone out for a walk." He took her hand and led her to the kitchen, placing the bag on the table before pulling Maggie toward him.

"Now I can greet you properly," he whispered as his lips found hers. She loved his kisses, which started soft and gentle and then deepened with more urgency as she responded. As the kiss ended he leaned against the kitchen counter still holding her close. "God, I can't stop thinking about you these days," he whispered into her hair.

Maggie pulled back to look up into his eyes. "Me, too. You're the first thing I think about in the morning and the last thing at night….and a whole lot of in between." She rested her head against his chest and listened to his steady heartbeat, savoring his arms around her.

She finally stood up straight and pulled away slightly. "I suppose at some point we should actually do some cooking, huh?"

"If I didn't like cooking almost as much as I like you I'd take offense at that thought." He flashed her that dimpled smile as he grabbed a couple of aprons from a hook by the back door and threw one at her. "Here, put that on. If you're gonna cook in my kitchen you better bring your top game."

She laughed as she tied it behind her. "I told you my mac & cheese was the bomb. Guess I'll prove it to you today."

They worked side by side, doing kitchen choreography that allowed both space when sharp objects were being used and close contact when passing items from a cupboard or the refrigerator. Stolen kisses found their way into the routine along the way, and Maggie had never been so happy sharing such simple tasks. Sharon had gotten home and said hello, but retreated to the front porch with a book as Carl dozed in his rocking chair.

Once things were in the oven, Tim led her out the back door. "Come on, I want to show you the office."

He led her around to the side door of the garage and opened it for her. The inside door that led into the office was open, and Maggie almost gasped when he turned on the light. While half of the room was jam packed with old and new items, the other half was set up with a desk and computer and a large drafting table. With everything cleaned out, the back wall revealed a beautiful window with a view of Carl's rose bushes out back. Tim's desk was up against that wall.

"Someone's been busy. I don't even remember there being a

window there when we came to pick up your grandfather's clothes during his stay at the Manor."

Tim smiled. "That's because the drafting table was on its side blocking the light. The piles still need sorting, but I have a functional work space for the time being."

Maggie walked to the cluttered side and surveyed the bins. "I take it some of this is your stuff and some your granddad's past stuff?"

He nodded. "I had driven up this week to grab a few things from my office in Danvers. They're keeping me on for a few jobs but okayed me working here most of the time. I told them I'd consider staying on, but wanted some time with a lighter load until the community center is complete."

"How's that coming along?"

"Right on schedule. The community response and support has been phenomenal. I have a committee almost complete, and clean out and renovations will start in another couple of weeks. I'll have to take you over sometime this week to show you the progress." He pulled her away from the dusty blueprints and kissed her again. "I'd love to carry you up to the loft and spend some quality time with you, but I don't think we'd impress my mom or granddad if we burned our first dinner together."

Maggie laughed. "I love a man with sense. And for the record, I'm planning on sticking around, so the meatloaf is safe. Shall we go and be sociable?"

He smiled. "Okay. But later on I'm gonna walk you home and stand on your front porch for a long good night kiss."

The butterflies in Maggie's stomach started up again. "You've got yourself a deal, mister."

* * *

A COUPLE OF HOURS LATER, Maggie sat around the dining room table as Sharon poured coffee for all of them. She had just brought in a delicious apple pie and placed it in front of Carl before fetching the coffee. Hints of cinnamon and nutmeg tickled Maggie's nose and she found herself hungry again even after a wonderful meal.

Carl sat beaming at his daughter and grandson, and Maggie's heart overflowed at the transformation in this man who had become a friend over the years.

"She bakes like her mother," Carl said as Sharon placed a heaping piece of pie in front of him.

Sharon blushed a bit. "I'm not sure I agree with that, Dad. For years I didn't even *want* to cook. Just ask Tim – I think he kept his mother properly fed for an long time." She patted Tim's shoulder as she handed him a piece of pie, and then smiled at Maggie as she placed a piece in front of her.

Maggie took a long whiff. "Cinnamon and apple is such a perfect combination."

"Thanks, Maggie. And I have to say, your macaroni and cheese was superb."

Tim cleared his throat dramatically. "A-hem…and my meatloaf? Was that worth even mentioning?"

Carl laughed. "Best meatloaf ever. Not too dry, and whatever that sauce was on top made it zesty. Have to admit I had my doubts when you put it on my plate."

Tim smiled. "That was a sweet and sour glaze, Granddad. And I'm glad you like it."

Carl shoveled a forkful of pie into his mouth. "I haven't eaten this well since your grandmother died. I'll put on twenty pounds with all this home cooked stuff."

Maggie shook her fork at him. "Not on my watch, you old curmudgeon. I have no desire to nurse you through another heart attack. In fact, after you finish that pie I think you need to take a little walk."

Carl scowled as he hid his smile behind his next bite. He looked over at Tim. "She's gonna be tough on all of us. You better hold on to this one."

Tim glanced over at her and winked. "Believe me Granddad – that's the plan."

Sharon smiled. "If anyone had told me a year ago that I'd be sitting here listening to you two banter back and forth I would have said they were crazy. Life is amazing sometimes."

Carl put his fork down and picked up his coffee cup, holding it up for a toast. "To family," he said with a smile. "Past, present....and future," as he smiled at Maggie.

"To family," they all repeated, and Maggie couldn't imagine another family she'd rather be a part of.

Sharon finished her pie and folded her napkin. "So Tim, how goes the project next door?"

He swallowed his last bite of pie before responding. "Going well. I have a committee almost lined up for planning and help with community support. In fact," he said as he turned toward Maggie, "I was hoping that you'd consider being a part of it."

"Me?" Maggie said with surprise. "I thought you were looking for business owners."

"I have a couple of those, but they also recommended some useful community liaisons. Brooke Martin suggested you when I stopped by her store the other day. You have the elder connection, and with Caldwell Manor right across the park it might be a strong connection for our seniors. I don't want to put any pressure on your schedule, and I'll understand if you're too busy, but at least think about it?"

"I can do that. So who else do you have?"

Tim mentally went through the list on his fingers. "Rich O'Sullivan jumped on board right away, and between his accounting background and his being on the zoning committee I grabbed him fast. Since then I've gotten Brooke, Ken Roberts, the librarian, and Amanda Clarke, who did some of the preliminary legal work for me."

Maggie nodded. "I haven't met her, but she's been in town for awhile and has a solid reputation."

"Yeah, I was pleased with the first couple of meetings I had with her. Oh, you might know Blake Newton – he runs an IT company and has agreed to be our technology guy. And then I hired a contractor named Jim Costanzo. His business is over in Brentwood but he lives here in Caldwell. I liked him and I haven't heard anything negative about him from anyone."

"Haven't met him, or Blake Newton – but it sounds like a productive team."

"Still need one more person – two if you decide you can't handle it. I'm hoping to have two community members – one that has a connection with the elderly and another with the younger people. Ken suggested the latter also have an arts background."

Sharon chimed in. "You could call the high school and ask them. They might suggest a teacher or even a student that could give a real perspective of what's needed for Caldwell."

Tim smiled at his mom. "Good advice – I had done that a few days ago, and they suggested a few names. One of them was Teagan, who works with Maggie. The other was Cassie, who Brooke highly recommends."

"Either of them would be awesome in terms of talent, but Cassie's plate might be a little full right now. She's just getting a handle on her own recovery and I'm not sure she could add too much to it."

"That's what Teagan's dad said, too. High school seniors don't have a lot of time to sit in planning meetings, or desires for that matter. But here's the thing. I might only need ideas from them initially; any actual art work won't take place until school is out – especially for the mural."

Maggie's interest perked up. "You had mentioned that in your initial presentation. An outdoor mural on one wall? I think that would be an awesome project for some of the younger people to help with. Until then, I think you're right about their attention being elsewhere."

Carl yawned. "I'm not bored or anything, but I'm a little sleepy after that meal. I think I might go settle down in my recliner with a crossword puzzle book for awhile."

Sharon stood up and shook her head. "Oh no you won't, mister. Not until you walk out to the roses and back. C'mon, I'll go with you. We can find another bloom for the living room. That one is starting to wilt a bit."

He shook his head, but Maggie spotted the twinkle in his eye. He loved having his daughter home, and she knew that he was in good hands with Sharon, who had a new lease on life as well.

She felt Tim's gaze on her and met his eyes. It might be nice to have a few minutes alone in the kitchen together while they were out getting their exercise. It might be very nice indeed.

CHAPTER 3

$\mathcal{C}$assie looked at the clock on the wall and popped another grape in her mouth. She had to finish her lunch and clean up before heading over to Caldwell Manor for Teagan's party. She'd been working at Brooke's Treasures since she got home from the Phoenix Center, and creating art had been a huge positive factor in her recovery.

"I can't believe how fast I ate lunch today," she said to Brooke, who sat across the work table dipping her carrot stick into a container of hummus. "There are times when getting through my meal seems to take forever, and the food seems endless."

"Been quiet today – that might have helped," Brooke replied. "I don't often eat my whole lunch in one sitting. Except for days when you're here – and even you got to sit and eat without jumping up and working the front of the store."

Cassie ate the last bite of her croissant sandwich. "Even when I have to watch the front, I still manage to eat without any stress. This place has the most peaceful vibes of any other place in town."

"You've been a delight to work with, Cassie. You're polite with customers, have a creative eye for displays, and create some gorgeous new pieces every time you're here. I've been thrilled to have you."

Cassie smiled as she packed her empty lunch containers back into her lunch tote, and then started to wipe down her side of the table. "This job has been wonderful, Brooke – and you're about the most perfect boss anyone could ask for."

"I know you'll be taking off soon for Teagan's party, but any changes to your schedule the rest of the week?"

Cassie shook her head. "Nope. I have counseling tomorrow morning, and then I'll be in right after for the rest of the day. I wanted to try and finish up the fall display items so I can change the window over in the next couple of weeks."

"I'd hold off until the week before you head back to school. I guess we need to wait and see how things go once classes start in terms of what hours you'll want to work."

"I'm still hoping to manage two days during the week and Saturdays – more if you need me and I can handle it."

Brooke took the rag from where Cassie had placed it and wiped down her side of the table. "Will you be doing any extra stuff this year? Dance, or the musical?"

Cassie sat back down on the stool. "No dance yet. I just got back to normal weight and my team wants me to wait another couple of months – I'm guessing I'll have to make a choice for the spring, but I'm leaning toward the musical. Much as I miss it, going back to dance might spark the competitive need to be thin. I need an outlet that lets me express myself without the need to compete."

"Makes sense," Brooke replied as she peeked out the door toward the front. "I think someone just came in, so I'll head back out. Thanks for getting those plaques painted today; I should be able to put them out tomorrow. They look awesome."

"Thanks, Brooke. I'll finish cleaning up here and be ready when Brian comes to pick me up. He's bringing Teagan's cake and said he'd swing by to pick me up on the way, but I might sneak out the back and meet him on the corner so he doesn't have to park."

"Give Teagan my birthday wishes – and have fun. I'll see you tomorrow."

"I will. And thanks again for being a great boss. I'm always in a good place when I leave here."

* * *

CASSIE AND BRIAN arrived at Caldwell Manor thirty minutes later, and Brian took the cake and went to hide out in Maggie's office. Cassie went to her grandmother's room where she found Ida working on a crossword puzzle.

"Hey, Gram, are you ready for the big event?" She leaned down to give the older woman a hug and noticed a mailing envelope bulging with homemade cards. "I take it 'Operation Birthday Card' was a success."

"I went door to door and I think I talked to every staff person," Ida said with a smile. "I think the number of cards is a reflection of how much Teagan is loved in this place. Did you come with Brian?"

Cassie nodded. "He took the cake down to Maggie's office. They'll come down when they hear our signal that music is about to begin. Unless Kitty or Melvin gave it away, I think we're gonna pull off the surprise."

"So far they've held it together. Granted, Kitty's about to burst from the excitement of keeping the secret, but Gladys has kept her in line. Melvin just walks around humming all day. I think Teagan will be thrilled." Ida reached toward the back of her crossword puzzle book and pulled out a pink card. "And I signed the card from us like you asked me to."

Cassie smiled as she took the card from Ida. "I have the tickets right here, and we'll put them inside. I don't think that Teagan has heard yet about Fiddler coming. All the senior stuff she's dealing with has been a helpful distraction." She looked at the clock and gestured toward the envelope with cards. "I guess we should get this show on the road. Can you manage those?"

With twinkling eyes, Ida picked up the envelope and tucking it in beside her in the wheelchair, and then draping her shawl over it.

"Master of concealment," she joked. "Let's go down to the singalong, shall we?"

Cassie pushed her down to an extra crowded activity room. Teagan smiled when they entered. "There you are, Ida! I was almost ready to come looking for you, but we got a few extra residents today and I've been finding spaces for all of them. Kitty has a spot saved for you." She looked over Ida's head at Cassie and grinned. "I didn't realize you were coming today – I thought you were working."

"I was, but had time to come up for a quick visit. Still making up for lost time for when I was at the Phoenix." She patted her grandmother's shoulder and positioned her next to Kitty, who was almost dancing in her chair. "So exciting!" the older woman said, putting a finger to her mouth while glancing at Teagan to make sure she hadn't seen anything.

Cassie spoke her rehearsed words. "Well, Gram, you guys are about ready to start, so I'll say goodbye for now." She winked at her grandmother as she headed out the door. Half way down the hall she found Maggie and Brian waiting with the cake, along with Teagan's boss Karen Drake and head nurse Charlotte Hurd. The latter had a bunch of balloons in her hand.

"Just gotta wait for our cue," Cassie whispered. Maggie nodded as she switched on the LED candles on the cake. "Even with fire codes we had to have candles."

From down the hall they could hear Teagan quieting everyone down. "You guys seem extra eager today; I guess that means you'll sing even louder than normal. What shall we start with?"

Cassie heard Ida's voice loud and clear. "Actually, we have a song all picked out that's perfect for today. A one, and a two, and a three….." As the residents began singing "Happy Birthday" the group in the hallway headed down to join the festivities with Cassie and Brian leading the way, Cassie with the balloons and Brian with the cake.

"What the heck?" Teagan squealed as the others walked in. The residents finished up the song with clapping. "Happy Birthday!" they all yelled as Brian came forward with her favorite mocha cake. She looked at him and Cassie and smiled. "You guys are the best."

"Whew! That was the hardest secret I've ever had to keep!" Kitty yelled. "I thought I was gonna burst!" Gladys nodded. "So did I. I'm not telling her any more secrets."

Everyone laughed as Brian and Cassie carefully took out the candles and turned them off. Karen Drake pulled a bag out from behind her that had paper goods and utensils. She handed Teagan a knife and gestured toward the cake. "You can make the first cut and then Charlotte and I can handle the cake while you open your presents."

"My what?" Teagan said with surprise. Several residents pulled small packages out from pockets or wheelchairs, and Ida pulled out the big envelope of cards. "These are from everyone; you can read them later."

Teagan spoke lovingly to the circle of residents. "You guys are like my second family. Thank you so much for the song and cards. And gifts, too? I feel so blessed!" She spent the next several minutes opening various homemade gifts, as well as gift cards from Karen and Charlotte. Brian helped hand out cake, and afterwards Ida handed Teagan a hand painted envelope. "This is from Cassandra, Brian, and I."

Teagan sat down next to her and admired the hand painted daisy border around the edges. "This is almost too pretty to open," she said. "But I'll do it carefully." Inside was a card about best friends, and when she opened the card she gasped before looking up at Cassie and Brian. "Fiddler's coming?!"

Cassie nodded. "I don't who was more excited – me or Gram. But this time we'll sit together to watch it. Brian's coming, too – he had to."

"I am so pumped!" Teagan said, clasping the tickets to her heart. "Thank you so much. And not just for the tickets, but all of this. I'm sure it was your idea."

Cassie pointed at Brian. "He's the guilty one – the rest of us were accomplices."

Brian winked at her. "Teags, you think we'd forget our best friend's birthday? Now put those down and eat your damn cake. You're practically salivating."

Teagan laughed as the residents chatted together. "I guess we won't be singing today, will we?" She picked up her piece of cake and grabbed a fork. "I guess I can settle for mocha cake instead." She took a bite and let the mocha flavor swirl around in her mouth. She opened her eyes and smiled. "Best cake in the world. Every damn time."

Cassie even picked up her plate and took a small bite of cake. "Hmmm. This is rich." She caught Teagan's gaze. "Here's to best friends. Every damn time."

CHAPTER 4

Saturday morning Maggie returned from yoga to find Liz and Lucy sitting on the couch eating breakfast sandwiches from the café. Tramp got up to greet her as she entered the townhouse. Watson, on the other hand, looked at her and wagged his tail, but turned his gaze back to the breakfast sandwich that Liz was biting into.

Liz laughed. "Hi Maggie. Sorry for Watson's lack of manners. Food wins out every time." She pulled a small piece of the biscuit off the sandwich and offered it to her German Shepherd.

Maggie reached down to accept Tramp's wet kisses on her hand. "That's okay, I have my guy here and he's making up for it."

Lucy gestured toward the kitchen. "Left one in there all wrapped up for you. Thought you'd be hungry after yoga."

"Yum. And you're right." She walked into the kitchen and poured herself some coffee, grabbing the plate with the wrapped sandwich and joining them in the living room. "My weekly treat." She took a big bite of her biscuit and savored the warm egg and melted cheese. "Thanks guys. This is so much better than the oatmeal I was gonna make."

"How was yoga?"

Maggie gave a thumbs up as she took another bite. Trying not to talk with too big a mouthful, she swallowed a bit before speaking in a muffled voice. "What's you guys doing today?" She chewed a little more before swallowing the bite completely. "And I apologize for the lack of proper grammar."

Lucy chuckled. "We're heading over to Carl's house in a bit. Liz is going to help Sharon with the roses and talk about a possible job for her."

"A job?"

"Just a possibility," Liz said. "I have no idea if she's even looking to work since she moved back. But the college kids are all leaving next week and we're hoping to hire at least one full time and one part time person. I thought of her since she was into gardening at some point."

"I can't say that she's even talked about work when I've been over there," Maggie replied. "She had to work when Tim was younger, but I'm not sure what she did."

Liz wiped her mouth and took a swig of coffee. "She might want nothing to do with it, but I thought I'd mention it. She also wanted a few pointers on the roses for the end of the season. Carl's not quite as energetic as he was before his heart attack, and she wants to take over their care at least for the colder weather."

"Well, what he lacks in energy he more than makes up for with personality. I swear, you won't even recognize him today. He's not our old curmudgeon anymore. Hell, he's *happy*."

Lucy smiled. "I'm so glad things worked out for him. And I suspect that you'll be spending a lot more time over there yourself."

Liz winked at her girlfriend. "Otherwise Tim will be here for breakfast some days."

Maggie laughed and threw her napkin across the table. "You guys are incorrigible." But she grinned as she took another bite of her sandwich. "I'm trying not to freak out over where this is heading."

"That's what love does, sis. Just enjoy the ride – and we'll be happy to buy a fourth sandwich when the time comes."

"Well, we're not there *yet*. But when you guys walk over I'll go with you. I'm helping Tim with his office set up, and he invited me to walk over to the abandoned hardware store to take some photos for the contractor and committee. He wants to do a photo journal of the whole process to show the community when it opens."

Lucy put her empty plate down on the coffee table, inviting Watson over to lick the crumbs. "I'm so glad that we won't have to deal with Sean McClean any more. Tim has become a hero at the town hall after buying him out; he's gonna be so much easier to work with."

"I'm glad you'll be there to keep all the single ladies away – nothing like having a sister on the inside in local government."

Liz laughed. "Yeah, because Caldwell's local government has always been a top news item." She got up and gathered the empty plates. "But it might be handy having Lucy fend off all the female competition for you." She bent down to kiss the top of Lucy's head as she passed by on her way to the kitchen. "At least I don't have to worry about *her* showing any interest."

Lucy chuckled. "Honey, even if I was straight, I wouldn't dream of going after my sister's boyfriend. That's part of some ancient sister code I think." She smiled at Maggie as she emptied her coffee mug and followed Liz into the kitchen.

* * *

AN HOUR later the three of them were on Carl Pritchard's front porch. Sharon answered the door with her father not far behind. "Well, if isn't my tomato pal and the rose queen," Carl said, "and someone else I haven't given a nickname to yet."

"I'm Lucy, Maggie's sister," she said, extending her hand.

Carl squinted at her for a moment as he shook it. "I know you. You're the town hall lady. So tomato girl's your sister, huh?" He then turned to Sharon as he patted Liz on the shoulder. "She's the one that kept our roses alive when I was stuck in the hospital."

Liz grinned at Sharon. Despite having met several times since she had arrived, Carl still insisted on introducing her every time. Sharon smiled back, and then invited them all in.

"Let's not have them standing outside, Dad; let's have them in."

Carl stepped back and Sharon gestured for them to come in and sit. When Maggie entered Carl looked for a bag in her hand. "What? No tomatoes today? I might not let you in, then."

Maggie chuckled. "You'll have them before the day is out, Carl. Tim and I are walking over next door to take some pictures and I figured we'd stop at the garden on the way back."

Carl nodded and gestured toward the garage with his thumb. "He's out there if you're looking for him. I told him not to throw anything away, but that big pile of stuff makes me wonder what he's planning."

"Tell you, what," Maggie replied. "How about I go out there and keep an eye on him for you? I'll make sure that nothing important goes into a trash bag, okay? And later on you'll have a bunch of tomatoes for sandwiches."

He seemed pleased with both suggestions, and opened the door again for her as she waved to the others seated in the living room. No doubt Liz was talking to Sharon about the greenhouse job, and then they'd head out back.

She opened the side door to the garage and then knocked lightly on the office door before opening it. "Safe to come in?"

Tim looked up from a filing cabinet next to the desk and his face lit up as he closed both the drawer and the space between them. "As long as you're okay with being kissed it is." She loved the way his arms enveloped her as he leaned in to greet her. "Hmmm…..I'll never tire of smelling your hair."

"I'll make a note never to change shampoos," she murmured, wrapping her hands around his neck and looking up into his eyes. "So Carl sent me out to make sure that you're not throwing away any of his valuables."

"Shhh. No talking just yet. We can talk when they head outside – right now I want to enjoy the privacy." Maggie no longer felt butterflies of nervousness when he kissed her; rather, a growing desire was yearning to be satisfied as she kissed him back. He ran his hands up and down her spine, and the fear of him touching her and being close was quickly vanishing.

She gently put her hands on his chest and took a tiny step backwards. "Much as I love these moments, I think we better put on the brakes. Your mother and my sister could walk through that door any minute."

He sighed, caressing one side of her face with his thumb. "Agreed – although I may need to do some renovations to the loft upstairs just to have a little privacy with you."

Maggie's gaze told him that she understood. "So what progress are you making out here? The space is shaping up."

He stepped away, but still held onto her hand as he guided her back to the drafting table. "The space works at this point. I've been working on some changes to the preliminary designs for the community center that I showed at the town hall meeting. What do you think?"

Maggie leaned closer to the blueprints and squinted. "I can grasp the basic floor plan, but all those little numbers are distracting."

"Lots of measurements, my dear. That's why I want to go over and take some photos today. I want to make sure the changes will work with the existing outer walls, as they're solid. I don't want to have to demolish any of it. I'm not sure if my mom or grandad were going to come or not – we'd have to drive if they did."

Maggie shook her head. "Nope – only us. Lucy and her girlfriend Liz are inside talking to your mom and grandfather. I think Liz might even have a job possibility for your mom if she's interested."

Tim grabbed his phone from the drafting table. "A job? How about you tell me about it as we walk over? We can walk through the park down toward the B&B –a little path near the gazebo cuts through to the property."

"Sounds like a plan," Maggie said as she eyed an empty grocery bag. "And can I bring this along? I wanted to stop at the garden on the way back to pick some tomatoes for Carl. He might even share."

They walked around to the park entrance and past the community garden. Several town residents were working, and they waved at Maggie when they passed. It was the height of harvest time as the nights were starting to cool down, and weekends were much busier as folks came to tend to their plots.

As they passed by the gazebo Tim reached out and took Maggie's hand, pointing toward a little pathway that led through the shrubs to the adjoining property. "You can tell that some of the teens must scoot over here from time to time. I found a little graffiti on one wall that we may need to paint over, and a few cigarette butts inside."

"If that's the worst of it then I'd say we have decent teens in Caldwell," she joked. "Although when I was young most of us just headed over to Brentwood when we got bored or wanted to be rebellious. I guess Caldwell *isn't* for everyone – just us dull folks."

Tim took out his key and opened the door to the community center. He then flashed his dimpled smile at her as he took her hand. "Well, if this is dull, then I happen to love it. Be careful coming through the entryway –some tree branches broke a few windows."

He walked her around, explaining each room in detail and where the walls would separate the space. At one end he pointed up to an open space about four feet higher than the rest of the floor. "If we take out this half wall this will provide a stage area. There are doors on both sides in the back, and I think the height would be just about right once we open it up. What do you think?"

Maggie nodded. "Looks like they just used it as storage for stuff – or office space where they could still watch over the store. You should bring your mom over sometime. She worked at the hardware store when she was in high school and could share details the about layout back then."

"I like the way you think," he said with a flirtatious grin, wrapping his arms around her. "Then again, I'm not sure you name a single thing about yourself that I *don't* like."

Maggie blushed. "You're pretty amazing yourself, mister."

"So how about we head back over and visit with my mom and granddad for awhile, and then hit Gino's for pizza?"

"Gee, a day with my favorite guy *and* pizza? I guess the only change I might make would be to stop by and pick up Tramp on the way and walk over to pick it up. We could either eat at my apartment or at Carl's."

"I think your apartment wins out. You can text Lucy and find out if we can pick up dinner for them as well. Sharon's making my granddad some pork chops."

"Sounds like Carl is adjusting to having his daughter home. I hope neither of them are feeling too smothered."

Tim shook his head. "Hey, I'm the one with a girlfriend and no privacy and even I don't feel stifled yet. Believe me, having family dinners and sitting around catching up on life is what the three of us want right now. I have to say that I'm grateful that my dad had partnered up with Sean McClean all those years ago. The first part of my life was lousy, but all that had to happen to bring us to where we are – and I think all of us are pretty damn happy with that now."

"I'm glad. I know I've never seen your grandfather as happy as he is now. You and Sharon coming back has given him his family back. I don't think he ever dreamed of that happening."

"I don't think my mom or I ever imagined it could happen, either. Let's face it – Caldwell is *home* now, and it will be for life. Besides, there's this lovely woman who also has this thing for small towns that I plan to spend lots of time with."

He flashed his smile as they walked hand in hand, and Maggie anticipated the future and all it might bring.

CHAPTER 5

It was the first day of her senior year, and Cassie arrived at Caldwell High in time to meet Teagan and Brian out front before heading in.

Teagan greeted her with a huge hug. "Welcome back, girl! Are you ready for senior year?"

Cassie shrugged. "I'm a little nervous – not gonna lie. Hey, Brian."

Brian reached over and gave her a quick hug. "Hey, yourself. It's good to have you back. And it's okay to be nervous."

"I don't want people to treat me differently because I had to do the last two months of school online last year. I guess I'm thinking that everyone will be staring at me."

Brian laughed. "Don't worry; most of us are way too self-absorbed to have even noticed you were gone."

"Hey! That's my best friend you're talking about!" Teagan teased, whacking him on the back.

"Teags, I'm kidding. Cassie, just be you. Some folks will come and welcome you back, and a few might say something awkward, and others won't care one way or the other. The main thing is that you're back, and some of us are thrilled."

"Thanks, guys. I'm lucky to have both of you as friends."

Brian's expression grew serious. "Listen, before we go in, I have some news. Cassie, I was out with Lou this past weekend and ran in to Mike and Julia. Since you and Mike were an item last year, I didn't want it to blindside you today."

Cassie bit her lip as the news hit her. "Julia never said anything during yoga, but let's face it – Mike wasn't the model boyfriend. Once I went inpatient I never heard from him again. But thanks for telling me." As the three of them headed toward the front door, she remembered meeting Mike the first day of school the prior year. She was new in town and alone, and he happened to be heading in the same time she was. *"He even held the door for me that day,"* she thought. *"But I'm not as pretty or thin as Julia which explains why he's with her."*

Teagan linked her arm through Cassie's as she saw the change in expression. "Remember your worth. The cute guys will come and go, but there's only one Cassie. Concentrate on her, okay?"

Cassie smiled and squeezed Teagan's arm. "Thanks. You always know what I need to hear."

"That's what best friends are for, silly. Now let's go find out if Mr. C. is gonna announce the show today."

The three of them headed to the auditorium where the rest of the theater class was seated in clusters. Most of the kids in the room were here to gain experience and confidence and practice the craft they loved before auditions for the musical were even scheduled. A few kids came just for the theater class with no intention of trying out for the show. Cassie found herself in the middle – wanting desperately to be a part of the magic for her senior year, but nervous about whether her recovery would allow her to do so.

As they sat down, several kids from "Kiss Me, Kate" – the prior year's show – had come over to greet Cassie and welcome her back. Julia and Kyleigh rushed over to hug her as Kyleigh let out her usual squeal, and Cassie didn't notice any tension from Julia as she genuinely hugged her. "I'm so glad you're back," Julia said. "You're so damn talented."

"Thanks," Cassie replied with a smile. "I'm glad to be back, too – and I hope that I can be on that stage again in the spring."

"You'll do it," Julia said. "You amaze me with the work you've put into getting better."

As the two of them found their seats, Cassie spotted Mike arriving in time to slide in next to Julia. The smile he gave her confirmed that he had moved on. *So why didn't she say something? Is she trying to mess with my head, or did Mike just tell her I was nobody?*

Teagan had jotted down words on her notebook and pointed to them: *"Know your worth"* was scrawled on the page. Cassie mouthed the words "thank you" to Teagan as Mr. Calabreschi stood up.

"Good morn-ing!" he bellowed with his theater director voice that projected to the back of the auditorium without a microphone. "I hope all of you had a great summer and are as happy to be back as I am. This is Theater 101, and if anyone here decided to take this class with the expectation of a high grade for minimal work," he said, gesturing toward the side door. "Then I'm sure you can find a basket weaving class down the hall that will be a much better fit."

All the students laughed as he continued. "Theater is not an easy class. Acting encompasses every fiber of your being – body, mind, and spirit. And if you commit to it, I can guarantee you'll be a better person for it. Theater is all about putting your egos aside and being willing to take risks. When you step into your character's head you'll learn to view the world with a perspective that might be different than your own. That teaches you empathy. And working with your class mates will increase your confidence, your creativity, your commitment to each other, and your ability to communicate effectively. Those are all qualities worth staying for – besides, we also have a lot of fun. Before we start today, are there any questions?"

Brian's friend Lou Donovan raised his hand. "C'mon, Mr. C. Don't keep us in suspense. What's the *show?*" Several other students nodded their heads and affirmed his question. The director leaned back against the stage and smirked.

"You think I don't know that half of you missed my whole mono-logue as you sat there going through the lists of every musical in your head? Am I right?" He chuckled as Cassie and her peers joined in. He was such an awesome teacher, and had the respect of every kid in the room.

He put his hands up in front of him. "All right, you win. I won't get anything out of you today if I don't tell you. For those of you that will be auditioning in November, the spring musical this year will be *Hello, Dolly.*" Cassie joined in the applause and glanced over at Teagan and Brian. "I love that show," she whispered with excitement.

Brian nodded in agreement. "And you, Teags, will make an awesome Dolly Levi." Cassie smiled back with shining eyes. "Couldn't agree more." She squeezed Teagan's arm and sat back as others chatted a couple of minutes. Her mind was going through the various characters in the show, and what the dance requirements might be. *"Maybe the show will work and let me dance just a little,"* she thought with excitement. She followed her friends up onto the stage, eager to start what she knew would be a favorite class.

* * *

A FEW HOURS later Cassie sat between Teagan and Kyleigh at lunch, and her confidence from theater was replaced by self-consciousness as she glanced down at her lunch. *"Mine is huge compared to Kyleigh's,"* she thought. *"I'll never finish before the cafeteria aide comes to check on me."*

She caught Teagan's eye, who recognized the fear. "That sandwich looks amazing," Teagan said. "What's in it?"

Cassie took a deep breath as she picked up her croissant. "Turkey with avocado and mayo," she said, taking a bite to be mindful of the flavors and textures. Lunches all summer had been a croissant sandwich with a few different fillings that were agreed on each week. Most of the time there was fruit and either a salad or veggie to eat as well. Cassie's biggest fear wasn't the amount of food, but the time given to eat it.

Teagan's lunch made her smile; she had a whole grain tortilla chock full of beef, beans, and cheese, as well as chips with salsa and some grapes. "That looks good, too. Might have to plan that for a dinner next week." Teagan grinned as she prepared to take a huge bite of her burrito. "Tell me the night and I'll be there to lend support."

Cassie took a deep breath and took another bite, looking around at the other theater kids at her table. No one was looking at her, and most could care less what she was eating, but her eating disorder tried multiple times through the meal to make her think it was a big deal. Bite after bite, she listened to conversations around her and made progress on her lunch.

Kyleigh brought her back to the present moment. "What did you think of psych? I think it will be a good class."

Cassie nodded. "Mrs. Barnes seems pleasant."

"What else did you have this morning?"

"Composition with Mr. Hendricks. I think he might be a little tougher, but English is okay."

Kyleigh nodded. "My neighbor had him last year. Said he was tough but fair. Turn your work in on time and answer a question now and then and you'll be fine." She leaned in closer to Cassie. "I'm assuming you noticed Julia with Mike this morning; you okay with it?"

Cassie nodded, not knowing what else to do. "Mike didn't stay in touch once I went off to the Phoenix Center. I guess it would have been stupid to assume he'd be sitting home waiting for me to come back."

"Julia wanted to tell you at yoga, but was afraid you'd think less of her. She ran into him over the summer at the mall and they started seeing each other. I hope it won't affect your friendship. She adores you and is so happy that you got the help you needed."

"Thanks, Kyleigh. I'll be okay with it. I don't do that well with sudden surprises, but Brian told me outside this morning." She looked around. "So where is Julia? Mike's over at the football table."

"She had a French Club meeting at lunch for the officers. She's the president this year."

"Well, if you run into her before I do, tell her I'll be okay with it."

Kyleigh grinned as she popped a piece of chocolate in her mouth.

"Whew! That's a relief! I don't wannna deal with any drama for my senior year."

"Not even on stage?" Cassie joked.

"Silly girl – that's totally different! Can't wait for rehearsals to start! Hey, that's the bell. Gotta run." In a second, she had shoved her lunch remnants into her container and stood up, brushing the crumbs off of her clothes. "Catch you guys later!" she said, waving to everyone at the table and then practically skipping toward the door.

Teagan chuckled. "That girl has so much energy and can be so goofy at the same time."

Cassie nodded. "But she's nice. I don't think she has a nasty bone in her body."

"Sounds like you gave Julia and Mike your blessing."

"Not sure it was a blessing, but I can't change anything," Cassie said, looking down at a bit of sandwich and a few grapes remaining. "I'm supposed to finish this but the kids for second lunch period are all coming in."

"Wrap it up and take it to study hall. You have permission to use that time to finish your lunch if you need to. Brian and I both have study hall with you, and I can guarantee we'll make sure you finish. Nothing's gonna keep you from being in this show with us, ya hear?"

Cassie smiled and followed Teagan's advice. A few minutes later she sat at the back of the room for study hall and unwrapped what was left of her croissant sandwich. "I'm kinda self-conscious eating in here," she whispered to Teagan.

"The school gave you permission to eat in another room."

Cassie thought for a moment as she chewed and then shook her head. "No, I want to learn how to live in the real world and still manage this eating disorder. I can't run and hide forever, and if I'm gonna audition for the musical then I have to show people I can manage it."

"Just don't put too much pressure on yourself, okay? You have a ton of people that are here to help you."

"Thanks. Now shut up so I can finish this lunch."

Teagan laughed and pulled out her psychology book. "As one who *always* finishes her meal, consider this conversation over." Cassie took a bite of croissant, licking a little avocado off of her finger. She loved Teagan's warmth and candor, and was learning from her the gift of loving herself no matter what size. She hoped someday she'd be just as confident in her own body.

* * *

THAT EVENING Cassie enjoyed her dinner. Her mom had made a tuna casserole that had become a favorite of hers, and conversation bounced back and forth between her and Philip about their first day of school.

Her mom smiled as Cassie stopped talking to take another bite. "I'm glad your friends were there to give you support today."

She swallowed and wiped her mouth. "I got texts from Molly and Juanita, too. They both knew I was starting today and wanted to check in."

"How are they doing?"

"Well, Molly starts junior year next week, and she's settling in now that she's back home. Juanita is starting college and seems to be in a healthy place."

"How about her roommate? Was her name Ellie?"

Cassie nodded. "She's still at the Phoenix – they both said she's still struggling. I think I'll make her a card this week and send it to her." She took another bite as her mom responded to Philip's request for another serving. By the time she finished her meal she was full, but not bloated. Her body was adjusting to the larger amounts of food, and most dinners had been pleasant in recent weeks.

As her mom got up to clear the table, Cassie took her own dishes to the sink. "Do you want me to rinse them and load the dishwasher?"

Her mom glanced at her husband and shook her head. "Not tonight, honey. I can manage by myself."

"O-kay," Cassie answered hesitantly. She almost always did this chore, as it was understood that she needed to stick around for twenty minutes after the meal. "I can bring my homework in and work on that for awhile."

Her father had stood up and was walking over to a stack of papers on the counter. "Actually, honey, I asked your mother for a little time with you tonight. Can we sit?" as he gestured back to the table.

The tension started at the pit of her stomach as she slouched back down into her chair. She recognized the pile. She'd been avoiding it all summer, and so far had been able to redirect to another subject or activity. Now her father had her cornered. College stuff.

"Dad, I need to do my homework—"

"Honey, what we *need* is to work through this stack together." Her dad sat down next to her and reached over to put his hand on her shoulder. "You've been doing so well, and I'm so proud of you. Looking ahead is a little scary, but there are deadlines coming up that we need to hit. Can we agree to sit for thirty minutes and then we'll stop?"

Cassie stared down at the table and nodded.

"The first major thing here is the SATs. I went ahead and scheduled you for early October, which is the last chance to finish them before application deadlines."

"So soon? Dad, I don't think I'll be ready. They're early in the morning and I have to eat breakfast first. What if I'm late?"

Eliana wiped her hands and came around to sit on Cassie's other side.

"Honey, you're doing better with scheduling every day. You're almost ready for the next level when we start letting you do more on your own. You can do this."

Frank had opened one of the folders that had several college names written on a piece of notebook paper. She remembered sitting with her dad last year right after the holidays coming up with a list of potential schools. Her eating disorder was wreaking havoc back then, and it didn't go well. She fought the temptation to push it away and run from the room screaming, but her heart was racing. *"You'll never be smart enough for college,"* she thought. *"Tell them whatever they want to hear so you can get out of here."* Her eating disorder whispered in her head, and she found herself rocking back and forth slightly to stay grounded in the moment. "Fine," she muttered. "What else do I need to do?"

Frank smiled at her. "Thatta girl. That's the warrior spirit you have inside. So here's the list we had made last year, which is a good place to start. We might add a school or two – or stick with these three—but we need to schedule visits this fall as well."

"Can't we just check out their websites instead?"

"That's like buying a new car without a test drive. You gotta walk around a campus before deciding to live there. We can either all go or I'll take you, but let's pull out the schedule and see what weekends are free, okay?"

Cassie nodded, fighting back the queasiness in her stomach. A day that had started wonderfully had come crashing back down. She wondered if she'd ever be free from the power that her eating disorder had over her.

CHAPTER 6

Maggie was eating her dinner before going to the library for her first planning committee meeting. As she finished her stir-fry, her thoughts returned again to Cassie, who had struggled repeatedly over the growing conflict with her dad regarding college. Maggie was still worried about her relapsing.

She sent a text as she cleared her dish into the sink. *"You need to have Natalie schedule a family meeting with your folks. This conflict won't go away, and you need help to face them on it. Your eating disorder will use every little detail to chip away at all the progress you've made with your folks since you got home. Don't give it the power."*

"Everything was going so well," Cassie texted back, *"and now I'm holding on by my fingernails."*

"Then keep holding on and make that call. I have a meeting tonight, but I'll check in when I'm done, okay?"

Cassie sent back a heart emoji, and Maggie reluctantly grabbed her bag and said goodbye to Tramp. She was tempted to call Tim and cancel so she could go down to Cassie's house, but knew that Cassie's parents would never give her the same respect that they'd give the counselor. She walked the short distance to the library, enjoying the crisp fall air that promised bursts of color in the days ahead.

When she got to the library she stopped at the circulation desk to check in. She recognized Teagan's friend Brian behind the counter. "So this is where you hide when you're not baking with the residents," she said cordially.

Brian laughed. "You got it – Maggie, right? Yeah, I've worked here since I was a sophomore. Only thing that would make it better would be if my boss would let me open a little café over there at the back of the reference area."

Maggie smiled. "I'd support that suggestion in a heartbeat! In fact, I'll try to grab your boss at the meeting as a concerned patron who needs caffeine with her books."

"Awesome! I should start a campaign! Anyhow, they're in the meeting room downstairs. You can take the elevator or the stairs."

"Thanks, Brian," Maggie said as she started past him, but stopped and turned around and leaned in closer. "By the way, is Cassie doing okay at school? She's having a rough time at home right now."

"Believe me, we know," he replied. "Teagan's been great with her, and she's getting some solid support from a few friends at school and Brooke at work. Hey, we feel the stress of all the college stuff and we don't have a damn eating disorder on our back – but so far, she's holding her own."

"Is she getting through lunch okay?"

"Don't worry. Teagan's on it, and Cassie trusts her enough to be honest. I think the only one she trusts more is you – well, plus her therapist."

"Thanks. I'm keeping close tabs on her, but I'm glad you guys have her back at school. I'm sure some family therapy will make a difference. I guess I better get downstairs. Thanks, Brian."

"No problem. We all want the same thing for Cassie – even her parents do. They just need to communicate better."

Maggie agreed as she headed past. She remembered back to her own recovery and how vital that communication was, and she gave thanks for how supportive her parents and sister had been in those early months. She was still deep in thought when she walked into the meeting room and almost walked right in to Tim.

"Well, hey," he said, flashing the dimpled smile that brought her back to the moment. "I'm glad I wasn't a wall; where were you just now?"

"Deep in thought, evidently. I'll tell you about it later. Hope I'm not late." She recognized most of the people seated at the table. She smiled when Brooke patted the empty chair beside her. Glancing back at Tim, she gave a little wink. "I'll go sit with Brooke so I'm not a distraction for you."

He smirked at her. "Honey, you are *always* a distraction when you're around – the best kind, I might add." He walked toward the head of the table as Maggie scooted around to the seat next to Brooke.

"Thanks for saving a seat."

Brooke was getting a pen out of her purse, but gave a slight nod. "Glad you joined us. You'll like the group. Tim will introduce everyone in case you don't know them, but the woman next to you is Amanda Clarke."

Maggie turned to a beautiful blonde with dark purple eyeglasses that framed striking blue eyes. "Hi, I'm Maggie Richmond. I think your office is right across from the dance studio?"

Amanda extended her hand. "Indeed it is – although I use the café as a landmark more than the dance studio. I'm not sure what that says about me. Nice to meet you Maggie." Maggie shook her hand before getting her own notebook out of her bag. She knew Amanda was the attorney that worked with Tim on the legal end for the community center. For a split second she wondered if the blonde was single, but then realized that she was secure about Tim's feelings for her. *"I'm not sure how I got so lucky to be the one,"* she thought, *"but I'll just enjoy it and perhaps gloat a little on the inside when I'm around attractive single women."*

One more gentleman arrived and grabbed the last chair; Maggie thought he looked familiar, and noting his more casual attire surmised that he might be the contractor that Tim had hired. Tim called the meeting to order, and introduced Maggie as the newest member of the committee. "Maggie, I think you've met most of the folks – Rich O'Sullivan is our accountant and also our zoning board contact, Blake Newton is our IT consultant, Amanda Clarke is our attorney, Jim Costanzo is our contractor, and Ken Roberts is the library director. You're joining him and Brooke as community connections."

He addressed the committee as he continued. "Maggie will be an asset in getting word out to the senior members of our community, as well as those that care for them. Considering that we want the community center to be inclusive to all residents of Caldwell, her input will be valuable when we start planning programs and space utilization."

Brooke spoke up. "At the last meeting we discussed rounding out the team with a younger person as well. Did you contact the high school as suggested for their input?"

Tim nodded. "I did, and stopped in to chat with one of their art teachers. She suggested a few names to consider. One was Teagan O'Sullivan." He turned to the gentleman to his right. "She's your daughter, isn't she, Rich?"

"She is indeed," Rich replied. "I can ask her, but she's busy with senior year – she has school, her job, and then the musical will take a lot of time once they start up."

Maggie jumped in. "I work with Teagan, and I think Rich has some valid points. However, I'd still give her the chance to make that deci-sion. She balances a lot on her plate with more grace that most adults, and I don't think the committee will be a huge drain on her time. Besides, I think she's looking at recreation therapy or administration for college, isn't she?"

Rich replied. "Hadn't thought of that. It would look impressive on a college resume. I can run it by her – unless you think you'd like to mention it," he said to Maggie.

"Why don't you ask her, and then I'll follow up with her at work. And if she doesn't work out, I'm sure she could suggest someone else that would."

Tim checked an item off his list. "Great! So I want to give you all an update on where we are. I thought I'd have Jim Costanzo give that update. Jim's the contractor I've hired to do the renovations. He's based in Brentwood, but lives up at the end of School Street here in town. Jim? The floor is yours."

Maggie liked his casual manner. He spoke professionally and knew his material, but he was similar to Tim in making everyone comfortable. Maggie was glad there was another single male on the committee as Amanda seemed to be listening extra intently. *"In case she's looking,"* Maggie thought, *"she'll have another target besides Tim."*

Jim passed out a written update as he spoke. "So here's the rundown on paper for each of you to keep track. Things will start moving quickly at the old hardware store at this point. All permits have been approved and we're ready to roll. The major clean out will begin next week, and we hope to have updates to the electric and plumbing completed by the end of October, as well as a possible new roof – we'll have it inspected, and either go for a new one or make any needed repairs on the existing one."

Rich O'Sullivan spoke up. "I think that roof is quite old. You might consider new right off the bat; it might save money in the long run not to have to make frequent repairs."

"I'm leaning that way, too," Tim added. "We'll take a look at the numbers this week and discuss possibilities."

Jim continued. "Inside renovations will begin in November, and we hope to have a community open house by next summer with an opening set for next August or September."

Maggie grew more excited as the plans were discussed in more detail. This had originally been an idea she had shared with Tim in a casual conversation, and it made her proud to think that the idea was coming to fruition.

As the meeting came to an end, she lagged behind to wait for Tim to finish up. Amanda was the last to leave, and Maggie watched from her seat as she said goodbye. "I'll have a few things for you to sign this week," she said, lightly touching his arm as she passed. "I'll call you when they're all set." She smiled warmly at him and then turned toward Maggie. "Bye, Maggie. Lovely to meet you."

Maggie flinched a bit in her seat, surprised that she'd react to a simple gesture that probably meant nothing. Immediate thoughts flashed in her brain. *"See? She is interested in him – and she's so much prettier and thinner than you. You'll never hold on to him."* She gathered her papers and shoved them into her notebook, determined not to let her eating disorder screw up her romance.

Tim missed her reaction. "Hungry by any chance? I didn't eat much for dinner and would love to take you down to the diner."

Maggie smiled and defiantly stood up to her eating disorder with her reply. "Even if I did eat dinner, I'd never turn down the opportunity for a waffle with strawberries and whipped cream. Lead the way."

* * *

MAGGIE'S WAFFLE didn't disappoint. She got through over half of it before sliding her dish toward Tim, who was finishing up an omelet and home fries. "You might have to help me with the rest of this – I'm getting full."

Tim grinned and grabbed a strawberry with his fork. "Happy to oblige. So are you happy that I dragged you onto the committee now?"

Maggie nodded. "It was neat to sit and listen to my thoughts becoming real, and they all seem congenial and on the ball."

"You must have known most of them."

"Yeah, most. Obviously Jim was new, but he seems honest and efficient – and excited about moving forward. I hadn't met Amanda but she was pleasant. The others I've at least run into a couple of times – and of course, Brooke, who's almost like a sister."

Tim took a swig of coffee as he finished his plate and moved it to the side to pull the remaining waffle pieces closer. "So, what's the likelihood I could drag you back here next week after the meeting to celebrate?"

Maggie smirked, knowing that he was referring to her upcoming birthday. "Hmmm, I wonder what you could possibly be referring to."

"You know darn well what I'm talking about. I had wanted to cook for you for your birthday, but that'd be a late start in your kitchen and I don't wanna impose on Lucy."

Maggie chuckled. "She wouldn't mind, but keeping your contact at town hall on your good side is probably wise."

"So can I at least treat you to dinner after the meeting?"

Maggie reached over to run her finger on the plate for the last dab of whipped cream. "How could I refuse? And how am I so lucky to be the woman in your life?"

Tim reached over and took her hand. "Honey, I'm the one who's lucky. I came to Caldwell hoping to have some kind of relationship with my granddad. Never in my dreams did I expect to fall in love with a beautiful woman kneeling in the dirt that day."

"Now you're making me blush."

"I mean it. You're the woman I've been waiting for – and the fact that you're so close to my granddad is just a bonus."

"I do love your grandfather – and am so amazed at how happy you've made him."

The waitress came with the coffeepot. "Any more, doll?"

Tim grinned, shaking his head. "You can bring the check. I think we're satisfied for now."

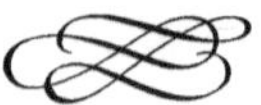

Cassie passed the popcorn to Brian, who took a huge handful to refill his bowl. Sitting with him and Teagan in the latter's family room watching *Hello, Dolly,* she was more peaceful today after a long therapy session with Natalie. Brian had suggested the weekend movie viewing, and Teagan had suggested the three of them rather than inviting other cast mates from the year before. Cassie was comfortable with these two, and was grateful for the chance to be away from her house for a few hours.

Brian pointed to the screen as he munched away. "Teags, there is no way you're not gonna be cast as Dolly Levi. No one else comes close."

Teagan threw a piece of popcorn at him. "Don't build my hopes up. I still think that Paula will be my main competition this year, and she was awesome as Hattie last year. I could end up as her friend, which is also a great comic role. I'd enjoy that one, too."

Cassie smirked. "Who are you kidding? Last year you nailed the lead. You're not gonna be happy with a small supporting role for your last show. I think Mr. C. had you cast when he picked this one."

"Spoken like a loyal best friend," Brian said as he reached for more popcorn. Cassie laughed and handed the bowl to him. "Why not just hold the big bowl, and we can use the smaller bowls?" He traded the big for the small. "Girl, I like the way you think! So what about you? Irene Molloy? Or Minnie Fay?"

Cassie squirmed a bit. "I'm not sure which roles to consider. I can't even think about the niece because she does a ton of dancing, but the other two both dance as well. I might have to settle for one of the minor roles that don't have to dance."

Teagan sat up straighter and shook her head. "I disagree. Yes, those two roles do have some minor dance, but they're not extensive – and choreography is easier to change for a lead than an ensemble member. And Irene has the singing that you can nail."

"You could talk to Mr. C. beforehand for his opinion," Brian said.

"I talked to Natalie a little and she said to hold off," Cassie replied. "I might be cleared for light dance by then anyway."

"How does that work?" Brian asked. "Do you need a doctor's note or something?"

"Not exactly. *Medically*, I'm okay to dance now, as I'm back to my prior weight and blood work is stable. But anorexia is a disease of the *head* more than the body, and exercise can be a trigger. For now I'm following Natalie's advice to avoid dance a little longer – the classes at the studio are designed more for competition."

Teagan used the remote to pause the movie. "But dance in musicals isn't competition, but part of the storytelling. Last year you got sucked into the excessive practicing, but you were well into your disease at that point. Things are different this year."

"I'm still a little nervous. The past few weeks have been kinda stressful at home, and I'm a little scared that my eating disorder will use the dance against me."

"What does Maggie think about it?"

"She said we'll deal with it closer to auditions. Right now the main conflict is still college stuff."

Brian paused in his eating. "Did you schedule the family session yet?"

"Natalie's calling this week to set it up. I hope my dad can take time away from his job for it. He's been working crazy hours, and then the only time he's home he wants to ram the college stuff down my throat."

"He *does* have some credibility, though. I mean, it sounds like he wants you to hit the deadlines coming up. Teags and I have gotten a lot of that stuff done."

"I'm not sure I *want* to start college next year. So the deadlines are important to him, but stressful for me. Even now, the tension inside is building."

Brian put his hands up defensively. "Hey, I'm not trying to upset you or anything – only trying to understand your dad's point of view."

Teagan laughed. "And here I thought you were going to be a cook, not a counselor."

"He's right, though. My dad has a different perspective."

Brian nodded. "And for the record, I'm shooting more for pastry chef than cook."

Teagan threw more popcorn at him. "Good; I don't want my supply chain for baked goods to ever be broken." She turned to Cassie and continued, "Natalie should have a better chance scheduling the meeting than if it was you asking. And resolving the issue will make auditions easier."

"Yeah, Cassie – bottom line is you're meant to be a part of that show."

"Thanks, you guys," she said caringly. "I think a gap year is the best choice for me, and others seem to be supportive of that. I wish I wasn't afraid to tell *him* that. It makes me think that our relationship isn't as healed as it could be."

"I think you might be surprised," Teagan offered. "Your head might be telling you he's going to react a certain way because it's the old pattern. But leave that to Natalie."

"So what do I do tomorrow when he wants to sit down and fill out applications, or practice for the SATs? It pushes every button, and my reaction is to restrict my food – which pushes lots of other buttons far worse."

Brian made a suggestion. "Look, why not sit down and go through the process for now. Even if you apply and are accepted, it doesn't mean that you have to go--but it might keep the peace until your therapy session."

Cassie considered Brian's idea. "Maybe. But for now let's focus on today. Brian, what parts are *you* looking at?"

Brian grinned. "I don't have a favorite. I love Horace, Cornelius, and Barnaby – so any of those roles would be awesome."

Teagan held up the remote. "How about we all just shut up for awhile and watch the rest of the movie? I think the hardest part is going to be waiting until November for auditions."

"A little different from last year, Teags. Even though the show was known early in the year, you just ignored it until the audition notices came out – then you stomped around for awhile before going for it."

Cassie leaned over toward Teagan and bumped her shoulder with her own. "Hard to believe that a year ago we hardly knew each other. After all the major ups and downs, I wonder if I'd even be here if it wasn't for you." She got a little misty eyed as her eyes met Teagan's. "I'll forever be grateful that fate brought us together."

Teagan squeezed her arm. "Me, too. Can't wait for the year ahead."

* * *

LATER THAT EVENING Cassie heeded her friends' advice as dinner came to an end. Her dad wiped his mouth with his napkin. "You had a nice visit with your friends today, so how about we sit down for awhile and pull out the college folder."

Cassie fought the knee-jerk reaction inside and took a deep breath. *"Remember what they said. Filling stuff out doesn't mean you have to go. Just go through the steps until we can talk with Natalie."*

She gave her dad a weak smile. "I guess that would work for a little while—but I do have homework I need to do."

Her mom wiped the table down in front of them. "Why not agree on a time limit?"

"Excellent idea, honey. Let's figure thirty minutes, and that will give you time for studying afterwards. Does that work for you?"

Cassie nodded, taking a sip of water to help her dry mouth. She considered bringing up the subject of a gap year, but decided against it. Instead she turned her attention to the piles that her dad was laying out in front of her and tried to focus in a calm manner.

Her father held up a list with three schools along with the catalogs that went with each. They had talked about possible schools last spring, and he had sent for the catalogs this summer while she was living at the Phoenix. She now tried hard to look at the three covers objectively.

"So if I was Cassie the college bound, which of these would be most appealing," she thought.

"These are the top three that we had talked about last spring," her dad said, "and the deadlines for all three aren't until December, so we have time. Unless you want to apply for early decision for one of them – then we need to move a little faster."

Cassie cringed inside, but put on a smile. "I don't think I'm ready for early decision, Dad. Let's stick to the December deadline, okay?"

She wasn't sure he was listening as he moved on to the next pile. "This is the financial aid pile, and I'll take care of all of this; I'll need the amount you've earned at Brooke's at some point. But this pile has the actual application forms and essay requirements for these schools. Plus we have to go online and update the CommonApp for the schools that will receive your SAT scores."

"Breathe," Cassie thought, checking the clock. "Doesn't the community college let you apply without the SATs?" she inquired. "Maybe I should start there."

Her dad patted her shoulder. "That's a silly reason to pick a school – besides, you're all set for SATs in a couple of weeks. And that reminds me," he said as he ruffled through the folder. "I picked this up for you this week to polish up a bit before the test."

Cassie took the SAT prep book from him. *"Yay. A whole book of tests to show how stupid I am,"* she thought. *"Talk about a waste of time and money."* She caught her dad's gaze and tried to give him a reassuring look. "I'll take a look at it later, if that's okay." She placed it on the table and picked up the catalog from Brentwood College. She knew that Teagan was planning to apply there, and it was close to home and even closer to Natalie if she needed counseling.

"I think Brentwood is still my top choice," she said quietly, and her dad smiled. *"Now if I can just survive until Natalie helps me tell you that I don't wanna go."*

CHAPTER 8

The clock read 3:30 as Maggie finished up her phone call with a resident's daughter. *"I wonder if I should work a little late tonight."* She was due to leave in an hour, but Charlotte had asked that the information be ready for the staff meeting the next morning.

Charlotte knocked on her door as she passed by. "You look deep in thought."

Maggie put her pencil down and leaned back in her chair. "Trying to find the energy to stay late and finish up my notes," as she gestured at the files in front of her.

Charlotte shook her head. "Don't stay. If they're not 100% done we can go on what you do have ready. Besides, the meeting's not until 11:00 – you might have time in the morning to finish them up."

Maggie glanced down at the files in front of her to assess where she was. "You might be right. I still have about three more family members I haven't heard back from, but I have an overall idea on most of the residents that do have family members nearby. Still, I hate relying on tomorrow to finish up last minute; anything can disrupt daily plans here– especially in the morning."

"Yeah, but you're always more prepared that you think you are, which is why we love having you here. So do you have any birthday plans lined up? Can I buy you a sandwich from the café after the meeting at least?"

Maggie smiled, wondering if Charlotte would remember. "Not necessary – but thanks. And it will be a quiet celebration. I have a planning meeting for the community center tomorrow night, but Tim's taking me to the diner afterwards for a quick bite. I think he was hoping to take me to Gino's for lunch, but we both have meetings that cut that time too short."

"That stinks. I could try to move the meeting up to 10 if that helps."

"Don't worry about it. I'll still spend the evening with him, and he said we'd plan a dinner over the weekend somewhere."

"I take it things are going well?"

"I think I'm finally believing him when he tells me that he loves me. I'm not as worried about him finding someone else more attractive or thinner instead."

"Tim's got good sense. He'd be crazy to think about dropping you for anyone. And I'm glad you joined the committee – you'll be a positive advocate for both our residents and the elderly in the community." She looked at the clock and stood up. "I have 4:00 meds to set up. Thanks for getting those notes together so quickly for me – and I trust your judgment on whether to stay late or not."

"Thanks. I'll see you in the morning either way. Have a good night, Charlotte."

* * *

THE NEXT MORNING Maggie woke up to her alarm, and the phone rang before she pulled off the covers. She smiled when Tim's name popped up. "Morning – a minute earlier and you could have been my alarm clock."

"I like the sound of that," he murmured. "Happy birthday, beautiful. I hope I got the first wish in."

Maggie's whole body smiled. "You were. Although I think I smell quiche, so I suspect Lucy has been trying to beat you out."

"I just wanted to wish you a wonderful day and tell you how grateful I am that you were born."

"I'm looking forward to spending the evening with you."

"I wish I could take you out for a romantic dinner – but I promise we'll get that in."

"I don't need a romantic dinner – I'm just as happy with a quick meal at the diner."

"Well, if we hurry the meeting along we can do Gino's instead. That's at least a step up. For now I'll let you go. Don't want you to eat a cold quiche, after all."

"I suspect Lucy will bang on my door when it's ready. But I guess I should get moving. I have a meeting at work this morning and need to arrive early – won't even make it over to the garden today."

"I could pick you up right from work and we could stop by then."

"Hey, you have your own meeting this afternoon – and Brooke said that she'd take care of my plot this morning, so we're good. I guess I'll see you tonight."

"I love you, Maggie – have a day as beautiful as you are. I'll be thinking about you."

"I love you, too. Have a great day yourself." Maggie hung up smiling, and wandered out to the kitchen where her place was set with coffee, quiche and fruit, and a card.

"Happy birthday, sis!" Lucy gave her a warm hug and gestured toward the counter.

"Now eat before it gets cold. I heard you talking and didn't want to interrupt the telephone love-fest."

Maggie sat down and reached for her coffee. "This smells wonderful. You made my favorite, I presume?"

"Onion, mushroom, spinach, and Swiss – only the best for a birthday breakfast. There are warm croissants in the basket, too." She sat down across the counter and extended the basket before taking one herself. "So how was it getting a birthday phone call first thing?"

Maggie took a bite of quiche and savored the warm cheese in her mouth. "Pretty wonderful."

"The quiche or the phone call?"

"Both," Maggie mumbled as she pulled the croissant apart. "Hmm....almond today."

"Café didn't have the chocolate ready yet, and I knew you were on a time crunch. Besides, if you didn't want them there would be more for me." Lucy slid the card over. "Now open your card and enjoy your breakfast."

Maggie grinned. It had already been the best birthday ever, and there was still plenty left.

* * *

A FEW HOURS later Maggie grabbed her files for the meeting in the conference room. Jason Johnson, the physical therapist, knocked outside the open door as she stood up.

"Hey, glad I caught you before the meeting. Eliana popped in to visit Ida and wanted to grab you for a minute before we got started. They're in the library."

Maggie immediately wondered if there was a problem with Cassie if Eliana was here this early. "Sure – tell her I'll be right there. I'll let Charlotte know that I might be a minute or two late."

"Why don't I fill Charlotte in," Jason replied. "You can head right down to the library."

"Thanks – I won't be long."

Maggie rushed to the library, hoping that Cassie hadn't had any kind of relapse. Expecting a problem, she was surprised instead to find many of the residents seated and most of the staff standing around a table with a birthday cake and balloons.

"What the—"

"Happy birthday!" Teagan directed the residents as they sang, even adding some harmony at the end. Charlotte laughed at the files in Maggie's hand. "I hope you didn't kill yourself getting those done. The meeting isn't until Friday – this is your birthday celebration."

Jason wandered in right behind her. "We gotcha! Happy birthday, Maggie Mae!"

Maggie stood there with her mouth half open. "Yeah, I guess you did. Thanks you guys – this is such a wonderful surprise." She glanced over at Jason and narrowed her eyes. "I take it the emergency with Eliana is bogus?"

"I suggested it," Ida chimed in. "I knew it would get you down here in a hurry."

Maggie turned to the older woman beaming from her wheelchair. "I'll talk to *you* later," she said as sternly as she could while smiling. She turned back to her fellow co-workers and shook her head. "I'm not often surprised. But thanks, guys."

Teagan stepped forward and handed her a knife. "Glad we pulled it off. Now hurry up and cut the cake – it's my breakfast today."

* * *

THE AFTERNOON FLEW BY, and Maggie headed out the door right at 4:30 to head home for a quick dinner. She had walked up to work today to enjoy the gorgeous fall leaves lining the street. As she passed by the park she marveled at the warm reds, yellows, and oranges that were even more vibrant with the afternoon sun shining directly on them. Against the blue sky the contrast was striking, and Maggie gave thanks for her favorite time of the year.

She peered at Carl's front porch as she passed by, but aside from cars in the driveway there was no sign of life outside. She looked forward to their committee meeting and dinner. As she rounded the corner and headed toward her apartment she spotted Lucy walking with Tramp up at the other end of the street. *"That's weird,"* she thought, *"she could have waited for me and we could have gone for a walk together."*

As she opened the front door, she was hit with the second big surprise of the day. Numerous candles flickered from every table, including a small table set up with a fancy table cloth, two place settings, and roses in a vase in the middle with two small tea lights on either side. Soft romantic jazz was playing in the background, and Maggie recognized the Harlem Nocturne from their trip to Gloucester and smiled. Tim stood in the doorway between the living room and the kitchen holding a single red rose in his hand. He approached her with that dimpled smile flashing her way.

"Welcome home, birthday girl. Are you going to close your mouth or the door first?"

He closed the distance between them and wrapped her in his arms, reaching out to close the door behind her as his lips found hers. Maggie never grew tired of the warmth of his lips and the smell of his soap on his skin. He pulled back and gazed into her eyes and brought the red rose to her lips. "Happy birthday, beautiful."

"What about the meeting?"

"Next week. Everyone got the memo – but I might have accidentally left your name off and mentioned to people not to say anything to you."

God, she loved that dimple. "This is the second time today I've been duped. And Lucy?"

Tim laughed. "She was my accomplice. She helped to decorate the place and set up the candles, and let me in an hour ago to start cooking. And I had my mom watching out the window at home to call when she saw you coming. That was Lucy's cue to take Tramp and book it."

"She didn't quite make it around the far corner – I wondered why she had taken him for a walk when I was due home at any time." She looked around the room at the romantic atmosphere and added, "I suspect she's not due home any time soon?"

Tim kissed her forehead. "Liz was parked down the street and they're letting Tramp and Watson have a play date together. I asked her not to rush home."

"I don't remember ever feeling quite so special," Maggie murmured. She placed her hands around the one holding the rose and took a long whiff of the aromatic bloom. "Mr. Lincoln, I presume? I guess your granddad is another accomplice in all this?"

Tim took the rose and placed it on Maggie's plate. "He sends his best wishes. And wonders why I didn't have you to the house for dinner." He led her to the couch and sat back, pulling her down beside him as his thumb caressed her cheek. "Somehow I didn't think he'd add to the ambience I was planning on."

Maggie responded eagerly when he kissed her again, softly at first, and then with more urgency. His hand running down her spine created almost an electric pulse. This sensation of desire was something new to Maggie, and she pulled back to catch her breath. "I'm not sure what button you just hit back there, but I hope you find it again."

Instead, Tim turned her body so that her back was leaning up against his shoulder, and he wrapped his arms around the front of her as he kissed her cheek and smelled her hair. "All in good time, my love. It took me twenty-eight years to find you, and I want to relish every moment along the way."

Maggie closed her eyes and sighed contentedly. "You make me feel so safe – and so loved."

"I hope I always can."

Maggie sniffed the air. "Whatever you're making for dinner is amazing. I still can't believe you did all this."

Tim kissed her hair in reply. "I've been thinking about it all week. And much as I hate letting you go right this minute, I suspect I should go and check on that dinner. I don't think it would help the romance if I burned it and set off the fire alarm."

Maggie chuckled. "Then again, a romance setting off a fire alarm might start some sensational gossip in the neighborhood."

Tim unwrapped his arms from around Maggie and sat up next to her. "Can I get you a glass of wine? Water?"

"I've never been much of a wine drinker."

"How about a wine spritzer then? Light on the alcohol, I promise."

Maggie nodded dreamily. "Do you need help?"

"Just sit here and miss me. I'll be back in just a minute."

"That'll be easy – shall I time you?"

Tim flashed that dimple as he stood up. "Give me five minutes or so." He returned with a glass of club soda mixed with a touch of wine. Strawberry slices floated underneath the ice cube, and one slice of strawberry adorned the rim of the glass. He handed her the glass, holding a glass of plain wine in his other hand.

"To the most beautiful woman in the world. Happy birthday, my love."

Maggie clinked her glass and took a sip of her spritzer. The bubbles tickled her tongue as the sweetness of strawberries enhanced a light flavor of wine. "This is perfect." She looked around the room before meeting Tim's gaze. "All of this is perfect."

He extended his hand, pulling her up as he kissed her once more. "Dinner, my love, is served. And I loved being able to commandeer your kitchen."

He led her over to the table and put his wine glass down as he held the chair for her with his other hand. Once seated, Maggie watched him walk into the kitchen and return with a small cart on wheels. "Where in the world did you find that – and how did you get it here?"

"It was up above the office in the garage. Rolled it around the corner with everything I needed to make dinner. And it doubles nicely as a serving tray." He gestured to the various dishes full of color and rich aromas. "I have a butternut squash stuffed with lentils, spinach, mushrooms, onions, and cheese; mashed potato twirls with garlic, and a loaf of Gino's bread with whipped cinnamon butter." He lifted one of the dishes over to the table to serve her. "May I?"

Maggie admired the gorgeous colors and smells of the stuffed squash and wondered by she'd never tried stuffing one before. Her stomach growled loudly enough for Tim to hear it and for a moment she was embarrassed. He gave her that loving smile, though, and next placed a swirl of garlic mashed potatoes alongside the squash. "I can tell that you're looking forward to dinner – I'm glad."

He placed the loaf of bread between them with a small dish of butter that had a pastel tint from the cinnamon, and then quickly served his own meal before sitting down.

Maggie noticed the small piece of steak alongside his squash and potato. "I'm glad you didn't sacrifice your meat on my account." Her eyes met his, and she felt his gaze reach in and kiss her heart. She picked up her fork and took a bite of her meal, allowing the flavors to mingle in her mouth. "This is amazing. Thank you for making my birthday so memorable."

Tim took a bite of his own squash and grinned. "I can't tell you how much I enjoyed having someone to do all this for. I think you're good for me, Maggie Richmond." He held up his glass again. "Here's to many more birthday celebrations together."

Maggie picked up her glass and clinked his, taking another sip of her wine. For a moment her eating disorder tried to interrupt the moment. *"He'll never stay with you that long. He'll find someone who's prettier and thinner—like that new attorney. Just you wait."* Maggie dismissed the old tape playing inside her head. *"Not tonight,"* she thought, *"Tonight you can take a hike, because I don't believe you. He loves me, and I'm going to enjoy every minute tonight."* With that, she took another bite of her fluffy potatoes, wondering what dessert might involve later on.

* * *

WHEN THEY HAD both finished their meal, Tim loaded the cart and wheeled it back into the kitchen before returning.

"I have a little dessert, but I thought we might work a bit of our dinner off first." That statement almost triggered another old tape in Maggie's head about the need to exercise right after a meal, but she was determined to trust the moment without having to take control. She did, however, raise her eyebrow in a teasing manner. "Just what did you have in mind, mister?"

He laughed as he pulled her close and kissed her forehead. "Honey, we're both way too full to consider that right now, but we can at least dance a bit." She fell into step as they moved to the music. "Not that I haven't been thinking about it," he whispered into her hair.

"Me, too." She swayed to the saxophone that melted her heart and felt more loved than she ever had. Most of all, she felt safe. And confident that nothing would take this away from her – especially not some pissed off eating disorder.

For several songs they moved together to the music, savoring the closeness while anticipating a future that promised even more. Maggie was almost disappointed when Tim stepped back and broke the full contact. "Much as I'd love to dance the night away with you, I do have a little dessert if you're interested. And there might even be a little birthday gift if memory serves."

"You don't have to give me anything," Maggie replied. "This whole evening has been magical."

"Not even if chocolate and strawberries are involved?" he teased.

Maggie ran her finger along Tim's lips. "Hmmm…..that might be motivation enough to stop dancing – at least for a little while."

"Get comfy," Tim said, gesturing toward the couch. "I'll be right back – I promise."

Maggie settled into the plush cushions, kicking her shoes off and pulling her feet up alongside of her. She leaned her arm up on the back cushions to face the spot where Tim would join her. She listened contently to the sounds of silverware and plates, and then the sound of coffee being poured into mugs. Within minutes Tim emerged from the kitchen with a tray in his hands, which he placed on the coffee table before sitting down. "Coffee or cake first?" he asked.

Maggie studied the slices of layered torte – alternating slices of chocolate and white cake were separated by strawberry filling, and the slice had a dollop of whipped cream, fresh strawberries, and dark chocolate drizzle across the top. "Oh my – that's gorgeous. Cake, please." Tim grinned as he handed her a plate and fork and then grabbed his own.

Maggie took her first bite and closed her eyes. "This is heavenly – the perfect balance of strawberry and chocolate without being too sweet. Is this your creation?"

Tim nodded as he chewed his own piece. "One I've been wanting to try for awhile, but my granddad's not partial to fancy desserts. He wants one flavor with one frosting. As soon as I got this night arranged I knew it was the perfect time to try it."

Maggie reached over to grab a sip of coffee. "Your confidence is admirable. What if it hadn't gone well?" she teased.

"Then I'd put my trust in the forgiving nature of the woman I love," he said with a smile. "But I'm glad you like it. Maybe I'll recreate it for Thanksgiving or Christmas. That is, if I can count on you to join us. I'm excited about having real family holidays this year."

"I'm sure this will be the best holiday season you've ever had. I'll work out the details as my folks are coming up for Thanksgiving. Lucy and I usually cook for them here."

"Have them all come – even Liz, if she's free." Tim's face grew more serious. "I want to meet your parents, and I'd like them to spend some time with my family." He grinned. "That sounds almost surreal, saying 'my family' – but I'm planning on lots of family celebrations in the future, and I'm sure hoping that you're going to be a part of those."

As they slowly ate their cake, Maggie's brain was spinning. *"Is he getting ready to propose? God, I'm not sure I'm ready for that yet. What if I relapse and all this magic falls apart?"*

Tim took her empty plate and moved both to the coffee table, and then reached under a napkin on the tray and pulled out a jewelry box and a card. For a moment Maggie held her breath, and then relaxed when she realized it was too big to be a ring box. Tim handed both to her. "Happy birthday, my love. I am so happy that life has brought us together."

Maggie opened her card first, showing a beautiful bouquet of roses with "Happy Birthday to the Woman I Love" on the front. After blushing at the prose and personal words inside, she carefully opened the jewelry box to reveal a heart shaped pendant in rose gold with a single red rose in the center. Several smaller red ruby stones trimmed the edges. Maggie traced the shape with her finger before looking up at Tim. "I can't think of a better symbol for our relationship than the roses – they brought us together, didn't they?" She carefully removed the chain from the corner slits that held them in place and held up the pendant. "Would you do the honors?" she asked as she turned around to face away from him.

"I'd love to," he answered, taking the two ends of the pendant and fastening them at the nape of her neck. "Hmmm, you smell so good," he whispered, kissing her neck as Maggie turned toward him to find his lips once more.

"I'm not sure I want to leave tonight," Tim said. "But I did tell Lucy it was safe to come home at midnight, because I have another idea I'd like to run past you."

Maggie ran her fingers through his hair, loving the soft texture. "You gave us a curfew?" she teased.

Tim's thumb caressed Maggie's cheek. "I don't want to pressure you in any way, but how would you feel about a weekend up in Gloucester at the end of the month? I'd love to fall asleep to the sound of waves outside."

Maggie's butterflies exploded inside, but more from excitement than fear. "I think I'm ready. Nervous, but not scared – and I can't think of any place in the world that I'd rather be when you hold me in your arms for the first time."

"That makes two of us." He leaned in to kiss her deeply. "And now I think I'd better go clean up the dishes before I change my mind about tonight." He got up and carried the tray to the kitchen as Maggie sat anticipating the magic that awaited.

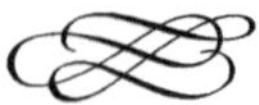

CHAPTER 9

Cassie sat at lunch staring at the remainder of her sandwich. She wanted to throw it away, as the lead balloon in her stomach had lingered throughout the morning. She casually started to wrap it up when she caught Teagan watching her. "What are you doing?"

"Look, Natalie's calling my mom today to set up that family therapy appointment, and my stomach's in knots. I'm gonna eat this later as my afternoon snack at work."

Teagan reached out to hold her arm. "Cassie. Listen to yourself – and then tell me how it sounds from my perspective."

"Jeez. It's not a big deal." She placed the sandwich back into her lunch bag and ate one of her grapes. "See? I'm not restricting – I'm eating my grapes, okay?"

Teagan didn't say a word. Cassie kept looking down, but every time she looked back up it was still there. The gentle, steady, stubborn gaze that refused to believe her justifications. "Why can't you just go to class? You don't have to sit here and babysit me through study hall. And who promoted you to be my food police?"

And still she sat. Cassie got angrier at her lack of response. "What the hell, Teagan? What's *wrong* with you?"

Teagan replied calmly. "Nothing at all. I'm going to sit here and love you, even when you try to push me away. Your eating disorder's screaming inside your head right now."

Cassie glared at her, picking up her water bottle and taking a drink. "I told you, I'm *fine*. At least I was until you started acting like my mother."

"Not your mother. More like Natalie." Cassie winced at the sound of her counselor's name, and Teagan saw it. "So tell me, what would Natalie be doing right now if she was sitting in my place?"

Cassie sat pouting, hating that the truth was clear to see. "She'd be doing the same thing you're doing," she grumbled. "And I hate both of you right now."

"No, you don't. Your eating disorder may hate us, and is trying like hell to win you back, but you're stronger now. And you have so many people fighting beside you."

Cassie's eyes filled with tears and she covered her face with both hands. "I hate this. I hate being scared again. I was so hopeful that day when I left the Phoenix. What the hell happened?"

Teagan moved her chair closer. "Cassie, the road ahead isn't always going to be easy. At the Phoenix you learned that there are going to be ups and downs that are normal. But they gave you all the tools to manage day by day – no matter what life throws at you. You have to trust the journey, okay?"

Cassie wiped the tears away. "Thanks. Why do you put up with me being so nasty sometimes?"

"It's what best friends do," Teagan answered with a smile. "Joanne never gave me the chance to help her, so I'm grateful that you keep letting me in. I promise I'm not going anywhere – even when you tell me to leave."

"What if I'm so much like Joanne that I push you away and end up dying like she did?" Cassie whispered.

"Hey, you may have tons of things in common with Joanne, but that's not one of them. She never admitted that she needed treatment, and lost out on the recovery available. You just keep remembering how you felt that day when you left the Phoenix – because that girl is who I'm looking at right now."

"Some days are just so damn hard."

"Life isn't easy. Handling the college stuff and family tension – plus recovery– is a lot to deal with."

"Sometimes I wonder if the eating disorder will ever stop screaming inside my head."

"I heard once that things scream loudest when they're dying. Maybe that's the right perspective to have on this one."

Cassie looked down at her lunch bag for a moment, then slowly reached in and pulled out the leftover sandwich and unwrapped it. When she caught Teagan's smile she rolled her eyes. "I hate it when you're right. But thanks." She took another bite of her ham and cheese croissant, and told her brain to shut up as she chewed.

* * *

LATER THAT AFTERNOON Cassie found some solace at work. She had the soundtrack to *Hello Dolly* playing as she worked on crafting grapevine wreaths with silk leaves and ribbons for the Thanksgiving display she was working on. The colors were all reds, oranges, and yellows, and their warmth gave her peace. She still missed dance, but art had fired her creativity and helped her body to heal as it needed to. She nodded approval as she finished up the last wreath. *"Not bad,"* she thought. As she went to put the ribbons away one of the songs from the musical began, with the character singing about wearing ribbons down her back, and she sang along as she pictured the slow choreographed movements she had seen in the movie. None of them were intense, and hopefully wouldn't be a trigger for her. She twirled around once and stopped, feeling both nervous and exhilarated. *"Not yet,"* she warned. *"It can't be Cassie dancing – it has to be Irene or Millie."*

She turned around to find Brooke leaning in the doorway with a smile on her face. "How long have you been there?"

"Long enough to know that you belong back on stage. But the dancing has you nervous, doesn't it?"

"Is it that obvious?"

"I know you a little bit better than most," Brooke replied, glancing at the table. "By the way, those are gorgeous. We'll put them out next week with all the other stuff you did. I hope they don't run out; you'll need to change focus and start working on Christmas stuff next."

"I forgot how far ahead you have to plan for everything here. Does it ever stop?"

Brooke smiled. "After the holidays. In fact, I close the shop down on the 23rd of December, and don't come back until after New Year's. A much needed vacation, believe me."

"But then doesn't it just start back up?"

"The only real rush is around Valentine's Day, and that tends to be more the fudge and candles – not as much of the homemade crafts. I'll actually have to cut your hours down then. I can't afford to pay as much when business hits its winter slump--but it's not a reflection of the work you do, trust me."

Cassie pondered Brooke's words, and a smile began to creep across her face. "I've been trying to figure out if doing the show was too much for me right now – but if you can't use me as much after the holidays, I might be able to handle it after all."

"I have no doubt. Hey, your mom will be here in a few minutes." She stopped in the doorway. "And Cassie, you made it crystal clear when I walked in here earlier that you need to audition. I'll even supply the ribbons for your costume."

After she left, Cassie twirled again once more before starting to put things away. Brooke was right. She needed to sing and dance one more time with the peers that had become her friends – and a few that were like family. And at least for the moment, she was excited about the year ahead.

As soon as she got into the car with her mom, her mood changed.

"Hi honey. Is everything okay? I got a call from Natalie today."

Cassie felt like the wind had been sucked out of her in an instant. For a couple of hours she had escaped into the magic of music and art, and now the world of college decisions and family pressures had barged in to bring her back to reality.

"She said she was gonna call this week," Cassie responded nervously. "What did she say?"

Her mom pulled out onto Main Street for the short ride home. "Why don't we table the discussion until after dinner? That way you can keep your peaceful routine."

"Whatever." Inside, her brain was spinning. *Peaceful routine – yeah, right, mom. What did Natalie say? And what will Dad say? Why can't you tell me now so I can be more prepared?* She looked out the window as her mom drove in silence.

Her mom tried to change the subject. "What did you work on at Brooke's?"

Cassie sighed. Her mom either had no idea that she had hit a trigger or was pretending ignorance to avoid the conversation. *"Fine. Two can play that game."* "Nothing special. Just finished up more wreaths for the fall display next week."

"You sure seem to like working there – it's provided a creative outlet for you."

"Brooke's been a great boss."

Her mom pulled into their driveway and smiled as she turned the car off. "I hope the job hasn't been too much of a stress on your school schedule. But we'll talk about that tonight. You can start on your homework until dinner time. Dad should be home soon, and we can sit down and chat afterwards, okay?"

"I guess. But why can't you tell me now about Natalie's call?"

Her mom opened the car door. "No point in having to go through everything twice; it's easier to wait."

"Easier for you," Cassie thought as she got out and closed the car door.

The next hour waiting for dinner proved impossible for studying. Cassie's brain had resumed the battle from earlier in the day, and she was losing this time. *"I won't go down for dinner; they can't make me."* She closed her laptop and considered doing some sit ups. *"You don't deserve to eat. Look at all the money your parents have spent on the Phoenix, and how much more college will cost – and you'll fail at both. Focus on the one thing you can control – and that's getting thin again."*

Cassie sat down on the floor and did five sit ups. *"Harder than it used to be? You've put on a ton of weight since you came home, and you're so out of shape. No point in trying out for the show because they'll never give you the role if you can't dance. Do more sit ups and you might have a chance."*

Cassie did a couple more before her gaze fell on the photo of her and Teagan together with her grandmother after the final show of *Kiss Me, Kate* the previous spring. Tears filled her eyes as she stood up and walked over to pick it up. *"Look at how much fatter you are now then back then."* Cassie could hear her eating disorder screaming in her head, but the longer she gazed at the photo the more she tried to ignore the voices.

"I need help," she realized, reaching for her phone. While her first instinct was to call Teagan, the contact she brought up was Maggie. Much as Teagan loved her and supported her in every aspect that she could, only Maggie could truly understand the battle going on in her head. She sent a quick text, not wanting to bother her, but praying that Maggie would call back.

The phone rang within seconds, and Cassie answered it with urgency.

"What's going on?" Maggie inquired.

"I'm having the crappiest day I've had since leaving the Phoenix, and I'm ready to lose it. I need help."

The care in Maggie's voice was immediate. "Where are you? Do you want me to come and pick you up?"

Cassie desperately wanted that – any escape from the place she was in. However, she knew that leaving right before dinner would only make things worse. "I don't know what to do. I'm up in my room and dinner's gonna be ready any minute, but I don't want to eat anything. I *really* don't want to eat. It hasn't been this strong since I first got to the Phoenix. It's like the last five months got erased and I'm right back where I started from."

"First of all, take a slow deep breath," Maggie instructed. "Like we do in yoga. Your emotions are *normal*. Recovery is gonna have those crappy days when you feel like a failure. But that's the lie talking. The stronger you get, the harder it has to fight. Sounds like you have something going on that distracted you enough to let the old voices out of their cage. So what's going on?"

Cassie took the deep breath, and then another. Maggie understood where she was. Knowing that was enough to offer hope. Maggie had years of recovery, yet still knew about the crappy days.

"My mom got a call from Natalie today to schedule a family therapy meeting. I knew it was coming, but all my mom told me was that we'll talk about it after dad's home."

"Giving your brain tons of time to hijack your afternoon, huh?" Maggie asked.

"I think it was on a roll all day. I had a tough time today. I tried to restrict my lunch, and was nasty to Teagan in the process."

"I suspect Teagan held her own and threw it right back at you, didn't she?"

"Yeah….she's damn stubborn," Cassie said, smiling a bit. "She got me through it, though. And work was fine until mom showed up, and then one line about the phone call triggered all this. I hate the idea of having to go down stairs."

"Do you want me to come up for the meeting? I could be the referee if you need one, but I think you're strong enough to manage on your own. Why don't you talk through what you're afraid of? It may be that your fears are unfounded."

"I'm afraid to tell my dad that I want a gap year. That's the whole reason for seeing Natalie. But how do I not say something tonight? And then when I *do* my dad will blow a gasket. He's been on me for days to finish all this college stuff."

"Why do you think it has to come out before your meeting with Natalie?"

Cassie pondered Maggie's question before answering. "They're gonna ask why I wanted Natalie to schedule a meeting. And they'll want to find a solution together – like they don't need Natalie."

"First of all," Maggie replied, "Natalie might not have said anything about you. Your folks might be wondering why Natalie has asked them to come in."

"But she'd have had to give a reason for a family session."

"That's true – but it might be a normal thing after several months to have a family session to share how things are going."

Cassie calmed down a bit. "I suppose that's possible. But what if they bring up college? It's all my dad ever talks about."

"How do you think Cassie in recovery would answer that?"

Maggie's questions were bringing Cassie back to the present moment. "I'd probably tell them that I'm stressed over various things right now and Natalie's perspective might be valuable in sorting it out. Does that sound somewhat rational?"

"Cassie, it's how you're feeling. Simply mention your stress and that you appreciate their willingness to continue supporting your recovery with another family session. Do you think you can do that?"

"I...guess," Cassie stammered. "But what if I have those sudden urges to refuse food again?"

"Then text me. I'll be in a meeting so be sure you text rather than call."

"I'll be okay. I wouldn't want to interrupt you if you're in a meeting."

"The hell you won't," Maggie replied firmly. "I don't care if you're in the middle of dinner. One text and I'll be there in ten minutes to help you through it... But remember that the person going down the stairs isn't the Cassie from five months ago. She's the Cassie who's worked her butt off in these early stages of recovery. Do you want to piss that Cassie off?"

Cassie knew that Maggie heard her chuckle. "Thanks. You always say the right thing. I promise I'll text if I need you. I guess I can manage on my own – even with the college crap – if our meeting with Natalie is only a day or two away."

"I think you can, too. And remember, taking steps in all the college applications does not automatically mean that you have to follow through on the results. Your head is trying to tell you that it's a done deal, and that's not true. You might be surprised to find your parents supportive of a gap year."

"Doesn't seem like it. My dad's been on my case for weeks."

"Again, his motivation is coming from thinking that you are going next year – and he sees the deadlines approaching. Once you meet with Natalie, he might loosen up when he sees that the deadlines aren't straight ahead."

Cassie heard her mom calling her for dinner. "Hey, I guess I gotta go. Mom just called up that dinner was ready. Thanks, Maggie. Sometimes you're a life saver."

"Text me anytime if you need me. And be sure to check in later to tell me how you're doing, okay?"

"I will. And thanks again." She hung up and took a deep breath, recognizing that it was okay to be scared, and that it didn't mean that a relapse was imminent. For now, that was enough.

CHAPTER 10

That night Maggie got to the library for the planning meeting to find Teagan chatting with Brian at the front desk. "I guess your dad got you to join us, huh?"

The redhead nodded. "Why not? It didn't sound like a ton of extra time, and it'll be an asset on my college applications. Are you on your way down now? I'll walk with you."

They both said goodbye to Brian and proceeded down the stairs to find only Brooke and Jim Costanzo not there yet. Maggie introduced Teagan to those she didn't know and they grabbed two seats together next to Blake Newton, who was like a second dad to Teagan.

Maggie grabbed Tim's attention and smiled as his face lit up. She held up her phone before placing it on the table. "I need to keep this in front of me tonight in case an urgent text comes through. Sorry."

Tim's expression changed to concern. "Everything okay?"

"A client I'm working with might have an issue that needs immediate attention. If a text comes through I'll have to leave to deal with it – I hope you understand."

He nodded as Teagan leaned toward Maggie. "Is everything okay? She had a rough day today."

"I think so, but I wanted to give her reassurance if she needed it. She said you really helped her through lunch today."

"I wish I could do more," admitted Teagan. "I'll be glad when the whole college thing is resolved."

At that point, Brooke and Jim both arrived, and Maggie was content seeing Jim take the empty seat next to Amanda. She greeted him with a smile as Tim began the meeting. After updates from Jim on the renovations, Rich O'Sullivan brought up the financial status. "We've gotten some solid community support from a few businesses, and there are a couple of grants likely to come in, but I think we need to look at some fundraising possibilities to involve more of the overall community. Any ideas?"

Several raised their hands, suggesting ideas including a bulk mailing, a bingo game, and raffle tickets. Brooke made the suggestion that made everyone in the room take notice. "What about a community Christmas celebration to bring the whole town together?"

Amanda agreed. "I like it – but would you sell tickets to make money?"

Brooke shook her head. "We could have donation baskets set up, but also do a huge basket raffle during the month leading up to it. Every business could create a basket and sell raffle tickets up until the event, and then bring the basket to a central spot – or if they'd prefer, they could sponsor a basket that someone else could create. I've seen it done successfully in other communities."

Tim nodded. "It sounds like a great project – but we'd need to coordinate it. Not just a basket raffle, but the whole community Christmas – that sounds exactly what Caldwell needs to support the community center." He turned to Jim Costanzo. "I don't suppose the renovations would be done enough to have the event right in the building, would they?"

"I'm reluctant to open it up with construction getting under way; that might bring some possible liabilities."

Teagan raised her hand. "I'm not sure I can offer suggestions at my first meeting, but what about having something in the park? Maybe sing some Christmas carols and set up a few tables for the baskets?"

"How about a visit from Santa for the little kids?" Amanda offered.

"And what about lighting a Christmas tree?" Maggie suggested.

All of a sudden everyone was talking avidly about possibilities, and Maggie could see how excited Tim was. By the end of the meeting the basic plans for a "Christmas in Caldwell" event were down on paper, and everyone had various tasks to complete. As folks left, Maggie watched Tim thank each person for their suggestions during the meeting and admired what a natural leader he was.

She and Rich O'Sullivan were the last two remaining, and as the latter had a couple of things he wanted to discuss with Tim, Maggie offered to wait up at the desk. She knew she'd find Teagan waiting for her dad as well, and proceeded upstairs to hear Brian's laughter. Sure enough, the two of them were chatting at the front desk with Ken Roberts, who was filling Brian in on the ideas from the meeting.

When Teagan caught Maggie's eye, she gestured to a table in the reference area. "Wanna sit and chat? They might be another ten minutes or so."

"I'd like that," Maggie replied, following Teagan to two chairs next to the magazine rack selection.

Teagan plopped down on one as she surveyed the now empty reference section. "Normally I'd introduce you to my personal table there in the back, but with only a few minutes before closing I figure these will do. So your phone stayed quiet during the meeting; I guess that's a good thing, huh?"

Maggie nodded. "I'm glad she got through the evening. I told her to check in tonight, so I'll give her a few minutes before contacting her. Her dad works late sometimes and I'd hate to text in the middle of their chat. Thanks again for being there during the day."

"I wish I could give her the strength to turn off those voices in her head – most of the time she's doing well."

"I agree," Maggie replied. "And I think Cassie will find it gets easier and easier over time to recognize the eating disorder thoughts and respond differently."

"She counts on you so much for guidance. You understand things so much better than anyone else can."

"Don't sell yourself short. You've been a rock for Cassie since she was first diagnosed."

"I think she has an amazing support team, doesn't she? Now if communication with her dad can improve she'll be even stronger."

"Couldn't agree more. So are you excited about seeing Fiddler this Friday?"

Teagan's eyes twinkled as her face lit up. "You have no idea! And I love that you and Tim's family got tickets as well. Ida was talking non-stop about seeing Carl again. I think those two built quite a friendship while he was at the Manor."

"Oh, it's mutual, believe me. Carl often brings up her name, and Tim and Sharon have walked him up to visit a couple of times. Hard to believe he had a heart attack just a few months ago."

"Ida says he's a different person now that Sharon and Tim are back in his life," Teagan replied. "Certainly not much of a curmudgeon these days, is he?"

"Far from it." Maggie's gaze fell upon Tim and Rich heading down the hall. "I guess the two of them are all set. I enjoyed chatting – I guess I'll see you in Brentwood on Friday night."

"Yup. Rehearsal tomorrow, and then I'll work on Saturday. And I'll check with some of the theater kids to see if they might like to sing Christmas carols for the big celebration in the park. That's gonna be one awesome event!"

Maggie smiled as Tim joined them. "Yeah, I have this awesome boyfriend who knows how to make this great little town even better."

Tim wrapped his arm around Maggie's shoulder. "I hear he's even planning on sticking around long after the event's over," he teased.

"Even better yet," Maggie replied with a squeeze. "Especially for me."

CHAPTER 11

The next day Cassie found herself in her favorite chair in Natalie's office; it was a big plush chair with soft paisley fabric, and most days she could sink into it and feel safe. Today, however, she wished the chair would envelop her and make her disappear, as her parents were seated on the loveseat to her left. Her mom sat closest to her, and nervously played with the tassel on the corner of the seat cushion. Her dad sat next to her, looking stiff and uncomfortable. He had always hated family therapy sessions, and didn't appear to be thrilled to be back at the Phoenix Center. Natalie sat to Cassie's right and gave her a reassuring smile before she addressed Mr. and Mrs. Durand.

"I appreciate you both for being able to come in on such short notice," she began. "Cassie's been concerned about increasing tension at home right now, and I thought a family session might help to ease the adjustments you're all facing at this time."

Frank squirmed a bit. "I thought family sessions ended when Cassie came home. I'm not sure I can be here every time there's a little tension at home; I have a busy job and am up for a big promotion."

Cassie squeezed the big cushion she held in front of her. *This was a huge mistake. He's never gonna listen, and now you've pissed him off for wasting his time."*

"The fact you could make the time today speaks volumes about the commitment you've made to your daughter's recovery," Natalie shared, "and I know Cassie wouldn't have made as much progress had you and Eliana not been there for her."

Cassie was amazed at how Natalie's gentle manner could break down the walls between them. While her dad was never a big believer in the effectiveness of family therapy, he had never missed a scheduled session. Now Natalie was giving him the same positive feedback she always gave to Cassie before delving into problem areas. Cassie had felt stress all day at school, and the last thing she wanted was for her father to shut down before they started.

Eliana spoke up. "We've tried to keep the structure we learned here at the Phoenix to give Cassie a sense of security. But we're also trying to give her more choices since she's been doing so well. I think returning to school and having the daily structure change has been difficult at times."

"That's an excellent insight," Natalie pointed out, and then addressed Cassie. "Perhaps you can share how you're feeling with the changes going on right now. I think your parents want to know where you're coming from so they can continue to offer what you need for recovery."

Cassie bit her lip as her parents watched her expectantly. For a moment the tapes inside her head screamed at her to keep everything inside, but instead she took a deep breath before answering. "I wouldn't be where I am if it weren't for all the support you both have given me. And the first month home was scary, but I felt safe. You guys stepped up and gave me what I needed."

Her mom reached over and patted her knee. "Honey, all we want is for you to get better and lead a normal life. We know you can do it."

Her father nodded. "We were scared, too – scared we might have lost you. But now you're finding your way. And knowing that next year you'll be off on your own we want to give you time now to start working on those goals. It takes time, but there are steps you have to take along the way to get there."

Cassie's stomach tightened as he talked. *"It's all about college to him,"* she thought. *"And I'll never be successful getting there."*

She knew Natalie had picked up on the subtle reaction, and she braced herself for the impending explosion. Natalie spoke calmly to her parents. "It's clear that you both want Cassie to move forward and beat this eating disorder that keeps trying to hold her back."

Cassie held her breath. *"This is it. She's gonna unplug the dam and open Pandora's Box."* She wanted to bury her face into the pillow she was squeezing, but she knew she'd have to speak in a moment.

Again, Natalie brought a sense of calm. "I know Cassie's high school graduation will be one of your happiest memories, am I right?"

Cassie's mom beamed at her. "Aside from her wedding day, I can't imagine anything more wonderful."

Frank echoed her enthusiasm. "It'll be one of the proudest days of my life when she gets her diploma and is set for next year – she'll be the first in the family to go to college, you know."

"But what if Cassie's dream doesn't quite match up with the one you have in your mind?"

Cassie's father scowled. "What do you mean? We've been talking about it a lot, and I know Cassie's a little behind in some of the planning, but I know she's excited about what lies ahead." He shifted his attention to Cassie. "Aren't you, honey?"

Cassie had been trying to breathe, feeling the panic rising inside and wanting to bolt. Afraid to look at them in the eyes, she sank down further in her chair and spoke the words she'd been wanting to scream for the past two weeks. "I....don't think I'm ready for college yet." She looked to Natalie who smiled with reassurance. "I want to take a gap year after graduating."

She saw her father's moment of disappointment before leaning back on the loveseat, slightly shaking his head. "A *gap* year? Why would you want a gap year? It's like going backwards in recovery."

Cassie's mom was more sympathetic. "Honey, I know it's scary right now."

Cassie's eyes filled with tears. "I don't think you guys understand how hard it is to get through the day sometimes. I was doing okay at first – you guys were always home. I hated you some days, but I felt safe."

Her mom reached over and patted her knee. "I know it hasn't been easy, honey."

Cassie hugged the chair cushion hard. "Since school started I've barely managed what my eating disorder's thrown at me; but having to look ahead? I'm scared it'll push me right into a relapse."

She watched her father, sitting with arms crossed and shaking his head. "Cassie, a gap year is like surrendering—you're letting the eating disorder win."

Natalie chose to offer some insight. "What I'm hearing from all of you is the common goal is for Cassie to succeed in college – and the huge transition involved. Am I right?" When all three nodded, she continued. "The conflict I'm seeing, however, is a difference in perspective. Frank, you and Eliana believe college is the next step after high school, and by not preparing right now Cassie is losing to her eating disorder. Is that an accurate summary?"

Eliana nodded. "We want her to be happy. She's come so far."

Cassie felt somewhat stronger hearing Natalie's calm and straight-forward manner. She watched her parents as her counselor contin-ued. "What I'm hearing from Cassie is she recognizes how big a step college is, but she's not feeling ready to take it quite yet." She turned to Cassie and gestured with her eyes to address her parents inde-pendently.

"Dad, I don't look at taking a gap year as a failure, or a step back-wards. I *do* want to go to college – but I want to go when I feel strong enough to make it." Once the words were out, Cassie's grip on the pillow tightened as she met her father's gaze.

Her father leaned forward. "But honey, meeting life's challenges is what *makes* us stronger. I don't understand why you're giving in to those fears—"

"Doesn't the fact my stomach turns to lead every time we sit down tell you I'm not ready?" Cassie spat out. "It's like every fiber in my being is screaming at me to *stop,* and those are huge red flags telling me there's stuff I have to deal with before I can move forward." As soon as the words were out, Cassie sank back into her chair. *"Now you've done it. He'll shut right down now and all this will be for nothing."*

As she watched her father tense up, Natalie gently intervened. "I think what Cassie is trying to explain is that recovery isn't linear. There's not always going to be forward movement. Perhaps a compromise you can all consider is to have Cassie take a break and give her a little peace right now. But then next year," she turned toward Cassie, "you might consider taking a class or two to see how it goes."

Cassie sat up a little straighter. She'd been looking at the issue in black and white, when maybe there was a little gray. "I hadn't thought about going part time. That….*might* work."

She tried to read her dad's expression. For a moment he seemed doubtful, but then she was surprised to see it soften a bit. "Honey, if starting out part time will help you, then we can look at that. And for now, we can back off a little getting applications out."

Cassie's mom chimed in. "Maybe pull them out again in the spring?"

Her dad put his finger up to grab her attention. *"But –* in the meantime, since we've already paid for it, would you at least be open to getting the SATs out of the way?"

Natalie smiled at her. "Sounds like they're trying to compromise; can you meet them halfway?"

Cassie thought for a moment. "I guess I could manage the SATs."

Her mom reached over and squeezed her hand. "I'm glad we came in today. It feels like some of the sessions before you came home. This was a good idea -- for *all* of us."

Cassie smiled weakly. Her mom was always the optimist. She bit her lip as her dad sat back and once again crossed his arms. *"I got through this battle, at least,"* she thought. *"But I suspect this conflict is far from over."*

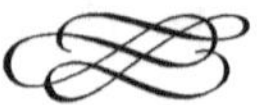

CHAPTER 12

*M*aggie reached for her phone as Tim turned down the music. They were on their way to Gloucester, but Maggie had told him Cassie would be checking in after her therapy session. She smiled at him as she answered the call. "How did it go?"

Cassie's voice wavered on the other end. "I survived – I guess that's something."

"That's a huge thing. I imagine your brain was screaming at you through the whole meeting telling you it was all your fault. Am I right?"

"I'm so glad you understand," Cassie replied. "I'm not used to confronting my dad."

"But you *did*. And I'm sure Natalie helped as referee?"

"I couldn't have done it without her," Cassie affirmed. "And she has me going back next week to talk things through a little more."

Maggie heard the relief in Cassie's voice. "So overall, how did your dad take it?"

"He was disappointed—and I still don't think he agrees with me—but he's okay with holding off on college stuff for awhile."

"I imagine you have a lot of mixed emotions right now?"

Cassie sighed on the other end. "I guess I was dreaming to think it would all go away, huh?"

"You're well aware the eating disorder won't slink away – but today was a huge win, so don't sell yourself short. How did the meeting resolve?"

Cassie's voice was stronger as she replied. "Natalie suggested starting with only a class or two in the fall."

"Sounds like Natalie – she's always steering you toward positive choices, isn't she?" She watched as Tim glanced her way and flashed that dimple. *Kind of like she did with me in suggesting this weekend,* she thought.

"I hadn't even thought it," Cassie said. "And yet it made perfect sense once she suggested it."

"How did your dad react to it?"

"I'm not sure he's entirely behind it, but at least for now he's met me halfway."

"Look, I know your brain will still tell you he thinks you're screwing up, but you have to recognize he and your mom are also being challenged to change long held beliefs. So be gentle with them as well as yourself, okay? And if you need to call me over the weekend, you know I'm only a text away."

She saw Tim raise his eyebrow a bit as Cassie answered. "Ah, knowing you're on your way to Gloucester right now, you'll be the *last* person I call in the next two days."

Maggie laughed out loud. "But if you should really need to—"

"I have both Natalie and Teagan on call for the weekend, and I'm feeling like I'll be okay. If nothing else, I know my dad is most likely working this weekend, so I'll enjoy the respite. Besides, I'll be thinking of you and smiling."

Maggie felt herself blush. "I bet you will, too."

"I hope you have a wonderful weekend. It's obvious Tim is head over heels in love with you – so don't *you* listen when your own eating disorder starts talking, okay?"

"I've coached you well, haven't I?"

"Hmm-hmm. So go and enjoy your romantic weekend. And tell Tim I wouldn't *dream* of calling," she teased. "Talk to you soon."

"Sounds good. And I'll tell him," Maggie murmured. "Bye, Cassie."

As she turned her phone off, Tim grinned. "Tell me what?"

For the second time Maggie felt herself blush. "She thinks you're awesome and she wouldn't dream of calling this weekend."

Tim reached over for her hand and brought it to his lips and kissed the back of it. "I must admit I'm looking forward to some quiet time with no interruptions from anyone." He glanced in the rearview mirror at Tramp relaxing in the back seat. "That includes you, by the way," as the thump of Tramp's wagging tail responded. He glanced back toward Maggie and smiled as he released her hand. "But I'd be lying if I said I wasn't a little bit nervous."

Maggie sighed. "Thank God; I was afraid it might only be me." She reached up to rest her hand on the back of his neck and curled her fingers into his hair. "But I can't think of anyone I'd rather be nervous with."

His dimpled grin calmed her nerves. "I hope you're okay with not going straight to the townhouse. I know we're both anticipating the evening ahead, but I'd like us to enjoy a romantic dinner and gorgeous sunset first if you're up for it."

"I wondered how I'd manage watching you cook without my brain screaming at me."

"There's another little jewel I wanna share with you while we're up here. It's a little hole in the wall, but they have outdoor seating and one of the best sunsets over the water you could ask for. And their onion rings and French fries might satisfy your appetite while I grab a few clams."

Maggie sat up a little confused and brought her hand back to her lap. "Wait a minute. How can we see a sunset over the water if Gloucester is on the *east* coast?"

Tim grinned. "Gloucester is part of Cape Ann, so there are beaches on both the east and west side. And up at the top there's Rockport-- which has a number of places I still have to take you to – including this little shanty restaurant right on the water. I hope you're up for it."

Her voice softened. "I'm not sure how hungry I'll be, but onion rings and fries sound perfect with a sunset thrown in."

"Tomorrow morning I'll cook you breakfast," Tim said, "although I can't promise we'll be up to see the sunrise." He reached over and squeezed her hand as he continued driving.

Maggie felt the butterflies start churning inside as she smiled in response.

* * *

NEITHER THE FOOD nor the sunset were a disappointment. Maggie reached for another onion ring as the sound of the surf lapping the rocks provided a steady accompaniment to the chatter of dinner guests and children returning from climbing the rocks. The salt air mingled with the scents of fried seafood, seaweed, and a faint whiff of tobacco from a pipe an older gentleman puffed on at the next table.

Tim had sat beside her rather than across the picnic table so they could both enjoy the masterpiece being painted in the sky. As the sun got lower on the horizon, scattered clouds unfolded vibrant pinks, oranges, yellows, and eventually pastel lavenders no camera would ever do justice to. Nonetheless, Maggie clicked several shots before a woman at the next table offered to take a shot of her and Tim together with the sunset behind them. Throughout it all, Tramp sat at her feet, content with the cheeseburger they'd bought him and the treats Maggie had brought along from home.

They now sat in silence aware of other diners throwing trash away as they headed back to their cars. Maggie finished her last French fry as she watched them go. "I must admit I envy them a little, being able to stop here for dinner as often as we visit Gino's.

Tim nodded. "His food might be the best in Caldwell, but he can't match this view. I used to come here after a rough day at the office; by the time the sun went down the stress had evaporated. I'm glad I got to share it with you." He slid his arm around her waist and she rested her head on his shoulder. "You warm enough?"

"For now. The waves sound louder now as folks are leaving."

"Tide's coming in," Tim responded. "It'll start cooling off quickly as twilight settles in, so let me know if you need my sweatshirt, okay?" He pulled her a little closer to him. "In the meantime, I don't mind keeping you warm."

His lips found hers and the smell of his soap mingled with the taste of salt on his lips. Maggie reached up with one hand to caress the side of his face until the kiss ended. He cupped her chin with his free hand. "God, I love you, Maggie Richmond. And I can't wait to hear those waves later on."

Maggie knew her eating disorder would invade her thoughts as the evening progressed, but for the moment she focused on the man kissing her eyelids, nose, and cheeks. By the time they found her lips again she was eager to respond. She pulled away and softly touched her fingers to his lips. "I love you so much," she said breathlessly. "And I think it's time to head back to Gloucester now." He kissed her fingertips and smiled just enough to tease her with a slight hint of the dimple she loved.

* * *

WHEN THEY GOT close to Tim's townhouse Maggie noted Tramp sitting up and looking out the window. "I guess he remembers being here," she said with a smile, reaching back to scratch his head as Tramp crossed from one side of the back seat to the other.

"Their sense of smell is so much stronger than ours," Tim added. "And I'm glad he's excited to be back – we'll have to let him run on the beach tomorrow."

By the time they pulled in to Tim's parking spot Maggie felt the butterflies in her stomach and the thoughts in her head getting stronger. She had tried to block them out with the quiet jazz on the way back from Rockport, but now with only the sounds of the surf they were tougher to ignore. *"You'll never make him happy,"* her eating disorder taunted. *"He'll find someone else who isn't fat like you are and knows how to control her food."*

"You okay?" Tim asked gently as they watched Tramp sniffing the flower beds and revisiting the landscaped hedges. "You've been quiet during the ride."

"I guess my nerves started to kick in," she said shyly, looking up into his eyes. "But I'm still glad to be here."

He wrapped his arms around her and held her for a moment, and Maggie tried to focus on his steady heartbeat as she took a slow deep breath. *"I can trust him,"* she thought, *"even if it means being honest about the conflict in my brain."* She followed him inside, admiring again the gorgeous view of Gloucester harbor from the huge sliding glass doors leading to the patio. "I'd forgotten how beautiful it was," she said as he unlocked the door and gestured for her to step outside.

"Why don't you enjoy the view while I make a couple of wine spritzers?"

Maggie shook her head as she gave him a smile. "Let me give Tramp some dinner first – and then I'll be happy to comply."

Within minutes, Tramp had chosen to curl up inside the sliding door while she and Tim were curled up outside on the glider with strawberry wine spritzers. Maggie had her legs curled up underneath her and tried to relax with Tim's arm wrapped around her under the quilt they shared. She sipped her wine and felt the bubbles tickle her tongue. *"Enjoy your drink,"* her eating disorder teased, *"but no amount of alcohol is gonna make him think you're beautiful."* She clenched her glass a little tighter and tried to focus on the steady sound of the surf.

Tim's quiet voice finally cut through the silence. "You wanna tell me what's going on? Because you've been noticeably quiet since we left Rockport." He put his glass down on the end table beside him and gently lifted her chin with his hand to meet his gaze. "You *do* know there's no pressure, don't you?"

Maggie's eyes teared up with the loving concern on his face. She took a deep breath as she sat up straighter to face him. "It's not what you think," she began. "I've been trying to keep the voices in my head at bay, and not doing a great job at the moment." She took another sip of her drink before turning to put it on the side table, and then faced him again. "It's not you – I promise."

He reached out and took her hand, resting both on her leg as he caressed her shoulder with the arm still behind her. "Honey, I can only imagine what your eating disorder might be trying to tell you tonight, but I'm sure it's not anything positive, is it?"

Maggie's heart warmed a bit hearing him recognize the problem before she could explain it. "I love how you know me so well."

"Look," he said gently, "I knew when we started dating you and your eating disorder were sort of a package deal. But I need you to feel safe enough to share *whatever's* in your head tonight, okay?"

Biting her lip, Maggie nodded. "I'll try, but it's ….not easy." As Tim waited patiently, she clenched her fists, summoning her strength to share her innermost fears. "No one's ever seen me naked – well, except the nurses at the Phoenix Center – and that wasn't exactly romantic." She saw Tim's slight smile and stumbled on, her heart pounding inside her chest. "My brain's been screaming at me that you'll think I'm fat and ugly and everything will be ruined…." Her sentence crumpled at the end as tears spilled over, and she buried her face in the crook of his neck as he wrapped his arms around her.

"Shhhh," he whispered into her hair. "It's gonna be okay."

As he stroked her hair Maggie listened to the sound of the waves and her heartbeat slowed to match his. *At least he knows now how screwed up I am…and he'll never want this package deal.*

Instead, Tim held her in silence until she could feel her body relax a bit. When he pulled back to look at her, she met his warm and steady gaze.

He brushed a few straggles of her hair back behind her ear. "First of all, thank you for trusting me enough to let me in – I know it wasn't easy. I hope your eating disorder is listening when I tell you how much I love you and how beautiful you are."

Maggie nodded, still holding his gaze. "I know it in my heart…..but try telling my head."

Tim chuckled. "I did……and I'll keep telling it the same thing over and over again as many times as you need to hear it. What is it you're always telling Cassie? You have to listen to the people you love and trust and rely on them to help you stop believing the lies?"

Maggie chuckled, snuggling in a little closer as her fears began to melt away. "I guess I should take my own advice, huh?"

"Look, I know you may never completely overcome the battles with anorexia, but I'm not going anywhere, Maggie. And I'll help you fight them if you let me….do you trust me?"

Maggie gazed into his eyes and trembled a bit. "I've never trusted anyone more in my life…or loved anyone more."

His kiss was warm as it melted away her fears and rekindled the desire. As their kiss deepened Maggie wrapped her arms around Tim's neck and pushed the eating disorder firmly aside. Tonight she was going to listen to the voice she trusted and loved. "Let's go inside," she whispered.

His loving gaze was all the answer she needed as he stood up and pulled her close.

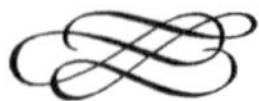

CHAPTER 13

Cassie woke up Saturday morning feeling more peaceful. With only a week before the SATs, she had at least found a compromise with her parents, lightening some of the pressure. She got up for breakfast, knowing her scheduled yoga class would give her the motivation to get through her meal. Her mom was seated at the table with coffee and plain oatmeal, and she gestured toward the stove when she saw Cassie. "I left yours in the pot so it would stay warm. Why don't you try scooping it out today and cutting up whatever fruit you want – it's the exact amount I give you every day."

Cassie approached the empty bowl on the counter with apples and bananas within reach, a dish of hard boiled eggs, some nut butter, and a still warm pot of oatmeal covered on the stove. She hadn't plated her own food since she'd been home, and found herself frozen in place staring at the pot.

Sensing her hesitation, her mom got up and came over to wrap one arm around her shoulders. "It's the exact amount you always eat – all you have to do is to put it into the bowl. I'll stand here with you if you want. But I think you're ready to start taking baby steps."

Cassie tried to conjure up some confidence. *"I can do this. It's not any extra food – it shouldn't matter who's holding the spoon to scrape it into the bowl. And I wanna go to yoga.*" She gingerly picked up the handle of the pot and lifted the lid. Warm steam filled her nostrils with cinnamon and apple pie spice. She took a deep breath and visualized herself eating each bite mindfully, knowing it was needed body fuel for a healthy life. She emptied the oatmeal mix into the bowl and placed the empty pot back onto the stove.

Her mom pointed to a small dish containing a glob of chocolate-hazelnut butter. "A quarter cup – all measured out – but ready for you to practice plating again." Cassie found her mom's voice firm but soothing, and scraped the creamy mixture on top of the oatmeal. She ignored the quiet voices inside pointing out the high fat content in peanut and nut butters and defiantly ran her finger along the bottom of the smaller dish and licked the remaining butter from her finger. She smiled at her mom. "I'm going to have a Granny Smith today." Simply stating her choice was empowering. She sliced the apple into pieces and arranged them around the outside of the oatmeal, noting how the nut butter was melting a bit with little rivulets forming over the oatmeal. She picked up the bowl and took a long whiff, holding the warmth in her hands as she brought it to the table.

Her mom brought her a cup of coffee and a hard-boiled egg before sitting down beside her. "I'm proud of you, honey. I knew you could do it. Now enjoy breakfast and I'll get you to yoga."

Cassie took her first bite of oatmeal, enjoying the sweetness of chocolate hazelnut with the tartness of the apple. "Hmmm, I love the hazelnut. I woke up hungry this morning."

"I'm glad you called Natalie to have us meet with you. We haven't had a family session in a long time, and I think we all needed it. How are you feeling this morning?"

Cassie took another bite and smiled. "Better than I've felt in weeks. I know it didn't solve everything, but I'm glad we found a compromise for now." She paused a moment, and then added, "I hope Dad wasn't too disappointed. I could see it in his eyes when I first told you."

"Honey, he'll be fine. We both want you to be healthy and happy, and if we need to change our expectations a bit we'll manage okay.

And you agreeing to the SATs meant a lot to him. He only wants the best for his little girl."

"I know that. And I do love him – even though I don't always show it. Where is he, by the way?"

"He drove Philip over to Seth's house before heading into Boston for the day."

Cassie shook her head. "He's working so much – now he's going in on weekends?"

"He really wants the big promotion coming up, and you know how your father is when he sets a goal. He'll give it everything he's got."

Cassie got quiet. "If he gets it, will we have to move again?" Memories of having to leave Houston and move to Massachusetts flew to the surface, and Cassie shuddered. "I don't know if I could do that again, mom."

Her mom came over and kissed the top of her head. "I asked him the same thing; I don't want to leave here either. This is the home I lived in when I was younger – and I want to stay close to your grandmother. He knows that. Go on, finish up now – you don't want to be late."

Cassie scooped out the last couple of bites of breakfast and decided to focus on the positive today. She rinsed out her bowl and went upstairs to brush her teeth. She caught her reflection in the mirror in the hallway as she came down the stairs and stopped to look at herself. After weeks of practicing affirmations every morning, she forced a smile at the distorted image she still saw. "Today I'm gonna be healthy, Cassie Durand, and there's not one damn thing you can do about it." With a defiant smile, she returned to the kitchen where her mom was waiting to leave.

* * *

YOGA CLASS WAS her favorite part of the week. Some of the poses reminded her so much of ballet moves, and while she longed at times to break out into a pirouette or an arabesque, she loved how yoga seemed to ground her – body, mind, and spirit. While ballet was an escape from loneliness for many years, it eventually became more of a prison as the eating order revved up her obsession with exercise. Today she felt healthy, appreciating every stretch, every balanced pose, and every prayerful affirmation. When class ended she whispered "Namaste" and sat for a moment enjoying the peace.

Kyleigh broke the spell as she and Julia twirled over to see her. "Earth to Caaaa-sssie," Kyleigh chanted. "Girl, you are in the zone!"

Cassie stretched up over her head and smiled. "I needed class today."

Julia smiled as she rolled up her yoga mat. "You're not as stressed as you've been at school. What's up?"

"I had an intense therapy session with my folks yesterday, and got the college thing out in the open."

"Woah!" Kyleigh replied. "Your dad was okay when you told him you didn't wanna go?"

"Disappointed, but okay, at least for now. And we came to a compromise – we agreed if things are going okay next summer then I might take a couple of classes over at Brentwood."

Julia's response was warm and caring. "That's awesome, Cassie. I wish you could come back to dance with us, but we'll settle for yoga for now."

"And theater – don't forget theater," Kyleigh added. "It's gonna be an awesome senior year for all of us!" She twirled back across the floor to fetch her own yoga mat.

"She's such a dork," Julia said. "A big, lovable dork! Have a good day – see you Monday in Psych." They waved as they headed out the door.

Cassie rolled up her own yoga mat, looking up to see Brooke chatting with Colleen. They both smiled as she approached them.

"Do you need a ride home?" Brooke asked. "Since your regular ride is off being romantic?"

Colleen chuckled as the rest of the students filed out of the studio. "I'm sure we'll hear all about it during the week."

"Not quite *all*," Cassie teased, "but I'm so happy for them. And to answer your question, I don't need a ride. My mom's due soon. I think I'll wait out by the door though to keep an eye out."

"That's fine," Colleen replied. "I'll be kicking both of you out anyway as my little cherub class should be arriving soon."

Cassie walked out into the waiting room and was greeted by one of the younger dancers who had rushed in with her mother. "Well, hi there. You all ready to dance today?"

The little girl was about four years old, and big blue eyes sparkled as she grinned. "I'm gonna be a ballerina today. Miss Colleen says any time we dance we can be ballerinas."

Cassie squatted down to the little girl's level and smiled. "Miss Colleen's right – it's almost like magic, isn't it?"

"I like to twirl," she answered, spinning around on her tip toes. "It's better with my tutu at home, but pretty soon I'll get my costume here for the big show."

Cassie had a momentary pang of sadness, knowing she might not share that special memory for her senior year. Not wanting to break the child's mood, she forced a smile. "I bet you'll be one of the prettiest ballerinas on stage. Remember to always have fun, okay?"

"Okay!" the little girl said, spontaneously stepping forward and wrapping her arms around Cassie's neck to give her a hug. "I gotta get my ballet slippers on now," she said matter-of-factly, and walked over to where her mom had sat down. When Cassie stood up, she noticed Colleen and Brooke watching her.

"What's that look for?"

Colleen smiled. "I was watching you with Tracey. I didn't realize how good you were with little kids."

"Something about their innocence, I guess. I remember how magical those first years were, memorizing all the terms and tripping over my own feet trying to learn the positions. I envy her a little bit – there's no competition, no drive to be better than everyone else -- only the sheer joy of dancing." Cassie swallowed hard. "I do miss it."

Colleen stepped close and gave her a hug. "We miss you, too. But trust that when the time is right you'll be back – okay?"

"I can do that. At least this morning, anyway."

Brooke had gotten her bag and noticed Cassie's mom pulling up. "Hey, there's your ride. Have a great day and I'll see you on Tuesday at work."

"Thanks, ladies; same to you." As she got to the door little Tracey waved vigorously. "Bye!" Cassie smiled and waved back. "Enjoy your dance class, little ballerina." The beaming face stayed with her as she headed outside, wondering if she'd ever get to be a ballerina again.

CHAPTER 14

Maggie woke up to the smell of fresh coffee and the sound of Tim moving about the kitchen. She sat up in bed, snuggled into the pillows behind her, and pulled the quilt up under her bare shoulders and smiled. The sun was shining through the bedroom patio door and off in the distance Maggie could see fishing boats sailing past the stone breakwater on the outside of the harbor. *"How peaceful,"* she thought.

A moment later Tim entered the room carrying a tray of omelets, avocado toast, and coffee. "Morning, sunshine," he said as her favorite dimple lit up his face. "I hope that smile means you're thinking about me."

"Actually, I was looking out your window and thinking what an amazing view it is to wake up to."

He curled up next to her and placed the tray on the bed between them. "That's funny," he murmured, "I had the same thought earlier when I woke up to see you curled up beside me." He leaned over and kissed her lips. "You're beautiful when you're sleeping, you know."

She touched her fingers to his lips. "I slept so well -- it was a magical night."

"It was, indeed, my love. I hope you're as hungry as I was when I woke up. I took the liberty of making us some breakfast." He reached for the two coffee mugs first and handed one to her. "But first, here's a toast to many more magical nights with the woman I love."

Maggie clicked her mug against his and took her first sip of coffee. "And *this* is a magical coffee blend......what is it?"

Tim chuckled. "It's called the Andrea Gail Blend – named after a local fishing boat that went down in a huge storm. It inspired the movie *The Perfect Storm.* I found it in a little coffee shop along the harbor and bought a pound to keep in the freezer here. Great way to start any day." He reached out and pulled the breakfast tray a little closer. "Of course, you might also like a certain chef's garden omelet – prepared with love."

Maggie placed her coffee on the side table and accepted the plate he handed her. The smell of Swiss cheese reached her nose first and her stomach growled as she took her first bite. The cheese was a warm and gooey contrast to the crisp peppers and sweet onions inside the fluffy omelet. "Hmmm.....so yummy. I'm hungry this morning."

He took a crunchy bite of avocado toast and grinned. "Can't imagine why," he teased.

She felt herself blush. They ate in silence for a few minutes, enjoying the peaceful sound of waves and utensils clinking against their plates. Tramp had wandered in and wagged his tail.

Before Maggie could say anything, Tim patted the bed beyond the breakfast tray and called him. "C'mon up, Tramp. This is a pet friendly bedroom." As the beagle hopped up, Tim offered the crust of his toast as a breakfast treat.

"Jeez, I don't even feed him in bed....no wonder he likes you." She reached down to scratch behind his ears. "Morning, sweet boy. I should take you out, huh?"

"I took him out earlier," Tim replied as he reached down to pat Tramp's head. "He told me he likes it here, by the way."

Maggie took another bite of her omelet. "He's not the only one.....and thank you, by the way, for taking him out."

"You were sleeping so peacefully when I woke up. I watched you for a little while, but then I heard Tramp moving around and figured I could take him out for a minute. Besides," he said with a smile, "now we don't have to hurry getting up."

Maggie took a sip of coffee and met his gaze with understanding. "I like the way you think," she murmured, placing her coffee back on the table. She reached out for the breakfast tray and placed it on the floor as Tramp jumped down to lick the plates. Giving him a pat on the head, she pulled the quilt back up as she snuggled close to the wonderful man beside her.

* * *

HOURS LATER, Maggie took one last stroll on the little beach at the bottom of the hill and laughed at Tim and Tramp playing fetch with a piece of driftwood. She breathed in the salt air as the sand warmed her feet. *I have never been as happy as I am right now,* she thought as Tim joined her with a radiant smile.

"Hope it was me you were thinking about," he whispered, "because I've never seen you looking so content."

"I suspect you'll be seeing this goofy grin for a long time. So get used to it."

"Believe me, I'm planning on it." He watched as Tramp trotted through the sand with the driftwood in his mouth. "I think he likes the taste of salt on his wood. Maybe he should bring it home."

Maggie sighed. "I guess at some point we *do* have to head back, don't we?" She reached for his hand as they turned toward the steps leading back up to the packed car. "It was so wonderful being here with you, I almost hate to leave."

Tim gave her hand a squeeze. "I predict a lot of weekend trips to Cape Ann this winter." He took a few steps and added, "But I've also been thinking about doing a little renovating up in the loft over the office. I think we're at a point where a little privacy might be needed from time to time." He turned and called for Tramp. "Come here, boy, Gotta have your leash on at the top of the stairs."

Maggie handed him the leash and watched Tim attach it to

Tramp's collar, smiling at the man who was helping her to believe she was worthy of the love she was feeling.

As they approached the car Maggie saw an attractive middle aged woman exiting the townhouse next door and walk toward the car parked a couple of spaces away. "Morning, Tim," she chirped. "What a perfect day for a walk down on the beach." She smiled at Maggie as she came closer and extended her hand. "I don't believe we've had the pleasure of meeting. My name's Betty."

Maggie accepted a warm handshake and smiled at the attractive redhead. "Maggie. Nice to meet you."

Tim came to wrap his arm around her waist as he smiled at his neighbor. "Hi, Betty. Wanna thank you again for keeping an eye on the place when I'm not here – and for cleaning it between rentals. You've been so helpful."

The woman's eyes twinkled when she grinned. "It was nothing – truly. My daughter did most of the work. She likes cleaning way more than I do. Looks like you're heading out. Do you need me to clean again?"

"Nope. We straightened up today, and there won't be many rentals through the winter. You might see us up here for occasional weekends – or my mom Sharon. She liked the place a lot."

"She was a delight to meet, and I hope she lets me know if she's coming up. Would love to introduce her to a few of my friends. Us older women have to stick together, you know."

Maggie recognized a slight southern drawl but didn't know if it was natural or not. Still, Betty was friendly and open and smiled at almost anything. When Tramp shook himself she laughed at the sand flying everywhere. "And look at this darling creature," she said, squatting down to give him a pat on the head. "What's your name, you handsome thing?"

Anyone the beagle liked got Maggie's stamp of approval. "His name is Tramp, and I'm so sorry if he got sand on your clothes. We were getting ready to towel him down before heading out."

The woman stood up and laughed as she brushed the sand from her jeans. "Don't you worry your pretty little head about it – I used to have a cocker spaniel and he loved sharing nature with me." She gave them a grin as she gestured toward the car. "Well, I'm gonna be late for my lunch date if I don't get moving; was a delight to meet you, Maggie. And Tim, let me know if there's anything you need while you're gone." She winked at him as she added "I can see why you'd rather be living elsewhere right about now."

Once they were on the road, Maggie found the jazz station she loved so much. "Your neighbor seems quite fond of you – should I be worried?" she teased.

Tim chuckled. "Hardly. Not about her anyway. I think at one time she had hoped I might like her daughter, but she wasn't quite my type."

"And was that a southern accent I was picking up? It seemed to come and go."

"Oh, she turns it on and off as she sees fit. She grew up here in Gloucester, but lived in Tennessee for years. Her husband died several years ago, and she moved back home to take care of her mother. I guess her husband left her well set financially – she fills her days with mostly social events from what I see."

"Must be nice."

"I'm sure it has its perks – but I think I'd get bored if I wasn't working. And you – you'd hate being away from your adoring fans at the Manor."

"Yeah, I think you might be right. I'm so lucky to have gotten a job I love. I can't imagine working at a job where you're watching the clock all day and hating what you do." She sighed and looked out the window. "Although I must admit I'm a little sad leaving all this behind to head back to reality."

Tim reached over and squeezed her hand. "Trust me, we'll be back. But I bet an older gentleman at the other end has been missing you while we've been gone. Or at least your tomatoes."

"We'll have to stop by the garden to see what's left. He might be getting the last few of the season. I hope he won't be too disappointed."

"Honey, you are the last person in the world he'd ever be disappointed in; he adores you – even if he still tries to hide it."

"Well, I adore him, too, although you and Sharon have taken away the old curmudgeon I grew to love. I can't believe the change in him since you've been here."

"Gino said the same thing last week, and he's known him for decades. Grandad still insists on getting dinner there every Friday, though. Some habits refuse to die."

"Hey, those Friday night dates with your Grandma were some of the best memories he has – I'm glad he's kept up the tradition. I imagine she must smile from above every Friday night."

"I guess we should pick a night to start our own weekly tradition at Gino's…..gotta keep those family traditions alive, right?"

"Weekly trips to Gino's? Name the day and I'll be there." She leaned back and closed her eyes, happy to dream about being a part of such a wonderful family in the future.

CHAPTER 15

The weekend passed quickly, and Cassie arrived at school Monday feeling less anxious than the prior week. She knew she had SATs the following weekend, but Teagan had said she'd help her study if she needed it. They spent all but the last couple of periods together, and today they spent lunch and study hall chatting about Fiddler, upcoming auditions, and college.

"I'm not triggering anything, am I?" Teagan asked, eating a few corn chips leftover from lunch.

"You're not – and that feels so good. It's amazing how much stress I was able to let go of after talking to my parents."

"I'm glad they were okay with it. And it might be awesome if you ended at Brentwood for a class or two. We could have study hall chats for years to come – that is, if I get in."

Cassie popped a grape into her mouth and laughed. "Teagan, you'll get accepted at every school you apply to. I'm a little selfish to be hoping you pick Brentwood. The others are both too far away."

"Might I remind you I'll still be here at home? I'm commuting no matter where I go; I don't wanna give up my job."

"You're so happy there – and they all adore you."

"I love them, too. They brought me back from the brink of despair when Joanne died. I got the job thinking I'd hate it, and now I'm going to school for a degree in therapeutic recreation. I suppose I better mail my applications this week."

Cassie pondered her friend's words. "I envy you – and Brian as well – both of you know what you wanna do with your lives. I'm glad the pressure's off right now, but at some point I still have to figure out what the hell I wanna do with mine."

"Let's focus on the SATs for this week, lady – your life's goals can be for next week."

Cassie pulled the study book out from her notebook and smiled. "I'm so lucky to have a best friend who's so grounded. Now let's see you explain the math portion of all this stuff."

Teagan groaned. "We might need to track down Brian for help with math, my friend."

* * *

Tuesday Cassie was finishing the new fall display in the front window as Brooke rang up a customer. As the woman left the store, she smiled at Cassie. "Your window is beautiful – this store has the best window displays in town."

"Thanks," Cassie answered, catching Brooke's grin from a distance. She picked up the scissors and fishing line she'd used to hang up falling leaves and returned to the counter.

Brooke was still staring past her toward the window. "Looks awesome. I'll have to go outside in awhile and take a photo from the other side."

"It's one of my favorite things to do here. I can't wait to start on a design for Christmas."

Brooke picked up a big box of candles she had brought in earlier. "I have another four dozen of these I made this weekend. Can you help me with the labels? They'll start to sell again with the weather getting colder."

Cassie pulled a rusty orange colored one out of the box. "Don't tell me – it has to be pumpkin spice with the color." She pulled the lid off and took a long whiff. "It smells like the pumpkin spice muffins they sell at the café. Has anyone ever tried to eat one of these?"

Brooke chuckled. "Not to my knowledge – but they'd only do it once. I might have mastered the chemistry of scents, but the thing still tastes like paraffin."

Cassie took the labels Brooke handed her – there were six different scents she had ready to go: vanilla, pumpkin spice, apple pie, gingerbread, hazelnut cocoa, and evergreen. "You can tell you're gearing up to sell a lot of Christmas gifts."

"These will be the main scents through the end of the year. There should be some left over after the holidays, and by the end of January we'll start pushing some floral and chocolate scents for Valentine's Day. All about marketing."

"Do you have a list of stuff you want me to start working on for Christmas?"

"I do. I'll go over them with you when we're done here. I also have an outside project I'd love you to help me with if you have the time; a lot of it you could do here at the store."

"Sounds intriguing."

"Well, you know I'm on the planning committee for the community center with Maggie and Tim – and Teagan recently joined as well. We're now planning a fund raiser for December to raise some money for the center, and Teagan suggested a community Christmas celebration."

Cassie's eyes got brighter. "A community Christmas? Sounds perfect for Caldwell! Makes you wonder why it hasn't happened long before now."

"I think it's mainly been a lack of space. The churches are swamped with Christmas preparations of their own, and the schools are busy with holiday concerts and sports. Next year the community center will be a perfect spot, but this year we thought we'd start with a tree lighting by the gazebo with caroling, Santa, and a basket raffle. I volunteered to be in charge of the baskets, so we might have lots of extra stuff to do this coming month."

"Count me in – well, after this week. I have to get through my SATs first. Then I'm all yours until auditions."

"How about we start with getting these finished, and then I can show you my list. Hopefully you won't get scared off; I don't think I would have taken this on if I didn't have you working here. You could do this for a living, you know."

A little bell signaled new customers, and Cassie watched Brooke as she headed off to greet them. *"I could do this for a living?"* she thought. *"Might be something to explore down the road. This doesn't even feel like work."*

* * *

CASSIE MADE it through until SATs and managed her stress levels by getting up earlier to eat breakfast. She ran into Barb Sanders and Paula Williams from theater and was grateful to at least see familiar faces. It was a long morning, but the tests themselves weren't as bad as she had anticipated.

Afterwards, she stood outside with the two girls while waiting for rides.

"How come you didn't drive yourself, Barb?" Paula asked, knowing she had her license.

"Mom needed the car. It's a juggling act some days at our house; there are four drivers but only two cars. Lately most of my driving is running errands or dropping Becca off at gymnastics. So how do you guys think you did?"

Cassie shrugged. "I'm glad they're over."

"Me, too. I took them in the spring, but wanted to try and get a higher score if I could. I want to go to Amherst, and there's better scholarship money if my scores are over 1300."

"Hey, we'll be close to each other – I'm planning on UMass – we should get together out there."

"Might make it easier for you guys to carpool when you're coming home for weekends or holidays, too," Cassie added.

"Good point," Paula replied. "So I heard you were taking a gap year after high school. I kinda wondered why you were doing the SATs today – did your plans change?"

Cassie shook her head. "My dad had signed me up, so I figured I'd get them out of the way. If I'm up for it next year I might look at part time classes over at Brentwood."

"I admire you, Cassie," Barb said. "My cousin struggled with bulimia for years, and she needed to take the time for recovery in order to get better. I imagine it's not easy – when most of us assume you're okay now that you're back."

"Exactly," Cassie replied. "I don't think many understand eating disorders are based in the head – which takes a lot longer to fix than the body."

"My cousin said the same thing. At any rate, I think you rock. Hey, there's my dad – see you guys Monday."

As Cassie watched her go, she smiled. *"Someone admires me for my recovery?"* she thought. *"I'll have to tell Natalie this week."*

"So you're still doing the show, right?" Paula's question brought her back to the moment. When she nodded, Paula continued. "I'm so freaking excited this year. I'm convinced Teagan will beat me out, but being able to try out for the lead as a senior is still awesome. My build is a little curvier than most romantic leads, and I suck at dieting." Paula had gestured down to her belly and hips, and then stopped short. "Oh my God, Cassie, I'm sorry – I didn't trigger anything, did I? Now I feel stupid for bringing it up."

Cassie had cringed a bit, but she recovered. "It's okay to talk about it. I have to get used to living in a world that's all about dieting and body image. If I can't learn to deal with everything society throws at me then I'll relapse back into it – and I *want* recovery. Most days, anyway."

Relieved, Paula nodded. "So what part are you thinking about for auditions?"

"My plan is to show up, audition and see where I end up this year. There's my mom. Is your ride coming soon? I can wait with you."

"I'm fine. My ride will be here any minute and there's still lots of kids around. Have a good weekend, Cassie."

"You, too. It'll be better now that we're done." She headed off to the car, grateful to forget about college applications for awhile and focus on the present.

* * *

SAT RESULTS WERE due out two weeks later, on the same day Cassie and Ida were taking Teagan to see Fiddler. Several other theater kids had tickets for the same performance, and at lunchtime Cassie joined in as a small group tried to sing the opening fugue about traditions.

At the end Cassie spotted Barb Sanders heading past, and the latter leaned down as she walked by. "Scores are posted – thought you'd be curious."

Teagan heard the comment and smiled at Cassie. "Go on. You know you wanna see how you did."

Cassie pulled out her phone and found the site. Within a minute her score popped up. "Wow. I never expected that." She held her phone up for Teagan to see. 1260 overall, with a 570 in Math and a 690 in Reading.

"That's awesome – considering you didn't have as much time to study for them."

"I guess my dad will be satisfied with these. Maybe he'll leave me alone about the whole college thing for awhile."

"Things are better at home?"

"There's still conflict to work through, but since meeting with Natalie they've been better. I think the key was my willingness to take the SATs and think about part time for next year. It keeps their dream alive for me to be in college, I guess."

Teagan popped a chip into her mouth. "And what about Cassie's dreams? Have you started thinking about the kind of life recovery can lead you to?"

Cassie sipped her water. "It's weird. Now the pressure is off and I find myself sometimes thinking about it. Usually late at night, when I'm going through my positive affirmations. I might incorporate art or psychology into my jobs down the road. Not sure which I'd end up with, but I think I have to find something other than dance as a career choice."

"You could look at art therapy," Teagan offered. "or counseling with an art minor. I can easily see you at a place like the Phoenix Center working with others who are struggling."

Cassie took her last bite of her sandwich. "Maybe. Or I might stay at Brooke's and find another part time job in town to make up the difference in hours." She crumpled the empty sandwich wrapper into a ball and put it back into her bag, then caught Teagan staring at her intently. "What's that look for?"

"Don't assume you'll never be able to dance again. I see it in your eyes – it's part of who you are."

Cassie swallowed hard. "It's certainly a part of who I've been. I guess I'm scared to think about a life without dancing. But at least I have acting, singing, and art – some would call me blessed."

"I still predict you'll dance again – and not only in the show. Keep believing."

"Thanks. I hope you're right. But for now, what time do I need to be ready tonight? I'm stoked to see this show again after all these years."

"Me, too. I've been driving my folks crazy the past couple of weeks singing all the songs. Show's at 7:30, so why don't you plan on being ready for 6:15. Then we can pick up your grandmother before heading over. How does that sound?"

"Perfect."

"What's perfect?" Brian asked, turning back from his conversation with Lou on his other side.

"You were next, buddy," Teagan replied as she elbowed him. "Tonight. 6:00. Be ready or I leave you behind."

"I'll be out front doing the Russian dance. Or better yet, I can do it down the street to your house and be waiting when you come out the door."

"I'm almost tempted to challenge you on that, but I don't wanna wreck your knees with auditions getting closer. Just be ready when I get there."

"You got it. And Cassie, I hope your grandmother is ready to be serenaded all the way to Brentwood tonight."

"It's all she's talked about the past few times I've been up to see her. She might even sing along. I think she's also looking forward to seeing Mr. Pritchard again."

"They got to be good friends when he was there for rehab," Teagan replied. "Maggie says he's excited, too. They'll be sitting right behind us tonight."

The lunch bell sounded, and Cassie grinned to see only two orange slices left in front of her. She was making measurable progress.

* * *

CASSIE SAT with Teagan to her right and her grandmother to her left. Brian sat on the other side of Teagan, and behind them sat Carl, Sharon, Tim, and Maggie. Cassie had grinned when she met up with the four of them upon arrival. They were a tight knit family unit despite being estranged for decades. She could also tell Tim and Maggie were head over heels in love, and the old man couldn't be happier about it. Maggie had brought so much healing to all of them.

She now sat watching the musical unfold, entranced by the songs and dances she had loved since she was a little girl. When Chava danced the ballet scene, she teared up, feeling the pain the character poured into her movements. *"God, how I miss it,"* she thought. *"Please let me get strong enough to dance again – to feel like that again."* Tears rolled down her cheeks as she mourned the part of her she missed most. Teagan reached out and squeezed her hand.

"Someday. Have faith."

Cassie nodded, feeling her grandmother's hand on the other side. They both had so much faith that dance would return without triggering her eating disorder. Maybe she could rely on their strength until she could be sure of it herself.

CHAPTER 16

Maggie swallowed the last of her coffee and left her apartment with Tramp soon after the sun came up. The crisp air beckoned as they walked to the community garden for the last time of the season. As they crunched through the leaves along the sidewalks Maggie listened to the morning chatter of birds and squirrels. Passing by Carl & Tim's house she fought the urge to stop in, knowing she'd be late in helping her friends pull the last of the garden plants and weeds. She loved this time of year as nature embraced the season of letting go and preparing to rest.

Brooke and Colleen were there ahead of her, and as she arrived she could see Barb at the far end of the park on her way. "Morning. Looks like you guys didn't beat me by much," Maggie said as she tied Tramp to his usual spot. She took out a small blanket she had carried with her and laid it on the ground for him to curl up on.

"Aww, what a nice thing your mom does," Brooke said as she gave Tramp a scratch behind the ears. "I guess I wouldn't want to lay on the cold ground right now, either."

She turned to Maggie and added, "So how hard was it to walk past his house without stopping?"

Colleen laughed. "We were sort of wondering if we'd see someone walking beside you heading back home."

"Maybe he's still there waiting for her to go back home," Brooke teased. As Maggie blushed, she added, "Seriously, love looks good on you, girl. You're glowing."

Maggie smiled as she pulled a dead tomato plant out of the ground. "You guys are incorrigible – but I'll admit it's sometimes hard to walk right past his house without stopping these days." She greeted Barb as she arrived with her rolling cart rattling with a couple of steel rakes and hoes. "Someone's ready for the last hurrah."

"Hoping to pull the last of my carrots and turnips this morning. It's been another great season, hasn't it? A few folks have gotten their plots done for the year."

"And then there's a few abandoned plots," Colleen replied, pointing to a few plots full of weeds and wilted plants. "I guess we'll have to get those cleaned out as well, won't we?"

Brooke spoke up as she yanked old tomato plants out of the ground. "We'll give them another week or two; the bylaws give the end of October as the closing date, so we can round up a few volunteers to help get them done before the heavy frost settles in."

"It'll only be a few plots," Maggie chimed in. "I doubt we'll have trouble filling them next year."

Barb grunted as she dug up some carrots. "If I had more time I'd take on another plot myself. The summer guests ate most of my harvest; my canning shelves look bare this year."

"That's what you get for being so successful," Colleen teased. "But we could all take on one extra plot between us."

Maggie nodded. "I know Sharon wants a plot next year, and Tim said he'd help with mine if he could put in a few plants. Cassie also seemed interested in trying to grow her own food."

"We should advertise a couple of plots as 'shared beginner' spots," Brooke suggested. "Let three or four people have a small section of a plot and run a class to teach them the basics; we might avoid the extra work in the fall with fewer abandoned plots."

"What a great idea," Maggie replied. "I wonder if the community center will be open by then; they could offer a hand on class right here."

Brooke laughed. "Hey, let's get through 'Caldwell in Christmas' first, okay? But why don't we put together a basket from the community garden with some seeds, tools, gloves, and a book?"

Barb's memory sparked a thought. "How 'bout some canning jars, too?"

"Why not make it extra special?" Colleen asked. "Could we afford to offer a small plot as part of the deal? Or at least a gardening class or tutoring session?"

"Brilliant!" Brooke said. "I'll add it to the list when I get to work later. For now, I suggest we stop talking and bust our butts a little if we're gonna be out of here in time for yoga."

Colleen groaned as she gathered a pile of weeds and old tomato plants to bring to the compost bin. "I think we'll all be ready for a nap at some point today."

* * *

AFTER FINISHING in the garden and then going to yoga, Maggie helped Lucy clean the apartment. By the time they were done she was sore and tired – and hungry. She opened the refrigerator to see what might be quick and easy to prepare, and pulled out various leftovers from the past week.

Lucy joined her in the kitchen as Maggie opened containers to take inventory. "Looks like a perfect stir fry waiting to happen," she asserted. "We have some frozen rice we could microwave as well."

Maggie loved her suggestion. There were small containers with leftover broccoli, mushrooms, peppers, onion, and corn, and another container with kidney beans. "Sounds perfect."

Lucy grabbed a frying pan out of one cabinet and some olive oil out of another. "Since you worked in the garden this morning *and* did yoga before cleaning, I'll do the cooking." She flashed a grin and added, "But you can throw all the empty containers in the dishwasher later on."

"Sounds fair. And now we'll have lots of room in the fridge for this coming week's leftovers."

Maggie rinsed out the containers as Lucy emptied them, so by the time they were grabbing their bowls only the frying pan was left in the sink. As Maggie sank down onto the couch she took a long whiff of the heaping rice and veggies she was holding. She had thrown some shredded cheddar and a little soy sauce on hers, and loved the salty flavor both brought to the food. "Kind of a cross between a stir-fry and a rice bowl…..I'll take it."

Lucy shoveled a forkful of food into her mouth. "I love refrigerator clean outs – always a delicious stir fry or soup by the time you're done." She took a sip of water and leaned back to relax. "So are you seeing Tim today?"

"Tomorrow. He's got stuff to do for work and says I'm a distraction."

Lucy giggled. "Yeah, I *bet* you are after last weekend."

"How 'bout you? Plans with Liz?"

"Nope – she's at the greenhouse today. She and Watson will be over tomorrow – we're gonna head over to the wildlife refuge and do some hiking. Supposed to be a sunny day."

"Did you ask her about Thanksgiving yet?"

"She said as long as there's turkey and pie she doesn't care where we eat."

Maggie laughed out loud. "One of the many reasons I love Liz. And I talked to mom last night and she and dad are fine with us all joining Tim's family. It'll be a little weird not having it here. We won't have to maneuver around the kitchen trying to get a whole turkey dinner cooked with too many people trying to help."

"True – although I suspect Carl's kitchen will be similar. You'll have to let us know what we can bring or do to help get ready." As Lucy took another bite of food, she added, "so I imagine Mom and Dad are eager to meet Tim and his family, huh?"

Maggie blushed a bit. "I hope they don't show how much. I think after all those years of wondering if I'd ever live a normal life they're extra excited to see me in a relationship."

"Well, you two *are* pretty tight these days."

"Yeah, I know we are – but you know how my brain works." Maggie grew serious for a moment. "It's like the eating disorder is determined to point out every little reason as to why Tim will eventually decide someone else is way better suited to him."

Lucy raised her eyebrow. "Anyone in particular we're talking about here?"

Maggie put her bowl down and took a sip of water. "I know it's stupid. But sometimes I look at Amanda Clarke at our committee meetings and wonder if she isn't flirting a bit with Tim. And then my head starts telling me she's way prettier and thinner and someday Tim will dump me."

"You *do* recognize how ridiculous that is, right? For one thing, I know Amanda and she's at least ten pounds heavier than you – so your premise is faulty. Besides, it's obvious Tim is head over heels in love with you."

"Thanks, sis. I need the voice of reason from other people. Makes it a little easier to tell my brain to shut up." She stretched her arms up over her head before grabbing her bowl for more food. "This is nice. Not too often we both get a day at home at the same time – anything you'd like to do?"

"Honestly? I'd love to pull out a couple of movies and have a lazy day with my sister. You game?"

Maggie stretched out and put her feet up on the coffee table. "Sounds perfect. Let's do it."

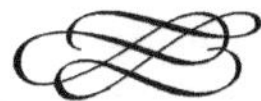

CHAPTER 17

The following week Cassie woke up super excited to get to yoga. After meeting with Natalie and her medical team at the Phoenix during the week, they agreed to slowly add dance back into her schedule. Rather than start in a class, Cassie had scheduled a private lesson with Colleen later Saturday morning. As Cassie packed leotards and ballet shoes into her bag the butterflies in her stomach fluttered like crazy. She was both nervous and excited to reach this milestone. But first, there was breakfast to get through – and then yoga.

Her mom dropped her off at the studio an hour later. "Good luck, honey. Remember to take it slow, and I'll pick you up at 1:00."

"Thanks, mom. See you later on." As Cassie entered the studio, Kyleigh and Julia were waiting for her.

"Are you beyond excited?" Kyleigh asked in her dramatic fashion. "Never mind, I can see it in your eyes!" She bounded across the studio to get her mat ready for yoga, twirling around once and calling back, "Can't wait till you're back in ballet with us!"

Julia shook her head, always quieter than her exuberant buddy. "You must be nervous, too. I hope it's everything you need it to be. I can't imagine not dancing, and I know you have that same place inside. I'll be praying for you later."

"Thanks. You get it. I may not be able to get back here right away, but I'm thrilled I can at least audition. I think I would have spiraled into relapse if I couldn't do either this year."

"The show wouldn't be the same without you. You were so amazing last year – and I can't wait to see where we end up this year."

The door opened and Maggie and Brooke arrived, and after quick greetings class got underway. Cassie's focus wasn't quite as strong as usual, but the class served as a warm-up and got her head in the right place. The girls wished her luck before heading out, and Maggie and Brooke let the other class participants leave before doing the same.

"Text me later," Maggie said as she hugged her. "If you need a coaching session tomorrow I'm free."

"What? No plans with Tim?" Cassie asked mockingly.

"Girl, every Sunday is spent with Tim these days. But he knows my schedule sometimes changes."

Brooke chimed in. "Hey, good luck today. And I'll see you Monday afternoon ready to work. The back room is looking a little chaotic right now with all the basket raffle stuff going on." She turned toward Maggie. "You tell Tim I might start dropping off finished baskets at his office this week if he has room. They're starting to invade our work space."

"I'll let him know – we're decorating the office before Thanks-giving since it will be a main spot for last minute raffle chances. The café will be the other one. They close early on Saturdays, so they were excited to get involved."

"With most people likely to park at the high school and walk right past, both spots are perfect," Brooke replied. "Hey, here come the cherubs; we better get out of here. Bye, Colleen!" The latter waved from the middle of the studio where she was setting up hula hoops around the floor.

"Can I help get anything ready?" Cassie asked Colleen as two cherubs entered the waiting room from outside.

Colleen paused for a moment. "You know, I could use a little help with this class if you're interested. We're doing a few different things at the same time, and I was going to park myself in the middle, but if I modeled the motions for one side you could work with a few of them. No pressure – if you'd rather sit and wait for your lesson I understand."

"And miss a chance to be around dancers? I'd love to help – tell me what to do."

"You can start by changing into your leotard and ballet slippers; another couple have arrived, so we're waiting on two more."

The last one to arrive was little Tracey, who recognized Cassie as she came into the studio. Her eyes got big and her smile beamed. "Are you dancing in my class today?"

Cassie nodded. "I'm Cassie, and I'm going to be Miss Colleen's helper today. I'm excited to see you dance."

"I'm Tracey – and this is my friend Taylor. Over there is Mary, Chloe, Stacey, and Lydia. She's kinda shy, so don't scare her or anything."

"I'll try very hard not to," Cassie said, trying to keep the chuckle inside.

Colleen called all the dancers together and introduced Cassie. "She's been dancing since she was your age, and today she's going to be my helper. We're going to try something a little different today, but I think you'll like it because you won't have to wait as long when you're taking turns. Are you ready?"

Five little heads nodded excitedly while the sixth ballerina nodded slightly, standing behind most of the other little girls. *"She must be Lydia,"* Cassie thought. *"Reminds me of myself when I was her age."*

Colleen pointed out the four hula hoops around the room, and demonstrated the four different movements for each circle. She asked Cassie to move around the room showing how the completed cycle would look, and for the first time in months Cassie found herself being able to do arabesques, plies, and pirouettes. The little girls watched in awe, clapping for each movement. When she got back to where she had started from, Tracey gave her a high five. "You're a really good ballerina – I bet you'll get a gold star sticker today!"

Cassie grinned. The next hour flew by, and she loved working with the little girls who were all eager to learn. They wanted to impress, but didn't care about competing. All of them danced for the sheer joy of being ballerinas. Even Lydia got excited when she did her first arabesque without falling over. When the class ended, she put the hula hoops away as Colleen handed out stickers. Lydia approached hesitantly as she held out her sticker. "I think you should have this today. You were a nice helper."

Cassie's heart melted as she squatted down beside her. "Thank you, Lydia, but I think you should keep it so you can tell your mommy about the arabesque you did. But I'll take another high five."

The little girl reached out and slapped her hand, and whispered thank you before running out to the waiting room. She caught Colleen's eye and smiled. "They are all so darn cute. Thanks for letting me help. I had a blast."

"So did they. But right now, how about we get your lesson underway?"

Cassie felt the butterflies again. Colleen chose some of the music she remembered from the previous year's classes, and worked through the warm up exercises. Her body was out of shape after months of destructive behavior and then the needed healing process, but it felt wonderful to move. Colleen had put together two short routines to cover most of the general movements needed in any audition. She had chosen two songs from *Hello, Dolly* to help set the mood, and Cassie grinned when she heard the second number – it was one of the songs sung by the character she was most interested in.

Colleen caught her expression. "It's almost like I know you or something. Your lines in the first routine aren't bad – I can tell you're rusty, but your technique is still there. You have to polish things a bit and you'll be fine for any dance in the show. This song is slower and more lyrical; I'm excited to see how you do."

As Cassie danced through the routine, her heart swelled. It was a simple dance, but one she could put her whole heart and soul into. By the time it ended she had tears in her eyes. "I didn't realize how much

I'd missed this," she whispered, overcome with a feeling of completeness.

Colleen came over and hugged her. "I've had numerous dancers over the years react much the same way after returning from an injury. It's like getting back to your innermost happy place, isn't it?"

Cassie nodded, wiping the tears away. "Exactly. I mean, art has helped a *lot* in filling my need for creativity, but dance touches my *soul.*"

"Remember how this feels today. No competing, no drive to use dance to punish or push yourself – simply using the music to help your soul connect with your body and mind. It's the same place yoga takes us to when we surrender – but dancers feel it most when they're moving."

"So do you think I'll be okay for auditions?"

"I think we should do one more private lesson to let you dance again beforehand. But yes, I think you're more than ready for auditions. I can't wait to see you on stage again this year."

"I wish I could be here, too – I'm gonna miss it more than I can say."

Colleen perched on the stool by her desk. "I've been thinking about that – and I have something to run by you. I know you'll have to talk to Natalie and your folks, and it might be too much once the show rehearsals start, but hear me out."

"O-kay…..I'm curious."

"I was amazed at how well you interacted with the cherubs today, and it was the best class so far this year as they could do more with an added teacher. I can't pay you, but if you needed volunteer hours for your senior year I'd love to have you help permanently with the class."

"You mean it? They were so much fun to work with – and I do need those hours before graduating."

"Why don't you talk it over with your counselor and your folks? You can let me know next week either way. And you can try it to see how it works if you'd like."

Cassie gathered her things together. "I'll talk to Maggie, too. She's been my recovery coach, and she might know me even better than Natalie these days."

"One more thing," Colleen added. "Since volunteering would be working here, I'd invite you to also consider doing a senior showcase in the spring recital – I think you've earned it."

Cassie's eyes filled with tears. "The showcase?" she murmured.

"Julia and Kyleigh are my only others seniors this year," Colleen replied, "and I think they'd love to have you join them as senior soloists. Granted, your medical team has to okay it. But I'd love to see you perform in your last high school recital. After all the years you've spent in spring recitals, I can't imagine how hard it would be to miss this one—especially where you missed last year."

Cassie was unable to speak. Last year she had missed performing in her first recital at Colleen's studio because she had gone inpatient at the Phoenix the week before. After years of dance, it had been the first spring recital she had missed, and this year she had assumed she'd miss her last chance to dance as a senior. Colleen saw her tears and smiled knowingly. "Now get yourself together and see if your mom's outside. And you can let me know about audition prep for next week."

"The senior showcase? This has been the best day ever." She met her mom with a smile not only on her face, but in her heart and soul as well.

THE FOLLOWING WEEK Cassie was in the back room at Brooke's finishing up another basket for the raffle. Brooke had left several for her to assemble, label, and decorate, and she was having a blast trying to make each look unique and inviting. As she attached the last bow on a kids' craft basket, she heard several voices heading her way from the front of the store. One sounded like Brian, and before she could identify the others Teagan, Maggie, Colleen, Julia, Kyleigh, and Brian appeared in the doorway with a big "18" balloon.

As they all began singing "Happy Birthday" Brian walked forward and placed a tray of individual angel food cakes topped with whipped buttercream icing and fresh strawberry slices. "For you, my lady!" he said with a flourish and bowed.

Colleen came over and gave her a huge hug and handed her a card. "I can't stay; I have a mom waiting with my next class so I could dash over with this – love you, girl!" Cassie returned the hug before Colleen left, tearing up at the other beaming faces around the table.

Kyleigh, as usual, was the first to speak when the song ended. "Eighteen!! I can't believe you're eighteen!" She handed her a card and grinned. "I got you a sentimental type card instead of one of those goofy ones – ya know, since you're an *adult* now."

Cassie returned the smile, opening both arms for hugs from both Kyleigh and Julia. The latter was more reserved as she handed her a bag with a ballerina on the outside. When Cassie opened it she found leg warmers and a dancer key chain. "Colleen told us you might be able to do the showcase, so I thought those might come in handy if you had to practice over the winter. We're *so* excited you might get to do senior showcase with us!"

"Thanks, Julia," Cassie replied. "I'm hoping it works out. I'll have to see how things go after auditions are over and the show rehearsals start up – and if I can only help with the little kids on their dance, at least I can be there one last time."

Teagan had come up beside Julia as Cassie finished. "Maybe *you* think that's enough, but all of us are convinced you'll dance on your own. You gotta believe." She handed Cassie a gift bag and gave her a hug. "Happy birthday, bestie. I'm so glad you were born."

"Me, too," Cassie whispered back. "And thanks for always being there for me." She opened the bag and pulled out a small musical snow globe with a dancer inside.

"She reminded me of Chava from Fiddler," Teagan said. "And I loved the music it plays."

Cassie smiled as she found the wind-up key and turned it several times. The melody of Whitney Houston's "When You Believe" chimed as the dancer inside moved in a figure eight pattern. Cassie noticed everyone had grown quiet as they all watched the tiny dancer's movements.

"Oh my God," Kyleigh whispered. "You should SO dance to this song in the showcase. It's *perfect* for you."

Cassie saw the others nod in agreement and then caught Teagan's gaze. "And we'll all be there to cheer you on, girl. Just keep believing."

Cassie wiped tears from her eyes with the back of her hand as she placed the music box on the table. "I'll try. But let's get through auditions first, okay?" She smiled at her friends who had become a second family to her and tried to lighten the mood. "Right now I want one of these cakes – homemade, I presume?" Her eyes sought out Brian for an answer.

"Girl, I wouldn't dream of serving anything out of a box. I think Teags made me promise about five years ago when I first started baking."

"Hmmm," Cassie said as she took her first bite. "A promise I'm glad you kept."

Kyleigh agreed as she took another bite. "I can't wait for you to open your own place someday. You'll put the café right out of business."

"Not a chance," he replied. "They have way more than simply baked goods. Besides, I'm thinking I might do better with a little coffee shop in Brentwood by the college. I'll keep a small used book shop at one end, but also cater to those who want to study and write with a steady supply of coffee and sugar."

"Sounds like a winning combo," Brooke said.

"That's the plan," Brian affirmed, "But first I have a year of culinary school to get through."

"Did you decide on Boston?" Julia asked.

"Yup. Cambridge School of Culinary Arts. I had considered the New England Culinary Institute in Vermont, but decided to stay home with my mom. It'll be an easy train ride in and they have the both the pastry focus and the banquet management tract to look at. I applied for early decision, so I might know before Christmas."

Brooke smiled. "Sounds awesome, Brian. And much as I'd love to have one of those gorgeous little cakes, I need to get back out front. Save one for me for later?" When Cassie nodded, she added, "and Happy Birthday. You guys can hang out back here until your shift is over – you worked hard today."

"Thanks, Brooke. I'll make sure I clean the table well before leaving."

As she and her friends ate their cake they chatted about auditions and college applications. For a moment Cassie felt the self doubt bubble up inside. *"See? Dad's right; they're all preparing for their futures and you're gonna fail because you don't have the guts to go for it."*

She caught Teagan's eye and smiled weakly, realizing the fallacy of her thoughts. *"That's crap, Cassie, and you know it. Teagan is also staying in Caldwell and going to school part-time. And she sure as hell isn't a failure. You're both choosing paths that work for you."* She glanced down once again at the music globe and smiled. *"Keep believing in miracles."* She took another bite of her cake, determined to listen to the more confident and reasonable thoughts she was starting to have. Recovery was the miracle she was determined to hold on to.

CHAPTER 18

*N*ovember flew by, and Cassie worked hard at taking little steps each day in her recovery. Natalie, Maggie, and her folks agreed to let her volunteer at the studio, and she was a favorite of both little Tracey and Lydia in the cherub class. Each class had her laughing as she learned to appreciate the crazy things the little girls had to say, and she loved watching the pride on each face as they completed each movement. Cassie made it her goal to reinforce each little cherub's inner worth and counter any competitive comments with the importance of lifting each other up. *"God knows they'll face it all as they get older,"* she thought one Saturday, *"Let them enjoy the magic dance creates at this age."*

* * *

THE FOLLOWING SUNDAY morning Maggie was slicing a banana bread when Cassie arrived for a short coaching session. "Hey, perfect timing! Warm out of the oven. Want coffee?"

"I had some at home – but I'd love some water."

Maggie gestured for her to sit on the couch. "Get comfy and I'll be right back."

Cassie curled up on one end as Tramp came over to greet her. She scratched his head as he yawned. "Did I interrupt your morning nap, buddy?" Tramp's tail woke up enough to wag his response, and he sank down next to the couch on the floor where Cassie could still reach down to pat him.

"You're spoiling him, I see," Maggie said as she returned with a tray holding banana bread, a glass of water, and a few small dishes with toppings. "I wasn't sure if you wanted anything on top, so there's peanut butter, cream cheese, and sliced strawberries. I also brought an extra banana if you want to slice it up. You can get yours ready while I grab my coffee."

When Maggie returned Cassie had grabbed some strawberries and a little peanut butter for her bread. "The cream cheese would taste better, but I'm trying to avoid dairy with vocal auditions tomorrow. Thanks, by the way, for not doing a quiche. I appreciate it."

"No problem," Maggie replied, grabbing the dish of cream cheese. "I know it can cause extra gunk in your throat while singing. Besides, I had some ripe bananas to use. So how are you feeling about the week ahead? Auditions, and then Thanksgiving dinner? That's a lot to deal with."

"Trying to take them one at a time. I guess I'm ready for auditions. Nervous, but that's normal. At least I get to *do* them. This fall I wasn't sure it would be possible."

"You've worked hard, and it shows. I think the show will be a much healthier experience for you this year. Did your lesson with Colleen yesterday go well?"

Cassie nodded as she took a sip of water. "She thinks dance can still work in my life if it's healthy. I'm trying to hold on to that idea. It was wonderful moving around yesterday. It connects inside way more than yoga does for me."

"I'm glad it went well. I know when I had to give up running years ago it was torture for awhile. I think the difference for me was I hadn't been running all my life, and while the endorphins were awesome, I think the behavior pattern was connected to my eating disorder from the beginning. You've been dancing all your life, so if you can connect back to *those* connections – before the eating disorder kicked in – then it might work to bring it back to some degree."

"I hope so. I know I have to be *willing* to give it up if it becomes a problem, but I'm praying it doesn't. For now, I'm concentrating on auditions. Colleen said I'd be fine with any role which doesn't have heavy dance requirements. I decided to indicate one role I wouldn't accept."

"The part of the niece?"

When Cassie nodded, Maggie continued. "It sounds like you're in a healthy place for the next few days. And I know Teagan and Brian will be there to keep you settled." She took a swig of coffee as her tone became a little more serious. "So let's talk about Thanksgiving. Are you ready for dinner at Caldwell Manor?"

"I think so. At least compared to last year. My disease was like a fast moving train to nowhere back then."

"It's helpful to remember where we were on key dates in the past," Maggie replied. "Then we can recognize the progress we've made when our eating disorder starts screaming again."

"Yeah, I know at some point between now and Thursday the brain will start up again. It's never totally gone, is it?"

"Not for me, but I do have long periods of time when it's quiet. I suspect Thursday might trigger some food thoughts simply from the abundance of it all. You should be prepared as well —especially facing a buffet."

"Yeah, mom and I talked about it. She offered to plate my food for me, but I don't want to be a coward. I can't have people plating my food for me forever if I'm going to be a functioning adult someday."

"I applaud your commitment to recovery. It's not easy, but learning to face each task is another step in the right direction. So what does this plan involve?"

"Mom's going to be right behind me in line. If I freak out she said she'd put stuff on my plate as I held it. People help each other all the time in a buffet line. And she'll try to guide me a bit in the amount I'm putting on my plate."

"You could put a teaspoon of stuffing on your plate and you'll think it's the same amount as the person across from you with a cup worth. Have you considered taking measuring cups if you need them?"

"Not at the buffet. But mom's gonna have one in her purse at the table in case I start obsessing over amounts."

"Can I give you one more piece of advice?"

"Always."

"When you get back to the table, look around at your family, and start a conversation with your grandmother. Sometimes we simply need a distraction to get our head away from the food in front of us. Then we can eat as we engage in what's going on around us. It doesn't ever make the voice shut up, but it takes some of the power away from the eating disorder and gives it back to us."

"Sometimes I wish I could find that switch and turn it off forever."

"It might be impossible to turn it off forever, but recovery does show us how to rewire our brains to respond like normal people." Maggie chuckled as she reached for her banana bread. "I'll let you know if I ever get there, by the way."

"So how are *you* doing? What's it like getting ready for Thanksgiving with Tim and his family?"

"Pretty damn amazing. Like you, I think back to last year at this time and I had no idea I'd be involved with someone at this point."

"Is that what you call it?" Cassie teased. "So how involved are you guys at this point?"

Maggie blushed a bit. "We've taken things to the next level; I spent a weekend with him up in Gloucester last month."

Cassie squealed. "Oh my God – that's huge!" Her expression grew more contemplative. "Has it changed things? I'm sure your eating disorder has been screaming at you after being so exposed."

"It was weird. A part of my brain was screaming at me through the whole process, telling me I was so fat, that he'd never love me, and I'd never be able to make him happy or satisfy him."

"I can totally see that happening."

"But it was only one little piece of my brain," Maggie said, "and so I focused on the healthier parts of my brain – and more so, I focused on the feelings and sensations. Tim was so gentle and loving, and I felt safe in his arms. I was also honest about the voices in my head, and he even talked to them a couple of times."

"Must have been a little strange."

Maggie smiled. "In some ways it was empowering to hear someone you trust tell your eating disorder all the ways we weren't listening to it anymore. I'm learning to follow the voices of people I trust – those are the healthy thoughts I want to associate with."

"Maybe someday I'll get there," Cassie murmured. "But I'm so happy for you and Tim. It's so obvious how much you love each other, and I know the old guy adores you. How's his mother with you guys, ya know—"

"Doing it?" Maggie joked. "Sharon is more reserved than Tim and Carl, but she's genuine. She's still coming to terms with being back with her father in her childhood home; I think she still has a lot of guilt to work through."

"I bet Thursday will be emotional with you all together for dinner, huh?"

"Absolutely. And maybe a little stressful – my folks are flying up from Florida to join us for Thanksgiving dinner."

"It really *must* be serious if the families are meeting."

Maggie swallowed the last of her coffee. "I'm gonna have to get going soon to go help Tim with some decorating over there. Do you need a ride home?"

Cassie shook her head. "My mom told me to text her and she or my dad could be here in ten minutes to get me. Let me text now – and if you have anything you have to do I can sit here with Tramp."

Maggie glanced down at Tramp snoring at Cassie's feet. "Yeah, he looks like he'll give you lots of attention right about now. Go ahead and text, and then we can chat for ten more minutes." She told Cassie about Ida and the other residents at the Manor and how they'd decorated the place with Teagan's help.

Cassie listened until her mom beeped outside. "There she is. I gotta go, but thanks so much for squeezing me in today. After chatting, I think I'm ready to face the biggest food day of the year now."

Maggie gave her a hug at the door. "Remember you can text me if you find yourself in a tough spot. Otherwise, text me later on Thursday to give me a quick recap. Oh, and be sure to send me a quick text when you find out what role you got for the show."

"And if you don't answer right away I'll assume you might be occupied, so don't rush anything for my sake."

"You have some real sass, you know that? Trust me, after eating Thanksgiving dinner I don't think Tim or I will have any desire for romance of any kind.....at least not until Friday."

Cassie waved to her mom as she closed the door. *I wonder if I'll ever have a relationship like that?* she thought. *For now, I'll focus on getting through auditions and that turkey dinner.*

CHAPTER 19

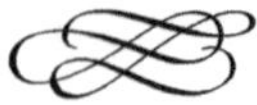

onday afternoon Cassie met Teagan at the end of the day and they headed to the auditorium. They made it to the front of the room and signed in, picking up their audition packets before sitting down in the third row. Cassie had signed in first and wondered why Teagan had let Paula go ahead of her, but when Teagan pointed to the number "1" on both of their folders she understood. They would now be in the same small group for auditions.

"I thought you were being polite," she whispered.

Teagan chuckled. "Couldn't imagine not having you in my group."

Someone tapped Cassie on the head and she turned to find Brian, Lou, and Jake right behind them. "Ready to rumble, ladies?" Brian asked with a smile.

"Ready as I'll ever be," she responded. Teagan nodded in agreement. "So excited, you guys. Hey, Beth!" She waved as Beth Newton and a couple other sophomores filed in next to Lou.

Beth leaned over Lou to give Teagan a hug from behind. "So glad you're here!" she whispered in her ear. "Hey, Cassie – I'm glad you're okay to be back. You were so phenomenal last year. How are you doing?"

"More good days than bad. Thanks for the cards you sent while I was at the Phoenix Center. I appreciated them so much."

"Wish I could have come to visit a couple of times, but I was off working as a camp counselor most of the summer. Good luck today."

"Thanks." Before Cassie could say anything else a tall brunette stood up near the front and whistled loudly using her thumb and finger in her mouth.

"Damn," Brian whispered. "That would scare a dog."

Teagan squeezed Cassie's arm. "Here goes nothing!"

Cassie felt a surge of energy as the young woman spoke. "Hey all, let's quiet down so we can get started. There's a lot of you here and we don't wanna be here all night. My name's Terry Monroe. I'm a junior this year and will be your stage manager, so come to me with questions. Depending on how well you follow directions you'll either love me or hate me by the end of the year. For now, turning it over to Mr. C."

A middle aged man with curly grey hair stood up and faced the group. He wore a faded sweatshirt that had "I'm a director – what's your super power?" written on it, and Cassie loved his smile. He was well loved and respected by almost every student, and only a few new kids that had come out for the show were unfamiliar with him. "Call me Mr. C. – short for Calabreschi, which is an Italian mouthful. Welcome to the toughest part of the entire production – not only for all of you, but for the creative team as well. Our stage can't hold the bigger casts; and sadly that means I can't keep all of you."

He held up a folder and pointed to the label in the corner. "On the front of your folders is a 1 or a 2 – everyone with a "1" will stay here and dance first, and anyone with a "2" will head across the hall to the music room for singing first. Afterwards you'll all come back here for the acting segment. Any questions?"

A younger girl in the front row gingerly raised her hand. "Do we try out for every part we want?"

"Excellent question," Mr. C. replied. "Choose the reading for the part you want most and show us what you've got. In callbacks I'll have some of you reading for several parts as I'll be looking for some chemistry between roles. Remember it's okay to be nervous, and try to have fun. All set?" With no extra questions, auditions got underway.

Cassie's small group included Teagan, Brian, Julia, and Beth Newton. As they gathered on the stage Cassie was both nervous and exhilarated. She was finally going to dance. She slid into the circle next to Teagan. There were a few new faces, but mostly the same gang back from last year.

Liz Patterson, the choreographer was back on the creative team. She was explaining the routine, directing those with less than five years dance experience to head to the center of the stage first. The more experienced dancers would watch the simpler routine, and then when it was their turn some more complicated movements would be added. Cassie remembered back to the previous year when she was so judgmental of Teagan standing next to her. *"I was so nasty to her, thinking that fat girls should never be in the same group as thin dancers. Boy, did she prove me wrong."* Almost as though she was thinking back to the same experience, Teagan glanced sideways at her and smiled.

When the first group was finished, Cassie took her place between Teagan and Julia, with Beth and Brian a couple of dancers over. Last year she was the new girl who only knew a few others, but she wowed them with her dancing and singing. This year they all knew her as the girl who had fainted and then left school after the show was done for treatment. A few had welcomed her back – the others most likely didn't care one way or the other if she was there.

Liz finished showing them the additional section, and then Cassie heard those wonderful words that she hadn't heard in months: "five, six, seven, eight!" As soon as the signal was given, Cassie lost herself in the dance, feeling more alive than she had since last spring. When the short routine was over she stood there frozen for a moment, closing her eyes and reliving the past minute over again.

Teagan came to her rescue. "You were awesome," she whispered as she clasped her hand briefly. "Kinda different from last year, huh?"

"For one thing, I don't hate you anymore."

Teagan grinned as Liz directed them over to the music room for singing auditions with Mrs. Kelly. This time, Cassie got to stand between Teagan and Beth Newton for the solo portion of the auditions. As each person down the line got to sing a few lines from the chosen song Cassie grew more confident. *"Please, God, help me nail this."* She spotted Mr. C. entering the room as Beth began to sing, and his reaction matched her own. *"Wow. She's even better than she was last year, and she's only a sophomore."*

When it was her turn to sing, Cassie gave it her all. While her breath control was not as strong as it could be, she knew she still had a voice that was lead material, and she pictured herself belting tunes in the back room at Brooke's as she sang. The music director gave her a smile when she finished, and then Cassie got to hear Teagan. Last year she was blown away that this fat girl could sing and dance the way she did. This year she was thrilled that her best friend sounded better than ever. *"No one in this group can beat her out for Dolly,"* Cassie thought. *"And no one deserves it more."* As the music director moved on to the last two singers in the group, Cassie squeezed Teagan's hand.

Before heading back over to the auditorium for the acting portion of auditions Julia caught up with Cassie. "Girl, you were *amazing* in there. I'd give anything to sing and dance like that!"

"Thanks. I had a couple of lessons with Miss Colleen; it was like being home. I've missed dance so much."

Julia cocked her head to one side as if deep in thought. "Does that mean you'll be coming back to the studio? We miss you."

Cassie sadly shook her head. "I can't handle the show and dance on top of my job at Brooke's. But I *am* helping with the cherub class – and *might* be able to dance in the senior showcase."

"Seriously?" Julia exclaimed. "That would be phenomenal!"

"I know. I'm trying not to raise my hopes too high, but I'm hoping it will work out."

"Kyleigh will freak when she hears – she was so bummed when you couldn't be with us this year."

"Time will tell. But if I can't do the showcase I can at least help with the little kids – and that's something, I guess."

"You've come a long way, girl. I'm so proud of your attitude." As they approached the front of the auditorium Kyleigh waved from the front row. "She saved me a seat," Julia said. "Good luck with the rest of today."

As Julia joined Kyleigh in the front row, Cassie saw Mike sit down on her other side and slide his arm around her. He leaned down to whisper something in her ear and Julia responded by looking up at him with a sparkle in her eyes and a warm grin. For the first time since she'd been back to school, it hurt. *"Last year that was me,"* she thought. *"Now he's moved on to someone who's way better than me."* She liked Julia, but couldn't deny the jealousy festering inside.

Teagan leaned closer. "You okay?"

"Thank God for Teagan. She knows. She always knows." She nodded, determined to acknowledge the emotion without letting it be a trigger. It was hard learning to recognize emotions again, and her eating disorder was always on the lookout for something to grab hold of and use against her. *"And Mike is certainly not worth that trade off."*

Before she could dwell any further, she heard the stage manager start calling names. This time they were just calling people in alphabetical order, so Cassie ended up on stage without Teagan or Brian. She stood with Brian's boyfriend Lou to avoid being next to Julia and Mike. *"Can't handle him with his new girlfriend?"* her eating disorder teased. She clenched her fists and focused instead on several girls she knew from classes and a few new ones she hadn't seen before. One in particular had been strong in both song and dance, and she studied her closely as they stood waiting. *"Not sure who she is, but I bet she'll be here for callbacks. I hope I'm there, too."*

Mike was one of the first ones to read, and he had chosen lines for the role of Cornelius. *"Great,"* she thought, *"I might end up opposite him."* Mike had some comic timing, and Cassie remembered him play opposite Teagan the previous year. She had been so possessive back then and wondered why. *"I'm not sure I loved him,"* she thought, *"but I sure needed him back then. As the new girl, dating him gained me acceptance from others – and let me be invisible when we were out in a group. I always felt so unworthy – no matter what I did. At least Julia treats him better."*

When her name was called, Cassie once again escaped into the magic of performing. She had memorized her lines for the character of Irene Molloy, the main romantic lead, and when she finished she was satisfied. *"I gave it my best, and now the waiting begins."*

Julia also read for Irene Molloy, and Cassie couldn't help but smile at how well she did. *"Maybe she'd be better as Irene; she'd have way better chemistry on stage with Mike than I would."* Much as she wanted to hate Julia at least a little bit, she couldn't. The girl was too damn nice, and she didn't ever want a guy like Mike to screw up one of the few friendships she had developed since coming to Caldwell. She caught Julia's eye after the reading was over, and gave her a thumbs up and mouthed the words "that was awesome," which was answered with a smile and a "thanks" mouthed back.

Once the entire group on the stage finished, they all filed back to their seats while the others auditioned. Teagan grabbed her hand as she passed. "You rocked it, girl. My turn now." Cassie winked at her. *"Go show us all what you've got, Teagan."*

It was clear that Teagan would have little competition for the role of Dolly. Cassie was also super impressed by Beth Newton's audition for the role of Minnie Fay. Last year it was Beth who had stepped in and taken over her role the night she fainted during tech week, and everyone had been amazed at how talented the freshman was. *"She might beat out some older kids for a lead this year,"* Cassie thought as she performed. *"I suspect she'll be getting a call back, too."*

By the time the last student had read, a quiet buzz of whispered conversations and critiques could be heard as everyone returned to their seats. Mr. C. got up to face the group before dismissing them. "Give yourselves a round of applause – each one of you put yourself out there, and that's never easy. No matter how the casting plays out, I commend all of you. For those not cast, I hope you'll consider getting involved backstage – we always need help with props, stage crew, lighting, costumes, and front of house. If you love theater, commit to being a part of this family, because every person plays an important role whether they're on stage or behind it. I'll turn it over to Terry to give you callback information – but thank you for coming out today. You guys are why I do what I do."

After a round of applause, Terry held up her hands to quiet them down. "With this being Thanksgiving week, the pace is fast and furious. Tonight – and it might be late – we'll be sending out a call back list for some of you to return tomorrow. If you don't hear from us it *doesn't* mean that you aren't in the show. The final cast list will be posted on Mr. C's door Wednesday before school lets out. I'll also email it to everyone. *Next* Wednesday will be our first rehearsal for those cast. For now, you guys are free to go. If anyone has any specific questions I'll be right here in front for the next fifteen minutes or so. Good luck – you all did great!"

Cassie took a deep breath and exhaled. Teagan had almost the same expression on her face. "And now we wait."

Brian leaned over from Teagan's other side. "We still on for the diner while we wait?"

"And miss a chance to celebrate your birthday together?" Teagan teased. "Of course we're on."

"Teagan's right," Cassie said. "Besides, I might go crazy if I headed home to be alone with my brain."

* * *

WITHIN THIRTY MINUTES they were seated at a table by the window at Caldwell Diner. Cassie chose the seat next to Teagan while Brian sat across from her.

"People are probably busy with Thanksgiving prep," he said while opening his menu. "Seems lighter than normal for a Monday."

Teagan agreed, taking the menu that Cassie handed to her. "It's still relatively early; I think auditions were done by 5:00. They went smoothly, didn't they?"

They nodded as the waitress returned with three waters. Cassie took a sip without opening her menu. Her brain was trying to hijack her dinner as she wasn't eating within the safety of home-plated meals, but she was determined to win this battle. She and Maggie had worked out options for situations like this, coming up with simple menu choices from a few of the local restaurants. Keeping choices simple gave Cassie a chance to practice independence with boundaries rather than letting her eating disorder take control of the endless possibilities. Without looking she already knew the three menu options that she'd agreed to with Maggie.

"You know what you want without even looking?" Brian asked. "I can't even decide if I want breakfast or dinner."

"I've found that keeping just a few options for each restaurant has made it easier for me to start eating out. Since I'm sort of in the mood for breakfast, which means bacon, a veggie omelet, and pancakes."

"Hmm……bacon sounds good," Teagan said. "Then again, when does bacon ever sound bad?" She grinned at both of them, happy that they'd chosen a table over a booth for her ample frame. "I might have breakfast, too."

Brian shook his head. "Nope, I made an omelet for breakfast this morning; I want something I can sink my teeth into. I think a burger is the way to go tonight."

"Damn, now I want a burger, too," Teagan joked. Cassie envied her friend's relationship with food sometimes. Even though Teagan had her own food issues to deal with, she was more comfortable with her real fat than Cassie would ever be with her imagined fat. *Maybe someday I'll be able to accept my body as it is. In the meantime, as long as I don't like my body size at any weight, I might as well have one that's medically safe and healthy instead of one that's trying to kill me.*

The waitress returned and Brian ordered a mushroom and Swiss burger with fries; Teagan ordered a bacon and cheddar burger with onions, and Cassie ordered an omelet with cheese, onions, spinach, and mushrooms along with two pancakes. As the waitress headed to another table, all talk turned to the auditions.

Brian took a sip of coffee and grinned. "I guess the role of Dolly is the easiest for Mr. C. to cast this year. You must be feeling confident, Teags."

"No less pressure, believe me. I was shocked last year, and I could easily be just as shocked this year if Mr. C. has another vision for Dolly. I'm simply hoping for a text to go back tomorrow, that's all."

"That's a smart mindset," Cassie said, "but you were born to play that role. How 'bout you, Brian? Feeling positive about Cornelius?"

"I think it'll be either be me or Mike," Brian replied, grinning. "I should have told Mr. C. it was my birthday Wednesday. That'd be a perfect gift."

"Gee, mine was this month, too," Cassie replied. "Does that mean we automatically get the parts we want?"

Teagan chuckled. "If only it were that easy."

They chatted about other auditions as they waited for their food, and Cassie mentioned how well Beth Newton had done. "Do you think she'll get the part of the niece? She's such an awesome dancer."

"I think Beth might be the big surprise this year," Teagan said. "She's only a sophomore, but she's got one of the best voices we heard."

"Remember how amazing Beth was last year during tech week when I fainted? I think you're right – Mr. C. will remember that performance. She might even be in contention for Irene Molloy."

Brian chimed in. "She's too young, but could definitely pull off Minnie – I still think you've got the strongest vocals for Irene. I guess Kyleigh and Julia would be the other contenders."

Cassie sipped her water. "I can't wait to see which role you end up with. Even though I hope you get Cornelius, it would be an awesome match up if you played opposite Teagan. You guys are so close."

"Speaking of awesome match ups," Teagan said, "Here comes our food."

The waitress brought a huge tray with plates of burgers and fries and another platter with eggs and pancakes. Cassie almost winced at the size of the omelet. *I'll never finish all that; they must use 3-4 eggs to make that thing.* She took a small bite and smiled. *Hmmm. The cheese is so melty.*

Teagan had just taken a bite of her burger and nodded in agreement. "Best part of a meal is all the cheese. Well, that and the onions. God, I love onions."

"Hmm-hmm!" Brian added, wiping his mouth with his sleeve. "This is gonna be messy, but so worth it. How do people not like diner food?"

Cassie chuckled to herself since diners were not always at the top of her list of places to eat. The servings were always huge and in the past she spent every minute trying to avoid all the calories in front of her. This one had grown on her, but it was more because of the people than the food. That being said, she took another bite of her omelet and admitted it was awesome.

Almost at once, three cell phones dinged revealing incoming messages which meant only one thing. "Call backs!" they all said in unison, wiping hands on napkins so they could grab their phone. Cassie reached hers first and held up her hand. "Let me read it."

"*The following students should report back at 2:30 Tuesday for callbacks. Please be ready to sing the song listed and be prepared for cold readings from the script. Please reply to indicate that you've received and read this memo.*" She grinned at the two still chewing their last bite and wiping their hands on napkins. "Entire list or just your names?"

"Us first!" Brian mumbled with some fries in his mouth.

Cassie turned her attention back to her phone. "Brian – callback for Horace Vandergelder and Cornelius Hackl. Mike has the same two, by the way." To Teagan she added, "Big surprise. Call back for Dolly and Ernestina. And you're only competition is Paula – plus someone named Anne Franklin."

"That was that new girl," Brian said. "The brunette in the first group. She was talented."

"What about you?" Teagan asked.

"Call back for Irene Molloy and Minnie Fay. Me, Kyleigh, Julia, and *Beth!*"

"I *knew* it!" Brian said with gusto. "That girl's going places!" He noted Teagan's silence. "You're thinking about Joanne, aren't you?"

Teagan nodded, her eyes a bit misty. "We spent so many years with Joanne assuming we'd all be here for our senior show together. She must be so proud of her sister right now."

Cassie reached over to squeeze her hand. "She's proud of you, too."

Teagan held up her glass to make a toast. "Here's to friends – old and new – who are more like family. Love you guys."

Cassie clinked her glass and shared the sentiment. "You guys really *have* become like family to me. I'm so glad that life brought me here to Caldwell."

"We are, too," Brian replied. "Now let's go kick butt tomorrow and get those roles!"

CHAPTER 20

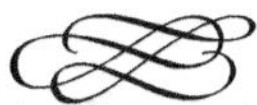

Even though the day before Thanksgiving was only a half day for school, it was the longest day of the year for any student involved in high school theater. Callbacks had gone well, and Cassie sat in psychology class waiting for Mrs. Barnes to pass back the quizzes from the day before. She sat next to Teagan who kept looking at the clock on the wall and rolling her eyes. Kyleigh and Julia sat just behind them, and Cassie could hear Kyleigh's constant nervous tapping of her pencil on the desk. Julia was quieter than normal. *"She's more like me, with the nerves on the inside."*

As soon as the bell rang she and Teagan headed out to meet up with Brian. Teagan had driven today, so they had decided to wait a bit before heading toward the auditorium. Most kids who took the bus would fly by and look at the list quickly before heading home for the holiday weekend. Brian had suggested they hold back so they could check it on their own instead of in a crowd.

"Last year Teags and I got there first and made it outside just before the gang arrived," Brian said. "So this year we catch the tail end. Are we ready to stroll over?"

"Jeez, I wanna run," Cassie said impatiently. "I swear this has been the longest hour of the year!"

The halls had cleared out quickly with students eager to have the next four days off. As they turned the last corner they saw two other cast mates sharing a high five as they headed out the door next to Mr. C's office. "Okay, the coast is clear," she joked.

As they got closer, Cassie stopped. "I don't think I can look – one of you will have to tell me."

Teagan laughed. "That was me last year – Brian had to be the brave one. I can look if you want."

"I'll go with you, Teags," Brian offered. "Cassie – have courage!" he kidded.

Cassie held her breath as the two of them walked arm in arm the last few steps.

"I *knew* it!" Brian shouted as he high fived Teagan. As the latter turned around Cassie knew immediately. "You got Dolly?"

"I did!" Teagan replied, her face beaming. "And you got Irene!"

Cassie wasn't sure who squealed first, but Teagan's arms were around her in a moment. "You'll be so awesome in that role," Teagan whispered, "I can't wait!"

Cassie tried to read Brian's smile. She had one gnawing question remaining. "Who's playing Cornelius?" The thought of Mike playing opposite her was nibbling away at her excitement.

Brian took a step forward and grinned. "I'm afraid you're stuck with me."

"Thank God!" Cassie blurted out as she wrapped her arms around Brian. "I was so afraid it would be Mike."

Teagan chuckled. "I handled him last year – I can certainly do it again with him playing Horace. It's kinda funny that I'm ace and aro and I'm playing a character who's a matchmaker."

"Let's check the rest of the list," Cassie suggested. She was thrilled that Beth Newton would play the role of Minnie – and Kyleigh had nabbed the goofy niece. She shook her head a bit. "Julia's the only senior without a lead. That's too bad."

Teagan came up behind her and put her hands on her shoulders. "Beth beat her out with her voice – and you guys had such great chemistry yesterday – I'm excited to see the two of you together."

Brian wrapped his arms around both of them. "This year is gonna be the best show ever!"

Cassie agreed. "And I've got my best friends right by my side."

* * *

THE NEXT MORNING Cassie woke up remembering the cast list and it made her smile. She sat up in bed, curling her quilt around her as she reached for her journal. She always tried to start the day writing down a few things to be grateful for – an exercise she had started when she first went to the Phoenix. *"I remember how hard it was thinking of anything to write down back then."* She thumbed through the pages until she found her very first gratitude list written back in late April. Cassie chuckled as she read through the required three items and nothing more:

- *I'm not as sick as most of the people here*
- *My roommate isn't a total jerk*
- *Teagan came to visit today (I wonder how long that will last)*

Natalie had told her that her list would change over time, and the pages she read as she thumbed through the now almost full journal reflected that. *"I really was as sick as everyone else,"* she thought. *"Thank God I've come as far as I have."* She picked up her pen and opened to the next blank page, and after thinking for a few moments, she wrote down her list:

- *I'm choosing recovery over my eating disorder today*
- *I have a recovery coach who helps me face every challenge that comes along*
- *I have a job and a volunteer gig that both nurture my creativity*
- *I'm healthy enough to be a part of the show this year – with some amazing friends*
- *I have a family that loves and supports me, even after treating them so horribly last year*

- *I might dance in the spring showcase*

Cassie read the last item on her list again. *"Not sure that counts as a gratitude, but just the idea that the possibility exists is enough for now, I guess."* She smiled as she read through the list one last time. *"Natalie was right; writing it down does help to note my recovery on days when I'm feeling lousy."* Fresh coffee beckoned from downstairs as she closed her book and put it on the table beside her bed. *"Time for Thanksgiving breakfast – and I'm even grateful for the chance to have dinner later with the family."* She was still smiling as she joined her parents in the kitchen.

"Morning," she murmured as she reached for a mug and poured herself some coffee.

"Happy Thanksgiving, honey," her mom replied. "Did you manage some sleep?"

"It took awhile, but I slept pretty well."

Her dad slid a plate of banana bread down toward her. "Want a slice? Dinner won't be until 1:00 at the Manor, so you'll want something in your stomach. And I hear congratulations are in order. Sorry I got back so late last night. I would have loved to have heard all about it when you got home."

"That's okay, Dad. You need to be putting in the extra hours right now." Cassie stopped to slide one arm down onto her dad's chest as she kissed the top of his head. "Besides, I'd rather have you working late at the beginning of the whole show than at the end."

Frank put his hand over hers and kissed her arm. "Nothing will make me miss your senior show, sweetie. Why don't you sit down and tell me all about who's playing what roles."

Eliana stood up as Cassie was sitting down. "You two have a nice chat. I have to bake a pie so we'll have something to eat tonight with dinner. Maggie assured me that each family would come home with a few leftovers, so I figure turkey sandwiches and pie will make a light meal later on." She tied her apron on and added, "You okay this morning in terms of food and the whole schedule change?"

Cassie nodded, cutting a small slice of banana bread. "Just having a chance to rectify what a jerk I was last year makes it a lot easier. I don't know if it will hit later on, but for right now, I'm okay."

"That's my girl," her dad said. "Now tell me all about auditions and how excited you must be."

Cassie took a bite of her banana bread. *"That's easy, today – at least for right now."* As her mom cut apple slices, she proceeded to reiterate the information she had shared the night before with her mom.

* * *

CALDWELL MANOR WAS BUSTLING when Cassie and her family arrived. Even though some residents went out for the day to visit family, there were quite a few families that opted to come and have dinner in the dining room with their loved one. Each family had a private table, with the other residents sitting in different spots to accommodate the different layout. On other days Cassie's grandmother Ida sat with Kitty, Gladys, and Melvin, but Kitty had gone to her daughter's home for the day, so Gladys and Melvin moved to another table with residents from the same wing.

The tables were decorated beautifully with centerpieces the residents made. Each table had a little cornucopia of silk leaves and small gourds, with a simple plaque painted with various quotes or questions about gratitude leaning against it. Cassie read the one at their table; it read "What are you grateful for today?" She smiled, wanting the chair directly facing the plaque.

Her grandmother sat to her right, and her mom sat on her other side. Philip sat on the other side of Ida, and Frank sat between him and his wife. Ida was beaming from ear to ear as they sat down. "I've been so excited to hear all about the show. You'll have to fill me in on every single detail, my dear."

Cassie was excited to tell her grandmother about auditions and the cast list. Last year she had insisted on keeping the whole show a secret from her, and it wasn't until just before the show that Ida even learned that she was involved at all, never mind as one of the leads. "Let's get our dinners first, and I can fill you in over turkey, okay?" *"That will be a strategy to keep my mind off the food I'm shoveling into my face,"* she thought. She had spotted the long buffet table along one side of the room. It was loaded with warming trays, baskets of rolls, and a big bowl of salad, and Cassie was nervous about having to walk from one end of the table to the other, filling her plate along the way. *"Of course the salad is at the opposite end – wish I could go the opposite way."*

Trying to keep the voices at bay, Cassie focused on the conversation. Philip was filling their grandmother in on school events, homework hassles, and weird things that teachers said in the classroom. Ida sat enrapt, drinking in all the information being offered. Cassie glanced at her mom and dad, who sat with content expressions as they listened. *"Focus on the question – I have so many things to be grateful for today, after all."*

Philip eventually ran out of things to talk about; Cassie noticed his gaze was constantly shifting to the staff as they carried the serving trays out from the kitchen. "Food's almost ready," he offered. "I don't know about you guys, but I'm starving."

Frank chuckled. "Just remember your manners and the other people behind you in line that might want to eat as well, okay?"

Philip groaned as he turned back to Ida. "Notice he only says that to *me,* and not Cassie."

"Ouch," Cassie thought. "Talk about a low blow, little brother."

"Jeez, I'm only kidding, sis," Philip retorted. "I'm kinda glad you're here this year. Last year I was bored being one of the only kids in the whole building. No offense, Grandma, but you live with a bunch of *old* people."

Everyone laughed as Ida responded. "Some are older than others, but we still know how to have a good time. I haven't had a single regret about moving in here – and that's sad, because there are too many here that do have those regrets."

"I bet you're a positive influence for them," Cassie said.

Ida reached over and patted her hand. "I try. If I can help one of them look for all the positive reasons to be here than I've lived with some purpose. Speaking of which, why don't we answer the question of the day before we head over for food?"

Cassie held up the plaque for everyone to see. Her father began. "I'm grateful to have a day away from the office – and to spend it with family."

"And football later," Eliana teased. "Don't forget football."

"She knows me too well," he laughed.

Eliana went next. "I'm grateful that we could all be here this year, and that Cassie is back with us and getting healthier every day."

Cassie blushed a bit. "I guess I'm grateful most of all for being alive, and believing that I'm worth fighting for. Plus all the people that help me to keep getting better."

Ida reached over and patted her hand again. "We're all grateful that you're here and getting better. I'm also grateful that I can look forward to another amazing musical in the spring." She turned to Philip. "So, young man, how about you?"

Philip's gaze was beyond his grandmother, but he'd heard her and he grinned. "Me? I'm grateful that they're taking the lids off the food dishes. Finally!"

As soon as Cassie reached the head of the buffet line, she froze. *"Oh my, God – there's too much food here. How will I ever know how much to take?"* "I don't know if I can do this," she whispered back to her mom.

Her mom's voice provided reassurance. "I'll guide you through it, and if you start to struggle I'll grab the serving spoon, okay?"

Cassie nodded, trying to swallow as her mouth suddenly dried up. *"Focus on the health. I'm not gonna listen to you, eating disorder. You can tell me that I'm taking too much potato right now, but I'm trusting mom's subtle nods when I have the right amount – even if I think you're right and she's wrong. God, that's a lot of squash....."* By the time she got to the salad, she felt like her plate weighed 100 pounds. There were small salad dishes next to the greens and Cassie wondered if she could even manage two plates.

"How about I help you with your lettuce," her mom offered. "Just hold your dinner plate and I'll fill your salad dish – you don't want to miss out on these tomatoes." Cassie watched her ladle ranch dressing over the salad, and then extended the smaller dish toward her. "Can you handle holding this in your hand while still grasping the dinner plate? Otherwise I can carry it for you."

"No, I can manage," Cassie replied hesitatingly. She made her way back to the table, sure that she'd trip and drop her meal everywhere. Surely every person in the room was watching her carrying this over-flowing plate of food back to her spot. *I probably took more than anyone else in the room. This might have been a terrible idea coming here today.*

Back at the table, Ida greeted her with a smile. "I can't wait for you to sit and tell me all about the show." As Cassie sat down she added, "and I'm so grateful that my Cassandra is back again – and just won another major battle in the last five minutes."

"Thanks, Gram. I think I needed to hear that."

Once everyone was seated, Ida raised her glass of water. "To family —a blessing to cherish."

Cassie reached for her own and clinked her glass with all the others. "To family," she joined in. *Both this one here and my second family – Maggie, Teagan, Brian, and the theater gang. I am pretty damn blessed.*

* * *

TWO BLOCKS away Maggie was mashing potatoes as Tim carved the turkey. She glanced down at the kitchen table, now loaded with serving dishes filled with squash, stuffing, green bean casserole, onions, gravy, and cranberry sauce. The blend of aromas filled the room and Maggie heard her stomach growl.

Carl wandered in to the kitchen as laughter followed from the living room. "That food almost ready yet? Some of us old folks are starving," he said, reaching out to grab a piece of turkey skin from the serving platter.

Tim turned toward his grandfather and raised his eyebrows. "You supposed to eat the skin?"

"Pffft," the old man grumbled as he licked his lips. "Today's a holiday – there are no forbidden foods on holidays." He smirked as he wandered around to Maggie's side of the table. "I don't like any lumps in those potatoes."

Maggie chuckled, taking a moment to tuck a lone wisp of hair back behind her ear. "Working on it, Carl. Sounds like you're keeping them entertained out there."

"Heck, no. Your dad and Sharon are having a reunion-fest out there; he's giving her the scoop on a bunch of old classmates."

"Yeah, he said last night that he remembered Sharon. He's a couple of years behind her, but Caldwell's a small town, after all. Hope he's not monopolizing the conversation."

Carl shook his head as he reached down to grab a small piece of stuffing with his fingers.

"Grandad, not with your fingers!" Tim teased. The old man's eyes sparkled as he grinned across the table. "It's tradition. Everybody does it." He turned to Maggie and added, "Ruthie used to hit my hand with the back of whatever kitchen utensil she was holding at the time."

Maggie held up her potato masher. "You better be glad you're standing next to me then and not Tim – that carving knife might take a finger off!"

Tim added another couple of slices of turkey to the plate and put the knife down. "Tell you what, Grandad – why don't you head out and tell folks dinner is ready. I could use a few extra hands to carry all this in to the dining room, but we're set to eat."

"About time," Carl answered, trying to hide his grin. "A man could starve in his own home waiting for you two lovebirds to put a meal on the table." He headed back toward the living room as Tim came around the table and leaned in for a kiss. "I'd hug you but I wanna wash my hands after carving. I don't think I've ever seen him so happy."

Maggie agreed as Carl announce dinner. "I doubt he ever thought he'd have a Thanksgiving celebration in his home again. What a difference a year makes."

Tim winked as he stepped to the sink to wash his hands. "Best year ever – for quite a few of us."

Maggie snuck up behind him and reached around him to place the potato masher in the sink, wrapping her arms around his waist afterwards. She leaned in and kissed his back, breathing in his scent through his shirt. "Hmmm….I'll go along with that."

They were interrupted by the bustle of hungry women entering the kitchen. Sharon led the way with Maggie's mom right behind. "I hear we're finally needed," Lisa Richmond said cheerfully.

Tim turned toward the older women as Lucy and Liz entered the kitchen as well. "Table's all set, so grab a serving dish and find a hot plate to put it on…..the big one will be for the turkey, but any of the others are fine for the rest of the food." He gestured toward Lucy, who was standing next to the refrigerator. "Could you and Liz pour the cider?"

"You got it, boss," Lucy replied, reaching in to grab two half gallons of cider and handing one to Liz. The two of them headed back into the dining room where Carl and John Richmond were sitting down. "You guys better hurry," Liz yelled back playfully. "Carl's gonna start banging his knife and fork on the table soon."

* * *

A FEW MINUTES later Maggie found herself sitting between Tim and Sharon. Her dad sat at one end with her mom across from Sharon. Lucy and Liz also sat on the opposite side with Carl at the head of the table. Once all the serving dishes had made their way around the table, Carl extended his hands out toward Tim and Liz. "Not much of a praying man, but I thought we might say grace – Ruthie always insisted on holidays."

Maggie's plate was brimming with stuffing and all the veggies and she gave thanks that her own eating disorder wasn't trying to interfere in her meal. *Thank you, God, for recovery, and all that it's brought into my life.*

Tim squeezed her hand and lifted his glass of cider. "To all the events that led my mom and I back to Caldwell, and for everything we've found since we've been home. To family!"

"To family!" all echoed, clinking glasses with each other. Maggie smiled as she looked around the table. It was wonderful having her parents up from Florida to visit, and she was thrilled with how well they got along with Tim's mom and grandfather. Lucy and Liz were keeping Carl entertained with stories from town hall, and Tim joined in the conversations at both ends of the table. Maggie caught his eye as he reached for his fork and smiled. She was rewarded with that dimpled grin.

"Love you," he whispered as he speared some turkey. "Now let's eat!"

She reached down to scoop some mashed potato on her fork. *"Let's eat, indeed. And thank you, God, for this amazing man."*

CHAPTER 21

The following Tuesday Cassie headed to work after school to help Brooke with more basket items for the big raffle. More completed baskets were piled on various counters; some had been donated by businesses and others by Caldwell individuals. Cassie was helping with basket accents and labels to make them all uniform. There were over fifty baskets done with two weeks still to go, and Brooke thought they might make it to eighty before the big event. "For the first year we're doing this, I'm thrilled with the community response," Brooke said as she showed Cassie the newest arrivals. "These all need labels. We have an Italian basket from Gino, a book and cocoa basket from the book store, and a kids craft basket from us – I threw that together over the weekend."

"These look awesome. I'll label them first, and then work on a few more of the ornaments we've been doing."

Brooke pointed to a bin that had several completed items in it. "Those are going like crazy. Especially the little trees with the Caldwell Christmas dated item. We'll have to make a different one each year from here on in – that was a fabulous idea, Cassie."

Cassie pulled out a box with plain wooden tree shapes from under the counter. "They were so easy to do – I'm glad they're selling. I should be able to finish another dozen today if that's what you want me to focus on."

"As soon as the basket stuff is done. I won't be able to help you much back here today; business is picking up with the holiday season underway. Any chance you could come in Friday this week? You're scheduled for Saturday, and I realize you have a rehearsal tomorrow and Thursday, but I'd love to grab you for a few more hours if you're open. No pressure, though."

"As long as my folks are okay to pick me up, I'll be here. I've been finding that having something to do every day has been helping. My eating disorder tends to make more noise in my head when I have a lot of down time."

"I guess the show will be a good thing for you, then? Even if I can only use you once a week after New Year's?"

"Having the reduced hours made the decision easy. I couldn't manage work, the show, and therapy if the hours were still three days a week."

"So how was your Thanksgiving?"

"Overall it went well. I had a short panic moment at the buffet table, but my mom helped me through it. I have another dinner tomorrow, but it's only a slice of pizza and salad this time, so I think I can handle that."

"Tomorrow's the first rehearsal?"

"Hmm-mm. The read through. We'll get our scripts and then read through the show cold for the first time. I'm excited – and so stoked to have Teagan and Brian as fellow leads. When I went to the Phoenix after last year's show I wondered if I'd even be able to do the show this year, never mind have the lead I wanted most."

Brooke smiled. "Recovery has some things worth fighting for, doesn't it?" As the older woman headed back to the front of the store, Cassie turned on her music and started working. *"It sure does,"* she thought, giving thanks to be able to sing and paint – and get paid for it.

* * *

THE NEXT AFTERNOON Cassie sat in a big circle on the stage between Teagan and Brian waiting for rehearsal to start. Julia sat with Mike, but seemed more interested in talking with Kyleigh on her other side. As Cassie studied Mike a younger ensemble member stopped to talk to Paula, who sat a few seats away from Mike. *"Jeez, is he checking her out? With Julia sitting right beside him?"* As the girl glanced over toward Mike he flashed her a grin. *"What a jerk,"* Cassie thought. *"Julia doesn't deserve that."*

She shook her head as Brian leaned close. "You saw that, too?"

"So it wasn't just me? I was hoping I was wrong."

"Hey, I may be gay, but I recognize a guy checking someone out. Never liked him, not gonna lie."

"I'm liking him less and less myself."

Teagan had been chatting with Beth Newton on her other side but heard Cassie's comment. "Who we talking about?" she whispered.

"Mike. He was just checking out that ensemble girl -- the one in the pink top."

Teagan looked over at the sophomore with a form fitting knit top that hugged her breasts tightly. "Yeah, I'm sure I can guess which parts he was looking at, too. What an ass."

Before Cassie could respond, Terry the stage manager got their attention. "Okay, folks, we are ready to roll! I'll be taking attendance. As your name is called, please come up for your scripts. Ensemble members, you can take one from either Mrs. Patterson or Mrs. Kelly – just be sure to sign your name next to the number on the sheet in front of them. Leads, your scripts will have your names on them. If you guys lose your scripts, you'll owe us fifteen bucks for a new one – and only use light pencil to make any notes! Got it?"

With everyone nodding, Terry began. Cassie noticed that Julia seemed a little quiet when she got her ensemble script, especially when Kyleigh returned with hers marked with the role of Ermengarde. When Beth Newton's name was called, some of the sophomores clapped loudly, including the girl in the pink top. Mike's attention seemed to stray again in her direction.

When Cassie's name was called, along with Brian's, the two of them headed up for their scripts – this time to some genuine applause from the entire cast. Cassie blushed a bit when she sat back down, not liking all that attention. It was one thing to perform in front of a bunch of strangers who she couldn't see, but amongst her peers who knew her, she felt more like she was under a microscope.

As soon as she sat back down Mike's name was called, and there was lots of applause. He strutted from the far end of the circle to the other, enjoying the attention. Just as he reached the table, Teagan's name was called, and the applause exploded. Cassie hid her smirk at Mike's reaction to the louder applause. He bowed dramatically to Teagan to regain some attention, and she responded with an equally dramatic curtsey before taking her script. Cassie loved that her friend wasn't taking any of Mike's antics.

Teagan sat down and whispered as Mike return to his seat. "Was he this arrogant last year with you?"

"I don't think so – but I wasn't a great judge of character back then."

As Mr. C. stood up, Teagan chuckled. "I like you way better now."

The first act flew by; Cassie loved reading with both Beth and Brian, but her favorite scenes were those where she interacted with Teagan. The chemistry between all the leads was amazing; Cassie couldn't believe how perfectly Mr.C. had cast the show. *I guess that's why he's such an amazing director,*" she thought.

When the cast finished the first act, Terry directed them all across the hall for a quick dinner break. Cassie found herself next to Beth Newton as they walked across the hall, and complimented the younger cast mate on the first half.

"I have never been so excited," Beth exclaimed. "Having a lead that lets me play alongside you and Brian and Teagan is like a dream come true. I love our scenes, by the way."

"Me, too. I'm excited for the year ahead."

Brian had run up behind Beth, and Cassie loved watching the two of them. She had never known the older Newton sister, but it was clear that Brian loved Beth just as much. "Hey kiddo, stop making all of us look bad, okay?"

Beth grinned at him and poked her finger against his chest. "Gotta keep up with the best, don't I? Hey, where's Teagan, anyway?"

Almost on cue, she entered the room from the hallway. "Right behind you, girl. And you were killing it as Minnie Fay." As Beth reached out to give Teagan a huge hug, Teagan continued. "Seriously, Beth, you have grown so much with your voice since last year. I got goosebumps listening to you sing. And the harmonies you had with Cassie – on the first time through? Unbelievable."

They had reached the buffet line and Cassie took a styrofoam plate and napkin. Her brain wanted to react like it had on Thanksgiving, but this spread was much more manageable. Plain pizzas and salad, with a plate of cookies at the end. *"This is just like dinner at home,"* she thought. *"Grab a slice and a bunch of salad, and you're all set. So screw off, eating disorder – I've got a meal to eat before rehearsal starts back up."*

When she got a table, she found herself seated with Teagan, Paula, Brian, and Lou. Kyleigh was over sitting with Julia and Mike with a few of the guys in the ensemble, and he was paying way more attention to them than he was to Julia. *"Something's not right between them,"* Cassie surmised. *"I'm glad she has Kyleigh to hang out with right now."*

She turned her attention to Brian and Lou, who were loudly reciting scenes from Hamilton in between bites. She and Teagan just laughed and shook their heads. It was like mealtime entertainment, and Cassie took bite after bite as she listened. By the time the dinner break was over, Cassie had finished all but the crust of her pizza and just a little salad left on her plate. She was full, but not stuffed. At home she often ate a second slice of pizza, but she had agreed with her mom to just take the one with the time allotment so limited. *"Overall, I'd call that a victory,"* she thought as she deposited the plates in the trash.

Teagan was right beside her, and gestured to the plate Cassie had just thrown away. "I'm so proud of you right now. You handled that dinner like a pro."

Cassie responded with a hug. "Let's head back over there and show them all who's gonna hear the most applause next spring, shall we?" Teagan grabbed her arm and led the way.

CHAPTER 22

The weeks leading up to Caldwell's Christmas in the Park kept Maggie extra busy as she had volunteered to help Brooke with baskets. With only a couple of days left before the big event she had stopped at Brooke's after work with five more baskets for the raffle in her trunk. The residents had put together two of them, and she had picked up items from the Catholic church, town hall, and one of the doctor's offices.

Brooke had told her to park out back to unload them, but Maggie had offered to pick up labels and bring them over to Tim's office herself. As she entered the store several customers were browsing, so she waved at Brooke on her way to the back room. She found Cassie working hard getting the last minute craft items finished for the Caldwell Christmas event. Brooke had bought another big box of the Christmas tree shapes and she and Cassie had spent every free minute painting as many as they could for the inaugural celebration.

"Looks like you've been super busy," she greeted Cassie. Holding up a tree ornament she added, "These are adorable. Hope you made a ton, 'cause they'll sell like hotcakes."

Cassie smiled as she painted delicate red ribbons on one tree in front of her, decorating each ornament in a unique way. "I'm just about done. Can you wait for about ten minutes?"

Maggie nodded as Brooke entered the room."Let's hope Mother Nature cooperates." She glanced down at Cassie's work. "I can't believe how many ornaments this girl has painted this month."

"They'll make some money," Maggie surmised. "You holding up okay?"

"It's been a little crazy between the baskets and regular sales, but I only have another week or so before vacation. Besides, I'm excited about how everything's falling into place. You guys are all set to work the baskets at Tim's office, right?"

"Yup. Cassie will help me, and you and Colleen can work over at the café's tables and give us a signal when it's time to head over to the gazebo. Teagan's helping the rest of the committee getting the gazebo area set up. Did we ever decide if we're gonna try and cart all the baskets over for the drawing?"

Brooke shook her head. "Tim agreed with me that it wasn't necessary. Most folks will be walking right past on the way back to their cars, so they can stop in and pick them up. We'll leave the gazebo as soon as things wrap up to be here to hand baskets out to the winners. Any leftover baskets that people forget to claim I'll bring back to the shop and they can pick them up before the 23rd."

Cassie finished up the last ornament and put her paintbrush into water. "Sounds like a plan. The whole thing sounds awesome; if anyone in town didn't like Tim before now they're gonna love him after this."

"I know of one that might particularly love him," Brooke teased as she winked at Maggie. She stopped Cassie from picking up the jar of paintbrushes. "Don't worry about cleaning up – I'll do it before leaving. I can't thank you enough for all the extra time and work you've put in. Hiring you was the smartest thing I've done since opening this shop."

Cassie blushed a little. "Really? 'Cause most of the time it doesn't even feel like work. Being able to paint and create has made it so much easier not being able to dance next door."

Brooke gave Cassie a little hug. "I'm almost hoping you'll decide not to go back when the time comes….but wherever you end up, you'll always have a job here if you want it."

"Thanks, Brooke. I wanna work here as long as you'll have me. You've become a good friend."

"I feel the same. Now grab your stuff and get out of here. I think Maggie's hungry." As Cassie got her coat Brooke continued. "Is Tim joining you guys tonight?"

"No, he has a meeting with Amanda and Rich O'Sullivan to go over some of the non-profit issues for the center. I'll catch up with him later tonight to drop these off, but I'm looking forward to hanging out with Cassie."

As the youngster returned they said goodbye to Brooke and headed across the street to pick up their meals at Gino's. As Lucy was off with Liz for the evening Maggie was looking forward to a relaxing evening at home.

The smell of mozzarella and garlic greeted them as the little bell signaled their arrival, and Gino's face lit up as he spotted them. "Buena serra, ladies! You must be here to meet that handsome man of yours."

Maggie's eyebrows went up for a moment with surprise; she had assumed that Tim's meeting was at Rich or Amanda's office, but it made sense that they'd be here as they'd be working through dinner time. She smiled back at Gino and shook her head. "Tonight is girls' night, so I'm picking up our order. The eggplant parm dinners and a salad."

Gino nodded in reply, wiping his hands on his apron before reaching up to grab one of the brown paper bags on the shelf. "Always a good choice. Enjoy your dinner, Maggie."

As she stood waiting for her change, Maggie glanced at the various people dining until one table grabbed her attention. She could see the back of Tim's head, but only Amanda was seated across from him, and she was laughing as she picked up her wine glass with one hand and flipped her hair back with the other. Maggie looked for some kind of file folder or any indication that a work meeting was in progress, but saw nothing but a bread basket to one side.

"Why did he tell me that Rich was part of this meeting? And why didn't he tell me that they were meeting here?" She fought the urge to go and confront them, standing frozen in her fears as her eating disorder chimed in. *"He's discovering how attractive Amanda is and how much they have in common.....and she's so much prettier and thinner than you'll ever be."*

As Gino handed her back her change his expression softened. "You okay, Maggie?"

She blinked back her tears and forced a smile. "Must be the garlic, Gino….makes my eyes water sometimes. See you next time." She grabbed her bag and turned to head for the door as Cassie followed.

Once outside, Maggie took a few steps toward the crosswalk before she noticed the concerned expression on Cassie's face. "What's that look for?"

"I saw him, too." As she took a step toward Maggie she spoke almost in a whisper. "I'm sure it wasn't what it looked like."

Maggie's gazed back toward Gino's window as her eyes filled with tears. "I don't know what to think right now – I just wanna get home, okay?"

As she drove the short distance her mind exploded into countless scenarios of Tim and Amanda together, laughing and drinking wine – at Gino's, in his office, at the community center, and even on the balcony of his townhouse in Gloucester. *"I told you you'd never keep him,"* her eating disorder chided. *"He'll always find someone more worthy than you are."*

As she parked the car she finally let her anger out, slamming her hands on the steering wheel. "Damn it!" she yelled. "JUST SHUT UP!"

The tears spilled over as Cassie spoke quietly beside her. "I can only imagine what those voices are saying – no, probably screaming – at you right now."

Maggie sniffled as she pulled a tissue out of her pocket and blew her nose. She gave Cassie a weak smile. "You probably know exactly what's going on in my head right now." She wiped her eyes and took a deep breath. "Let's head in before your dinner gets cold, okay?"

As they reached the door of her apartment Maggie was greeted by Tramp's wagging tail and excited dances around her feet. She reached down to give him a scratch behind the ears. "Hey, boy. I'll take you out in a minute, okay?" She received a wet kiss on her hand from the one who would forever love her as she was.

Cassie also greeted Tramp as Maggie carried the food to the kitchen, then followed her in to find her reading a note on the counter. "Lucy took him out before she left, so we can stay in." She reached into the cabinet and pulled out two bowls, sliding one over to Cassie as she took the food out of the bag. As she reached into the drawer to grab utensils she saw Cassie's concern. "I'll be okay. You go ahead with your dinner before it gets cold." She methodically opened her own container with eggplant parmigiana as her mind took her back to Gino's and the image of Tim sitting across from the smiling Amanda – the thin, attractive Amanda who was clearly flirting with the flip of her hair.

As Cassie watched, she angrily grabbed a fork and scooped some eggplant and pasta, almost banging the bowl as she plated the rich and gooey cheese laden food. "I'll be *damned* if I'm gonna let her derail my recovery." She opened her salad container, stabbed some greens, and filled up the other half of her plate as tears filled her eyes again. "DAMN that woman!"

"It's okay to be angry. That's what you're always telling me. But Maggie, I still think your head is trying to convince you to believe the lie. I *know* Tim loves you. Everyone can see that he's the real deal. Your own eating disorder is feeding you a load of crap, that's all."

Maggie stopped and looked over at her younger friend. "I've trained you well, haven't I? Let's go in and get comfy. I'm gonna force myself to eat this meal." As they settled on the couch her brain screamed at her to put the food down.

Cassie held up some pasta on her fork. "To recovery," she said before blowing on it and sliding the fork into her mouth. She nodded toward Maggie and mumbled, "The sauce is a tad spicy tonight."

Maggie faced the strongest test in her own recovery as she defiantly shoved a forkful of the pasta into her mouth and swallowed without noticing taste or texture. *"Just eat."* She gave thanks for the friend beside her. "I guess tonight showed you that it never truly goes away. If you weren't here I suspect this food would still be sitting on the counter and I'd be in bed crying my eyes out." She forced another mouthful. "So thank you."

Cassie twirled her fork around the piece of eggplant and spaghetti as she watched the stringy cheese wrap around the fork as she went. "Ya know, you're the one that taught *me* the need to separate the thoughts from the process of eating. I remember lots of meals when I shoveled food into my mouth like a robot. But now I'm sitting here smelling the cheese and tomato and garlic, and enjoying the textures in my mouth. Is your brain rewired enough at this point to be able to eat mindfully in times like this, or is it simply a repeated action? I don't have the recovery that you do to know exactly what you're going through right now."

Mindful eating. Seemed like a foreign concept all of a sudden, but Maggie forced herself to slowly smell the mix of cheese and balsamic dressing on the salad, and she followed Cassie's suggestion and twirled some pasta and cheese around her fork. Instead of chewing and swallowing, she took the time to recognize the tastes and textures in her mouth before swallowing. "Thanks. That helped a lot." She took another bite – this time of salad – and paused to crunch on lettuce and onion. "It's almost surreal to be honest. My head is screaming at me to restrict and push the plate away, my body is trying to follow the steps I've learned by shoveling the food in and swallowing it, and now you've made my mind aware that this isn't an automatic action like brushing my teeth. It's become a normal activity again in my life – one that's been filled with wonderful meals." She paused to take a sip of water. "I can't say that I'm enjoying the meal, but I'm at least aware of it. I guess that shows a little progress over the years."

Cassie reached over and squeezed her hand. "You've made a *ton* of progress over the years – and you'll continue to do so. I'm glad I could be here tonight; I might have helped you, but you're still teaching me through your struggle."

Maggie took in a deep breath and exhaled. "This is the closest to a relapse that I've ever been – last time I was lucky enough to have Lucy stop me from heading out for an unhealthy run." She shook her head sadly. "And both of those times come back to Tim."

"You *do* have to talk to him. Otherwise it's gonna keep eating away at you from the inside."

Maggie nodded as the churning in her stomach began again. "I know – and every time I think about it I feel like I'm gonna throw up."

"So let's look at this from Natalie's perspective," Cassie suggested. "Having the same therapist has some perks, I guess." She continued as Maggie chuckled. "She'd tell you to look objectively at what you observed and then weigh it against the history you and Tim have shared – and *then* assess which scenario is more likely to be true. Is it the one your eating disorder is screaming at you, or what common sense and history would tell you?"

Maggie's eyes brightened a bit. "You should consider going into psychology. You're sounding an awful lot like Natalie right now."

"Well?"

Maggie sighed. "If I'm smart I'll listen to the latter, because it hasn't failed me. And my eating disorder *only* tells me lies. So on one level I should push this aside and laugh at it, finish my dinner, and forget the whole thing, right?"

"Hell, if you can do that then you're way farther along in recovery than I may ever be. But at least you're vocalizing the voice of Maggie in recovery." She took another bite of her meal. "I imagine it still hurts like hell, though. Emotions don't always listen to logic, do they?"

"No, they don't. And I guess that's why it hit me so hard. I know Tim loves me – I truly do – but attractive single women like Amanda are always gonna attack my insecurities. I guess that's what I'm most afraid of. Will my own insecurities end up destroying my relationship?"

"Is this is where Natalie would remind you of the need for open communication?"

Maggie put her plate down. "Yeah….that means I have to talk to him later tonight or tomorrow first thing."

"Well, my mom's picking me up at 8:00, so you can always head over with all those baskets tonight. Unless you'd rather wait to face him, in which case I could help you carry the baskets in here and label them."

"I think I'd like that. I don't want to leave the stuff out in the trunk overnight in case it gets cold, and it might be smart to finish them ahead of time. I'm not sure I'll be in a crafty mood later. Are you sure you don't mind? You must be sick of them all by now."

Cassie shook her head as she put her empty dish down. "I've had a blast working on all of them. C'mon, I'll help you cart them in."

Maggie grabbed the two dishes and took them to the kitchen. It would be a welcome distraction for the next couple of hours. *"God knows I can use all the help I can get,"* she thought, dreading the impending confrontation with Tim.

* * *

BY THE TIME Cassie's mom arrived they had the baskets finished and back into Maggie's trunk, and after saying goodbye, Maggie knew that she had to talk to Tim about what she had seen. Her hands trembled a bit as she texted him to find out if she could drop baskets off at the office that evening.

His reply came quickly. "Sure, come on over. We're just finishing up here." He had added a heart emoji, but Maggie's brain wanted to cast that aside and just focus on the fact that he had said "we". *"Why did they leave Gino's and go to his office? For privacy?"*

She jotted a quick note for Lucy and addressed Tramp. "Wanna come along? I might need some moral support." The beagle understood that he was invited, and trotted toward the door wagging his tail. She smiled as she squatted down to pat him and attach his leash. "Thank God I have you. You'll always love me, won't you?" His answer was a warm lick to her face and a tail that thumped against her legs.

Tramp seemed confused when she opened the car door. "We have stuff to deliver, boy – but I need you on a leash if my hands are gonna be full." She smiled as he jumped in, always trusting her in anything she asked. She knew he'd be sitting there with anticipation until she walked around and got in, responding to her arrival with tail thumps against the seat as she backed out of her spot.

When they pulled up in front of Tim's office his response got more excited as Maggie's anxiety grew. "I'm glad you're with me, boy. Let's go see what's going on, shall we?" She opened the trunk of the car while holding Tramp's leash, grabbing one of the smaller baskets to carry in with her.

As she opened the side door of the garage into the stairwell she could hear laughter inside the office. She knocked on the door and saw Tim approach through the sheer curtain she had helped him put up. As the door flew open she was greeted with his dimpled smile and open arms reaching out for the basket.

"Let me take that," he offered as she nervously stepped in behind him. She was surprised to find not only Amanda, but Rich O'Sullivan as well. Both were seated around Tim's drafting table, which he had pulled out from the wall for better access. Rich got up to greet her first. "Hey, there! You should have joined us!" Amanda followed behind. "Hi, Maggie. Nice to see you again." Maggie nodded at the two of them, all of a sudden full of doubts over her earlier suspicions.

She had released Tramp's leash when they entered, and he was now basking in a belly rub from Tim. "How's my favorite guy, huh?" He smiled up from his squatting position. "Any other baskets to come in?" She stood there and nodded, not quite sure what to say. He gave Tramp one last pat. "You stay here, boy. We'll be right back." He turned toward Rich and Amanda and gestured toward the table. "You guys can wrap up the final notes; Maggie and I will grab the others real quick." He flashed her a smile as he reached for her hand and led her outside.

Once outside the door, he pulled her toward him. "Besides, I wanted a chance to say hello in private." As his lips found hers Maggie felt her previous fears replaced with guilt. *You were wrong,* she chided her eating disorder. *"And I was wrong to ever doubt him."* She shivered when he released her.

"You warm enough?" he asked with concern. "You can wait inside if you want."

"I'm fine. Just a little adrenaline in the system, I guess. I'll tell you about it later."

After opening the trunk she handed off the two big baskets to Tim, and then grabbed the two smaller ones that were left before awkwardly reaching up to slam the trunk door shut. Luckily her baskets were light and they were back inside in no time.

Tim gestured for her to put the baskets on his regular meeting table that had been moved toward the front of the office by the garage door. It was now covered with a holiday table cloth and numerous other baskets. Around the outer walls there were two other tables set up and filled with baskets, along with a row of bins piled two high – these were each covered with plastic tablecloths and ribbons to make them look like stacked presents. Maggie estimated that there had to be close to thirty at this spot alone, and the café would have even more room for their half of the display.

"Sorry we've sort of taken over your office," she said. "I guess that explains why you had pulled the drafting table out." She pulled out little ticket containers that went with the baskets they'd carried in and placed them in front of each.

By now Amanda and Rich had wandered over to look at the newest additions. Amanda smiled at the one donated by a local doctor's office. "Band-Aids, a thermometer, a first-aid kit..." she read the items listed. "Oooh! And a day at the Brentwood Spa? I'll be stuffing a bunch of tickets into this one."

"Brooke had a fantastic idea with this raffle," Rich said. "Now let's hope that people stop in to bid on all of them."

Amanda held up the ticket container from the basket she'd been looking at and shook it. "Judging from how many are here from the doctor's office, I don't think we'll have to worry. Besides, when Tim opens up these doors folks will be walking right past on their way to the park."

"And we'll have signs at the other end of the park reminding people to stop down before the tree lighting," Tim added.

Rich glanced at the clock on the wall. "I guess I'd better be getting home. I think we covered a lot tonight; I'll present the notes to town council next month to keep them up to date, and we can meet again after the holidays."

Amanda had put the basket down and headed for her coat draped over a chair. "I'll check on those two questions you had regarding the grants and that large donation." As she put her coat on, Maggie noticed a flirtatious look toward Tim as she pulled her hair out from inside the back of the coat. "And where would you like me for Christmas in Caldwell? I'll do whatever you'd like me to do."

Maggie took a deep breath as Amanda glanced her way and smiled before locking her eyes back on Tim. She watched for any change in his expression and found none as he replied. "You could help either here or at the café doing baskets, or up at the gazebo helping to set up for the main festivities. I'm glad the committee is all on board to be there to help."

She buttoned up her coat and reached out to pat Tim's arm when done. "Put me down for the gazebo – I'm sure you'll have a bunch of little things that need tending to." She again smiled toward Maggie. "Good night, Maggie." As she and Rich headed for the door, she turned back one last time toward Tim and flashed a wide smile. "And thanks for dinner – I had such a lovely time."

Maggie recognized the last look that Amanda sent her way. She knew without a doubt that the attractive attorney was clearly interested in Tim and intended to pursue him. The challenge was on – even if Tim might not be aware of it yet. *See?* her eating disorder teased, *I was right. She's gonna steal him right away--you can't compete with someone like her and you know it.*

Maggie bit her lip as Tim give a final wave from the door before closing it and facing her again. "Finally," he said approaching her. "I thought they'd never leave." He reached out his arms toward her but saw her expression and instead rested his hands on her shoulders. "You okay? I know that look – what's wrong?"

"Can we sit and talk?"

Tim nodded with concern. "Let me clear off the loveseat – or we can go upstairs – whatever you prefer."

Maggie gestured toward the loveseat covered with a couple boxes of files. "Here's fine. I can help with these." She picked up one of the boxes and followed Tim's lead in placing it on the floor. She curled up one leg underneath her and faced him as he sat down next to her. Not knowing where to begin, she just blurted out her biggest fear. "You *do* know that Amanda has a thing for you, right?"

Tim leaned back. "So I'm not crazy?" He reached one arm out on the back of the loveseat toward Maggie. "Cause all night she's been making me as uncomfortable as hell. Thank God you came when you did. I was terrified that Rich might leave me alone with her." He saw the concern on Maggie's face. "And may I address your eating disorder that's giddy with excitement to tell it to shut up and go away?" He leaned in close. "You have *nothing* to worry about."

Maggie's eyes met his as the fears began to fade. "I spotted the two of you at Gino's when Cassie and I picked up our food…"

Tim's eyes registered understanding and he finished her thought. "And you didn't see Rich because he was running late." He reached out to pull her toward him. "I wish you'd stopped by the table. I might have begged you and Cassie to join us." As she settled in next to him, he caressed her hair as he intertwined his fingers with hers. "I can only imagine what kind of evening you might have had. I'm so sorry, honey."

Maggie, feeling secure again, spun around so that she was curled up on his lap facing him. Wrapping her one arm around his neck, she focused on his steady gaze. "Just kiss me," she whispered. "My eating disorder can go to hell."

He pulled her close and granted her wishes eagerly.

CHAPTER 23

A couple of days later Cassie got up a little early to make sure she had everything ready for the "Christmas in Caldwell" celebration that evening. She still had a yoga class and the pre-ballet class at the studio to help with, and then she'd meet Brooke at the shop for a quick lunch and to load up the last of the baskets to bring over to Tim's office.

Her dad was sitting at the table with coffee, toast, and the newspaper when she entered. "Morning, sweetie. Your mom just dropped Philip off at Seth's and she's doing some handbag deliveries this morning so she'll be set for tonight. You okay with breakfast? She left warm oatmeal on the stove."

"Not a problem," Cassie replied, grabbing an apple off the counter and slicing it onto a small plate. "Mom and I sat down last night and planned out my food for the day. I have lunch and dinner all packed and ready to go, and I've been getting my own breakfast for almost a month now."

Her dad put his paper down. "I imagine you're getting excited about tonight."

Cassie smiled as she scraped the oatmeal into a bowl and arranged the apple slices on top. She opened the cabinet and added a spoonful of peanut butter to her breakfast and joined her dad at the table. "I can't wait. I think the whole night is gonna be awesome."

"You've come so far since being back home. I'm so proud of you, sweetie."

"Thanks, Dad. I wouldn't be where I am if it hadn't been for you and Mom. You guys have been my rock…I was pretty nasty to both of you last year at this time."

Frank took a sip of coffee. "Those were rough months for all of us." He got quiet for a minute before continuing. "Your mom was worried about you all the time – and I worried about both of you, because she had to handle most of the battles on her own while I was at work." His voice softened. "We were both so scared of losing you. I know I didn't help by yelling at you sometimes, but I was so frustrated when I couldn't fix it."

"At times I hated you guys. Even at the Phoenix, I had so much anger."

"That wasn't you, sweetie – that was your eating disorder."

Cassie put her spoon down for a minute. "I'm sorry for all the pain I caused both of you. I hope someday I can make it up."

Her dad patted her hand. "You are – every day you fight the anorexia and chalk up another day of recovery. We're glad to have our daughter back." He smiled weakly and added, "And I'm sorry if I still push sometimes. I know it's not always what you need, but I'm trying."

"I know you are, Dad – even more so since our session with Natalie. I like being able to talk again – like now."

"I agree. And I'm learning to trust the process, hard as that is for a goal oriented guy like me. So how's the oatmeal?"

Cassie gave him a thumbs up. "So are you coming tonight?"

Frank finished his last bite of toast. "Sure hope to. Gonna work from home today so I'm not stuck in the city on a project."

"Still haven't heard anything about your promotion?"

"I think it'll be after the holidays. Don't worry, you guys will be the first to know."

"Will…..we have to move again? If you get it?"

"I've asked a couple of times and they've said no, so hopefully that won't change. They did say I'd have more travel, but I can handle that as long as we stay in Caldwell."

"I love it here, Dad. Feels like home."

"It *is* home. Heck, your mom lived right in this house when she was your age. And we all love being close to your grandmother."

"I wish Gram could come tonight, but I told her someone would tape us singing."

"The weather's a little chilly for the folks at Caldwell Manor to be out – and besides, Teagan and Maggie are both super busy, so who would bring them over?"

"I guess you and Mom couldn't wheel her over, huh?"

Frank got up to clear his dish. "Dealing with wheelchairs is not my strength, sweetie – you know that. But your Gram can hear all about it the next time you visit."

"I'll be going up tomorrow. Some of the high school kids are coming to do some caroling with all the residents. I think Mom and Philip are coming along, too. If you're free you could –"

"Won't be free tomorrow. I'll head in on the early train for the day. Should be quiet on a Sunday and I have a big presentation to prepare for this week. You let me know when you're ready to go, okay?"

"Will do," Cassie replied as her dad left the kitchen. *"At least he's coming tonight,"* she thought, wishing he could spend more time with all of them. Therapy had helped them grow as a family unit, and since getting through the college conflict, things were better between them. *"I just hope that the promotion won't screw things up again,"* she thought, scraping the last bit of apple and peanut butter out of the bowl. *"Not sure my eating disorder could handle that."*

She rinsed her dishes and the one her dad had left in the sink and put them into the dishwasher, then reached into the refrigerator and pulled out her lunch and dinner bags. *"For today, I have the food I need to stay healthy, and I'll be busy doing stuff I love with some of my best friends. And that will help in shutting down the chatter in my head, because today I'm gonna choose recovery again."*

* * *

175

Hours later Cassie and Maggie finished setting up the basket display in Tim's office. He had opened the garage bay door giving access to all that walked past the house on the way to the park. The rest of the office was decorated for Christmas, including a small tree with lights and the "Christmas in Caldwell" ornaments. Raffle baskets covered tables and stacked bins, and in the corner one small table held a lockbox for money and a computer with a slideshow of the community center construction progress. A small space heater provided needed heat to take the edge off with the front of the building open. Music of Nat King Cole, Bing Crosby, and Frank Sinatra filled the space with Christmas classics as Maggie placed the last basket plaquard in front of the Broadway themed basket that Colleen's studio had donated. It contained a sparkly gold top hat filled with six different films of the shows *Chorus Line, Chicago, RENT, My Fair Lady, Newsies, and Hello, Dolly,* along with two boxes of microwave popcorn and a coupon for two free tickets to the high school musical in the spring.

Cassie came over to admire the unique wrapping, using the hat upside down to hold the films. "I'm gonna buy a raffle ticket for this one – *RENT* and *Newsies* are two of my favorite shows."

"What? Not *Dolly*?" Maggie teased. "I think there will be lots of tickets added for this one. The ticket can has a lot in it from being at the studio for a couple of weeks."

"Some of these baskets are gorgeous – and so creative."

"Considering how many you put together I'm not surprised, but I know you're talking about the ones assembled by other businesses. The community got behind this project. And all the money will go to the community center to help with renovations and decorating. I think most of the costs for tonight were donated, so the raffle will be all profit."

"Brooke's donating all the money we make from the ornament sales, too," Cassie said, "and I think we ended up painting well over a hundred."

They were interrupted by the first few residents on their way to the park. "Are you open for business yet?" the woman asked.

"Sure thing, come on in," Maggie replied. "And be sure to stop by the café as well; the rest of the baskets are over there."

The three women strolled along the rows of baskets, admiring them as they went. "Here's one from Gino's!" one of the woman called out. "A colander with a box of linguine, spaghetti tongs, sauce, and a gift certificate for dinner!"

One of the woman pulled out her wallet. "How much are tickets? I want to stuff a ton of them in that can!"

"They're five dollars each," Cassie said, "or four for fifteen."

The woman smiled as she handed her forty dollars. "Give me eight tickets – and then I'll take a couple of the ornaments as well. They're beautiful."

"This young lady is the one that painted most of them," Maggie chimed in as she approached. "You can pick the two you'd like as they're all a little different."

"Clara, look at this one," another of the women said, "it has all white ornaments with little blue lights painted on it. It matches the tree you have in your den." She looked toward Cassie and added, "You painted *all* of these? They're so detailed."

"Thanks," Cassie replied. She still wasn't used to getting compliments on her art, even though more and more people were admiring her work at the store.

The woman named Clara called her two friends over. "Hey, come here. They have a slide show of the community center here."

As they began to watch, the youngest of the three pointed to the screen. "Hey, it's that guy from the courtroom. The one in charge of the whole thing. God, he's hot."

Cassie caught Maggie's gaze and grinned as the ladies chatted. "I hear he's taken," one of the other women replied. "Amanda was telling me yesterday that she was sending him all kinds of signals this week and he didn't bat an eye."

"Wow," her friend replied. "If someone like Amanda can't entice him then none of us stand a chance. Too bad--he's so damn attractive."

Maggie's heart fluttered as the two nodded, watching the

slideshow. "The building looks great," one said to the other. "I remember going there as a kid when it was still a hardware store. Can't wait to check it out next year."

The next hour brought numerous residents as they traveled past; more and more tickets filled the raffle cans as the pile of Christmas ornaments dwindled. Maggie pointed to the clock. "Cassie, you better head over to meet up with the theater kids. Don't you start in ten minutes?"

"I can't believe how fast the time went by. Are you okay by yourself here?"

"You bet. I'll wait until 6:45 and then lock everything up and walk over with the raffle lists and ticket cans. Make sure you don't do your solo until I'm there to hear you."

Cassie felt the butterflies in her stomach, just like she always did before dancing in a recital or acting on stage. "That's not until after Santa arrives.....we'll be doing Christmas carols beforehand."

"Good. I'm sure I'll hear them from here with everyone singing along. See ya soon."

Cassie pointed at her two bags with empty lunch and dinner containers. "Can I leave these here and come back later for them?"

"Sure. Tim and I will hustle back to hand out winning baskets so you don't have to rush. Now get going."

Cassie walked out in the cold, crisp air toward the entrance of the park. A large crowd gathered by the gazebo and kids were running around the grassy area filled with anticipation of Santa's arrival. Above, the stars twinkled as patches of clouds rolled past. *"Maybe we'll have snow later – it's clouding in."* She pulled her jacket tighter. She may have reached a normal weight again, but she still felt the cold more than most people. *"Glad I have warm boots and mittens tonight,"* she thought. *"I'll be freezing by the end of the night."*

As she got closer she spotted the theater kids gathered next to the gazebo which was decorated with red ribbons and white lights. A red wing backed armchair perched in the middle waiting for Santa's arrival. Brian spotted her first and waved. "There you are! We saved a spot for ya!"

He wrapped his arm around her as she squeezed in between him and Teagan. "Don't worry, we'll keep ya warm, kiddo."

Teagan's eyes sparkled as her cheeks glowed from the cold. "I think most of the town is here. We should have done this years ago!"

Cassie agreed. "I'm glad we're here together," she whispered, as Beth, Kyleigh, Julia, and others shouted greetings. Mike approached them from her end and started squeezing between Cassie's row and the one behind her to reach Julia near the other end. As he passed behind her, he pressed in close and whispered in her ear. "Looking good, beautiful."

Her stomach knotted up. *"Did he just hit on me?"* she thought. *"Or is he making fun of how much weight I've gained?"*

She wasn't sure if Brian had heard it as he was talking to Lou on his other side, but Teagan saw the reaction on her face as Mike continued by. "What happened?" she asked.

"I'll tell ya later," she mumbled, not wanting anyone else to hear. She watched Mike as he reached Julia, bending down to kiss her firmly on the lips. She didn't know whether to be angry or jealous, but the knot in her stomach told her that it was a little bit of both.

Luckily, it was time to sing. *"Clear your head,"* she told herself. *"Don't let him bother you like that. He's clearly not worth it."*

Tim stood up in front of the crowd and took the microphone provided by Mrs. Kelly, the music director. "Good evening, everyone! Such a great turnout for our very first Christmas in Caldwell." He waited for the applause to die down before continuing. "I want to thank all the businesses and citizens that made this night possible. For those that donated baskets and equipment for tonight, and for all of you who bought raffle tickets, we thank you. All the proceeds will go toward the community center, which we'll utilize for next year's celebration." More applause. "I'll turn it over now to the music and theater kids from Caldwell High, who will lead us in some carols. Be sure to sing along; I hear that Santa might be in the area and he might stop by if he hears us all singing. We'll even light the tree in a few minutes to help him find us."

Cassie watched the little kids as Tim talked. When they heard the name of Santa some giggled, some hopped up and down, and others looked up at the sky trying to spot his sleigh. She spotted a couple of the little cherub dancers in the crowd; Tracey and Lydia stood side by side next to their parents. She scanned the crowd for her parents and Philip, but didn't spot them. *"I hope my dad made it,"* she thought as they began to sing.

The crowd indeed sang along--even Carl, the old curmudgeon. He stood next to Tim and Sharon off to the side closest to their property. Tim glanced back and at one point Cassie saw him leave his mom and grandad to walk back toward his office. In the distance Maggie was meeting up with Colleen and Brooke as they entered the park with a rolling cart of basket raffle cans, each of them on one side of the cart to be sure that there were no mishaps. *"That's so romantic that he goes to meet her."*

Shortly before Santa was due, the committee gathered beside the gazebo and the kids stopped singing as Tim once again took the microphone. "I want to thank the committee for all their hard work in helping to plan this night, and I think we should give special recognition to this lady for spearheading the amazing basket raffle. Brooke Martin, I'll turn it over to you."

The crowd cheered as men fumbled in their pockets for tickets and ladies took off their gloves and mittens to retrieve them from purses and pockets. "Thanks, everyone. And before we start picking raffle winners, let's all give a round of applause to Tim Collins for heading up this entire event."

Loud cheers and applause erupted. Brian put two fingers in his mouth and offered a shrill whistle which made the theater kids laugh. As committee members began approaching Brooke with the cans, the crowd quieted down quickly. "We'll choose one ticket from each of the baskets and record it here. If you have the winning ticket, be sure to stop by the café or Tim's office to pick it up on the way home. We have your name and phone number on the back here, so if you forget we'll give you a call and you can pick them up at my shop during the next week. Without further delay, let's pick the first winner!"

One by one, numbers were called with names written on the back of each ticket, and various winners cheered throughout the crowd. When the last basket had been awarded, Tim again thanked the everyone for coming. "And now, I'm going to ask everyone to help me count down for the tree lighting. Ten.....nine.....eight...." Everyone joined in, and when the lights went on Cassie heard numerous "oohs" and "aahs." The theater kids began a lively rendition of "Rockin' Around the Christmas Tree" before segueing in to "Here Comes Santa Claus."

She wasn't sure who spotted his arrival first, but soon most of the kids were pointing toward the street as a police car drove into the park with blue lights flashing. Behind it was a small horse drawn carriage with a local farmer and Santa Claus himself. Strings of jingle bells rang rhythmically to the sound of horse hooves, and as the carriage got closer the kids in the crowd got louder and more excited, jumping up and down and chattering with their friends. A line formed in front of the Christmas tree on the other side of the gazebo, and Cassie enjoyed watching them jockey for the best position in line.

Santa climbed out of his carriage with a big red bag stuffed with small Christmas teddy bears and made his way up into the gazebo. As the police car and carriage departed, the theater kids began to sing background music as kids took their turn climbing the two short steps to visit with Santa. Cassie smiled as Lydia approached shyly to Santa's beckoning gesture, and then stepped down beaming as she held her teddy bear out to show her mom. Tracey jumped up the stairs with enthusiasm, climbing up onto Santa's lap with animated chatter. *"I'm trying so hard to live more like Tracey,"* she reflected, *"but no doubt I'm more like Lydia in meeting new challenges."*

As the theater kids finished singing "Have Yourself a Merry Little Christmas" the first snowflakes began to fall, and Cassie hugged Teagan's arm. "Look! It's like magic!" She whispered, pointing to the flakes around them.

"Just in time for your song, bestie. Go ahead – keep the magic growing."

Cassie felt the butterflies in her stomach as she took her place in front of the microphone. As she began singing "O Holy Night," a hush fell over the crowd as they stood to listen. Cassie closed her eyes for a moment to focus on the music and lyrics. All of a sudden she heard the voice of Tracey calling out. "Mommy, look! Miss Cassie is singing like an angel!" As chuckles were heard among those gathered, Cassie opened her eyes with confidence for the remainder of her solo, and then stepped back into line with Teagan and Brian squeezing both hands on either side of her.

She continued singing with her friends, feeling the magic as the snow fell. That's when she spotted them. Her parents stood in the crowd a few rows back, with Philip standing beside them holding his phone up high as he recorded the song. Her cheeks warmed as she saw her dad's arm wrapped around her mom, who was wiping her eyes with a tissue after her solo. *"I am so lucky,"* Cassie thought. *"I have two families that love me – the one at home, and my theater family."* She glanced sideways and caught Teagan's eye as her own grew misty. *"And little by little I'm starting to believe in myself the way they believe in me."*

CHAPTER 24

The morning before Christmas Maggie had invited Cassie over for a short brunch and coaching session prior to holiday festivities. She carefully picked up the tray laden with their meal and carried it into the living room.

Cassie sat cross legged on the floor with Tramp resting his head on her leg as she scratched his ear. The white lights on the Christmas tree made the tinsel sparkle in front of her. "Your tree is so lovely," she said as she sipped her hot chocolate.

Maggie sat on the couch and handed her a plate with homemade quiche and a slice of banana bread with cream cheese. "Here you go. The quiche is my recipe, and Lucy made the banana bread this morning; it's still warm. And feel free to take his pillow away and sit on the couch if it's more comfortable."

"I'm quite comfy," Cassie replied. "I find it calming to have a dog resting his head on my lap." She smelled the quiche. "Hmm.....ham and cheese – and onion?"

"Always onion. I put onion or garlic in almost anything I make."

Cassie used her fork and took a bite of quiche, savoring the sharp taste of cheddar mixed with the saltiness of the ham. "This is delicious." She put her plate on the coffee table beside her. "I've never told you how safe I feel eating here. It's one of the few places where I never freak out when the food is around."

"I'm glad. I remember the first year or two of recovery when food would sometimes scream at me out of the blue."

"Right? I mean, sometimes I can leave therapy after a productive session and head over to the mall with Mom for a cinnamon roll. And ten minutes later – ten freaking minutes – when I'm standing in front of the case, I look down and think I can't possibly eat all those calories. Drives me crazy sometimes."

Maggie took a swig of coffee. "I'd love to tell you that someday it goes away, but even now after years of recovery I still have those moments. The difference now is that I recognize them as eating disorder crap and ignore them. It will get easier, I promise."

"Eating disorder crap. I like that. Is it a professional term?" she teased.

"I'm sure you've heard Natalie say it a few times – so yes, I guess that makes it professional. So are you ready for Christmas tomorrow?"

Cassie stretched her legs out in front of her as Tramp snored away. "Doing okay. Yesterday was my last day of work at Brooke's until after the show. I'm gonna miss it a lot."

"You guys have been swamped, I'm sure."

Cassie nodded. "Especially the past week. After Christmas in the park everyone was coming in to buy gifts. The ornaments we made sold out."

"Glad I bought one early," Maggie said, glancing at the ornament on her tree. "That night was so special. One of my favorite memories of the year."

"And how many of those memories involve a certain handsome guy?"

Maggie's cheeks blushed as she answered. "Most of them. The past seven months have been amazing with not just Tim, but his family, too. Watching them all reunite this summer was something I'll never forget."

"I bet that house is full of Christmas cheer."

"It's like night and day from last year. Carl sat in that cold empty house all alone, and now there's a tree up, decorations all over, and fresh baked Christmas cookies every time I walk in the door. He is so grateful to have his family again."

"Seems like they've made up for a lot of lost time."

Maggie agreed. "They have. At first I questioned if the wonder of it all would start to fade after they were living together for awhile, but they all seem to respect each other's space – and they recognize the gift they've been given to be a family after all these years."

"So are they respecting Tim's space when it comes to being with you?" Cassie teased.

"We've been managing. He's always welcome here, and he renovated the loft above the garage which is a little more private than the house. I haven't stayed over in his room there yet – that still seems a little awkward."

"He's in the master bedroom, right? Surprised Sharon didn't take that one."

"She wanted her old room. Granted, she did a total makeover, but she said she had so many happy memories in that room that she wanted it to be her space again."

"What about Tim?" Cassie asked. "Did he do a total makeover of the room his grandparents had shared?"

"Very little so far. He admitted the other night that he's afraid of making any changes in Carl's old room – he thinks it might bother his grandad."

"I suspect his living there is temporary – I mean, at some point won't you guys want a place of your own?"

Maggie took a bite of banana bread and pondered the idea before answering. "I guess time will tell; at least I'm not worried about Amanda's pursuit anymore. She's almost amusing now that Tim and I talked."

"I suspect there are other women besides Amanda who envy you as well. He *is,* after all, one of the most eligible bachelors in town."

Maggie smiled as she placed her empty plate on the table. "Then aren't I the lucky one?" She glanced at the clock and walked over to the tree. "Hey, your mom should be here soon, and I wanna be sure to give you this." She reached down and picked up a sparkly red bag with green ribbons and tissue paper. "Merry Christmas. The card's inside, and you can read that later."

Cassie untied the ribbon as Maggie sat back down. She reached in to pull out a beautiful leather bound journal with a phoenix design on the cover, along with a quote that said *"Accept who you've been to become who you'll be."* Cassie hugged it to her chest. "I saw this in the book store and loved it. The phoenix is so perfect."

"Teagan told me you had loved it. She was going to buy it for you for Christmas, but thought it might mean more coming from me. I bought one for myself as well."

"Thank you – so much. My other journal is almost full, so this will be perfect." Cassie reached into her bag and pulled out a flat box wrapped in red and gold. "A little something to thank you for being the best recovery coach I could ask for."

She handed it to Maggie, who carefully untaped the edges and took the paper off before opening the box. Inside was one of the gardening plaques that Cassie had painted, with a wire attached for hanging. Underneath the plaque were several packets of vegetable seeds.

"Gardening season is still way off, but I wanted to make you something personal, and I almost feel like one of the plants you've nurtured this year."

Maggie ran her hands over the vibrant colors of painted tomatoes, peppers, squash, and lettuce that Cassie had painted, along with a quote about planting seeds for a better tomorrow. "I love this – I think I'll hang it in my office at work so I can look at it every day. And I'll put the seeds right into my gardening bag for the spring." She came around and leaned down to give Cassie a hug. "Thanks so much for this – and for coming today."

Cassie gave her a squeeze. "I needed it before tomorrow. I'm glad we're keeping things a little quieter than Thanksgiving at the Manor. I think one holiday buffet a year is all I can handle right now."

Maggie sat back down and finished her coffee. "So are you guys doing anything special?"

"We're going to church tonight, and then we'll go up to visit Gram tomorrow with a few gifts and have a quiet dinner at home afterwards. A *lot* less stress. How 'bout you?"

"I'll be at Tim's tonight and again tomorrow. They invited Lucy and Liz for dinner again. By the way, I'm giving Carl that painting you did of Caldwell Cemetery – I'm sure he's gonna love it."

"A painting of his wife's grave for Christmas?" Cassie teased. "Sounds a little morbid to me."

"He still goes up there to sit on that little bench – not weekly like he used to, but at least once or twice a month. And sometimes Sharon or Tim will walk up with him. It's a peaceful place for him – and now he'll be able to look at it every day."

"You'll have to tell me what he thinks of it. And what did you end up getting for Tim?"

"I think he'll love his, too. Liz had taken a family photo of him with Sharon and Carl at Thanksgiving. I had one framed and matted for him. I can't wait for him to unwrap it."

"That will go up over the mantle, no doubt," Cassie replied. "Of course, I'm *dying* to know what he got for *you*."

"You and half the town," Maggie replied as she glanced out the window. "Luckily for me, your mom has perfect timing and I don't have to answer." She stood up and stretched before giving Cassie a hug. "Thanks so much for coming today."

Cassie put her journal back into the bag before grabbing her coat. "Thanks for *having* me. And for breakfast. And for this," as she held up the bag. "But mostly, thanks for believing in me – especially when I couldn't believe in myself."

Maggie smiled. "Have a great Christmas, Cassie. I love watching you bloom."

* * *

LATER THAT AFTERNOON Maggie got a text from Tim as she gathered the gifts for his family. "How 'bout a quick walk before dinner tonight?"

Maggie typed a quick reply. "I'll grab my scarf and mittens. Heading over in a couple of minutes."

"Grandad said to bring the 'dang dog' so he wouldn't be home alone for the holiday."

Maggie laughed as she put her phone in her pocket and called Tramp. "The old curmudgeon is missing his favorite buddy – you got an invite, boy." She quickly grabbed Tramp's feeding dish, a can of dog food, and a couple of chew toys. "That should keep you from going after any presents under the tree. You ready?"

As soon as Tramp's leash was attached Maggie picked up the bag with his food and the larger bag with gifts and headed out the door. It was a short walk around the corner and Maggie enjoyed the crisp cold air. Most of the snow from the Caldwell Christmas celebration had melted, leaving only a few patches here and there in shady spots. *"I wonder if we'll be lucky enough to have more snow tonight or tomorrow."*

Tim was waiting on the front porch when she approached, and Maggie chuckled as Tramp's pace picked up when he spotted the familiar smile. He bounded down the stairs to take the big bag with gifts. "I would have been more than happy to walk over and carry this for you," he said. "And let me take the other one draped on your shoulder." As he peeked inside to hear what was rattling he grinned. "Planning a late night, Tramp old buddy? She's got your dish and food all set." He winked at Maggie and added, "Might even be enough for breakfast."

Maggie reached up to caress his face with her mitten before meeting his kiss. "Merry Christmas," she whispered, her eyes sparkling.

"It's even merrier now that you're here," he replied. "Let me put these inside and we can take Tramp for a walk before dinner."

"Should I go in and say hello first?"

"Nope," Tim replied as he opened the door. "I told them we'd be back soon."

He placed the bags just inside the door and closed it again, turning to flash his dimpled smile as he joined her on the walkway and reached for her hand. "Want me to take over leash duty?"

She passed the leash handle over, content to hold his hand and watch Tramp explore the world as they walked toward the park entrance. "I'll never tire of this walk," she said. "Even though we sometimes head up and walk through the cemetery, this is still our favorite route."

"Grandad still watches for you every morning. Do you know that he often stands inside the door until he sees you coming around the corner before heading out for his newspaper?" Tim glanced over and grinned at her. "Not that I blame him or anything."

"I remember times when he'd be at the mailbox a little early and stand there reading the headlines until we passed by. I looked forward to his grumpy greeting every morning."

"Well, that old grump is crazy about you," Tim teased. "and he's not alone."

As they approached the community garden, a splash of red caught Maggie's eye. "What the heck?" she asked, catching the grin on his face as she let go of his hand to check out her garden plot. A gorgeous bouquet of red roses with bits of baby's breath sat inside a clear glass vase that sparkled in the afternoon sun. "Tim, these are beauti—"she stopped short as she turned to find him down on one knee with Tramp sitting beside him. A moment later she laughed out loud. "Why are you holding a packet of spinach seeds?"

Tim flashed the dimpled smile that she had loved the first time she saw it. "The first time we met I was walking over to look at my grandfather's house and I found you kneeling here with a bunch of spinach in your hand. Little did I know that you'd be the one that would bring my grandad and I back together – or that I'd grow to love you as much as I do." As Maggie's eyes teared up, he held up the hand with the spinach seeds. "Spinach symbolizes both simplicity and strength – two qualities that I love in you...." As he continued, he turned the seed packet over to reveal the gleam of the ring taped to the back. "They're also perfect qualities to bring to a marriage." As his eyes met hers, he continued. "Maggie Richmond, will you marry me?"

She closed the gap between them as he stood up, wrapping her arms around him as she nodded through her tears. Tim had removed the ring and now slid it over her finger before bringing her hand to his mouth and kissing her fingertips. "I love you so much. And you've made me the happiest man in the world right now." He cupped her face in his hands and kissed her. "Of course, you haven't said the word 'yes' yet," he teased.

"Yes!" Maggie shouted loudly with a sparkle in her eyes. "I'll tell the whole world!" Tramp sensed her excitement and barked. "I guess he's saying 'yes' as well."

Tim reached down to pat his head. "Glad you approve, buddy – 'cause I love her as much as you do." He gestured toward the roses. "Should we bring those back with us before they freeze?"

Maggie took a step toward the roses and stopped. "Wait a minute – when did you bring these over here? That's why you texted, isn't it?"

Tim grinned. "Couldn't leave them out in the cold for too long. Besides, I didn't want anyone else coming along and stealing my fiancée's flowers. I waited on the porch afterwards until you came around the corner."

Maggie admired her left hand. "I simply *love* this ring. I don't think I've ever seen such an exquisite setting."

Tim's eyes were misty as his gaze met hers. "It was my grandmother's ring. My grandad wanted you to have it when I told him I was proposing."

Maggie's eyes filled with tears as the ring's added significance hit her. "Oh Tim....I will treasure this forever." She smiled through her tears as she reached for his free hand. "Come on – I can't wait to show it to him."

Tim laughed as he glanced back at the house before taking her hand. "Trust me, they've been watching all of this through the kitchen window. Should we wave?"

Maggie pulled him back toward the paved roadway. "No, I think they've waited long enough. I still can't believe he gave you Ruthie's ring. I feel so blessed."

"Trust me, I'm the one who's blessed. This year I have my family and a home….and now I have you to spend the rest of my life with – not to mention the best dog in the whole world."

"And *that*, sir," Maggie teased, "is one of the many reasons I said yes."

They got back to Carl's house in minutes, and Sharon was there to open the door as they climbed the porch steps. "Congratulations!" she blurted out as she gave her son a hug as they entered. She turned to Maggie and opened her arms. "Thanks for making him so happy. Welcome to the family." Maggie embraced her as Tim placed the roses on the table by the door before hugging Carl.

When the old man turned to her his eyes got misty as she held up her hand. His wrinkled hand took hers as he smiled down at the heirloom on her finger. "She'd be so happy right now. Come here, tomato girl." Maggie stepped in to his warm embrace, tearing up yet again. "Thank you so much for such a special ring," she whispered in his ear.

He nodded as they parted. "I should be thanking you – I never thought I'd have the chance to pass it on." Before the sentiment could get to him anymore, he stood up straighter. "Now are we gonna stand here blubberin' all day by the door or are we gonna *eat* at some point. A man could starve in his own house, I tell ya."

Maggie grinned. "We certainly can't have this wonderful man starve on Christmas Eve – shall we head to the kitchen and get dinner finished?"'

Carl patted Tim on the back. "See? I told ya she was the one!"

"Dad, I think he figured that out all by himself," Sharon replied. "Now let's leave these two lovebirds alone and you can help me with that crossword puzzle until dinner." She smiled at Maggie. "Give me a holler if you two need any help – I got the table set earlier. I left a spot for the roses as our centerpiece."

Maggie returned the smile as Tim came alongside and wrapped his arm around her. They glanced in at the old curmudgeon who was grinning as he sat down with his crossword puzzle book. Sharon curled up in the seat next to him before looking up at Tim. "And thanks for making *him* so happy. This will be the best Christmas he's had in decades."

Tim kissed her forehead. "Hey, this is best Christmas for *all* of us. Now let's go in and explore cooking as an engaged couple, shall we?"

Maggie patted his chest, her ring sparkling in the light. "I like the sound of that." She picked up the roses and followed him into the dining room, stopping only long enough to place them on the table. "They're not quite as elegant as your grandad's roses, but they're a perfect color for Christmas." She followed Tim into the kitchen. "Now where's my apron?"

CHAPTER 25

The Christmas break flew by, and instead of heading back to Brooke's to work after school, Cassie found herself immersed in rehearsals four afternoons a week. She stood on stage as Irene Molloy, who owned a milliner's shop. Beth played her store assistant Minnie Fay, and Teagan played Dolly Levi, a vibrant busybody who liked to play matchmaker. Brian and Peter played the roles of Cornelius and Barnaby who were hiding under tables and in the closet during the scene, as Mike, who played the part of Horace, tried to flirt with Irene. In the end, he stormed out, leaving Dolly to then convince the boys to take Irene and Minnie out for dinner and dancing. She then proceeded comically to teach both of them how to dance as they all sang the next number.

It was one of the few scenes that Cassie had to perform with Mike, and after his exit she grinned at Brian as they began to dance together.

"What'd I do?" Brian whispered.

"You're not Mike, that's all," Cassie replied. "I can't tell you how grateful I am you got this part and not him."

Brian twirled her around as he sang his line, his smile telling Cassie that he understood. When Teagan took over singing again, he quickly responded. "Glad I make you feel safe, kiddo. Now sing!"

Cassie almost laughed, but caught herself in time to make her entrance. By the time they were finished, she felt exhilarated for having been able to dance. She stayed on stage as the others went down to sit and ran through her solo where she danced with one of her hats. It was a slow ballad with some graceful lyrical movements, and Cassie's voice was even stronger than it had been the prior year. *"Recovery is good for me,"* she thought as she twirled around the stage. *"I'm not dizzy and my heart's not racing."* When she finished, her friends applauded her.

Beth was the first back on stage. "That was awesome! Your voice is perfect for that song!" She was followed by Teagan and Brian, who hugged her at the same time. Cassie laughed at being sandwiched between the two of them, but her heart was full. *"This is like a second family,"* she thought, *"and they love me so much."*

"You need a ride home?" Brian asked.

"Thanks, but Maggie is picking me up for our weekly session. We're swinging over to meet Tim at the arts center; she said he wants to talk to me about something. Can't imagine what for, but afterwards we're heading to Gino's for dinner."

"Hmmm…..Gino's," Teagan said. "Now you've gone and made me hungry."

"Me, too," Brian chimed in. "Teags, you think your folks would mind you bailing on dinner? I could go for some calzone after all that strenuous dancing."

Cassie slapped him lightly on the arm. "Strenuous?" she joked.

The glint in his eye revealed his exaggeration. "Okay, so it was easy – but any excuse I can find for Gino's is legit, right?"

Teagan laughed. "Hell, the fact that it's Wednesday is all the reason I need for Gino's! Let me text my mom to check with her, but I can't imagine she'd have a problem."

While Teagan texted, Brian turned to Cassie. "So, do you want a private coaching session with Maggie, or would you wanna join us? We could grab a table if you want."

"Can we play it by ear? I'm not sure how long we'll be, or if Maggie has stuff she wants to go over."

"Gino's shouldn't be too busy mid-week, so we'll ask for a bigger table in case you decide to join us. If you end up just stopping by before grabbing your own table that's fine, too."

Teagan gave him a thumbs up as she put her phone back in her pocket. "Calzone, here we come! I love it when a plan comes together."

As they were leaving, Mike was heading out the door just ahead of them. He opened it first and held it for them, smiling at Cassie as she exited. "You nailed that song. I was backstage listening."

He flashed a smile and Cassie remembered him holding doors for her in the past. She gave him a weak smile in return, confused by some of his recent flirting. "Thanks." She was surprised that Maggie's car wasn't parked outside.

Teagan noticed as well. "We'll wait with you. And Mike, you were almost convincing as an old grump in there today."

"Wasn't my top choice, but this guy beat me out this year," Mike replied, playfully slapping the back of Brian's head. He then grinned at Teagan. "I guess fate decided we belonged together – like last year."

"I think it's more likely that Brian's range is a little higher than yours."

Mike stepped back dramatically. "Ouch! You know how to hurt a guy's ego, don't ya?"

Teagan patted his arm. "Save the drama for the stage, pal. You're doing an awesome job as Horace."

Cassie loved how easily Teagan could tease Mike. "You guys don't have to wait – Maggie should be here any minute. I'd never wanna keep you from your calzone."

Mike's eyes lit up. "Calzone? Now you're talking my language. I'd tag along if I didn't have a paper due tomorrow. But hey, I can wait with Cassie till her ride gets here."

For a moment Cassie felt uneasy, but she smiled at Teagan. "Mike's right. Maggie will be here any time. You guys go on ahead, and I'll see you when we get there."

Teagan glanced at Mike and back to Cassie. "You sure?'

"I'll be fine. Go on."

As Teagan and Brian headed down to the student parking lot Mike winked at Cassie. "Don't worry. I'll take care of ya till your ride gets here. I kinda like having a few minutes alone with you. Reminds me of some old times."

If Cassie had wondered about whether he'd been flirting with her before she was now convinced. "So how are things with you and Julia?"

Mike flinched a bit. "Why do you always have to bring her up?"

"Julia's my friend – and besides, she's good for you."

Mike's gaze traveled down Cassie's body. "So were you – maybe even better."

Cassie was grateful to see Maggie's car pulling up. "My ride's here." Before hastening to the car, she quickly added, "Don't screw things up with Julia, okay?"

Mike snickered. "That might be the actual problem." He nodded toward Maggie's car. "Enjoy that calzone. It's looking mighty fine on you these days."

Cassie got into the car and tried to fasten her seatbelt with clenched fists. "Get me outta here," she hissed.

Maggie drove off as Mike waved. "So what the hell was that all about? I can tell you're upset."

Cassie took a deep breath and exhaled through clenched teeth. "The guy's a jerk. He was hitting on me – even though he's dating Julia. And then he just called me fat."

"He what?"

"He called me fat – or implied it. He said the calzone's looking good on me these days."

Maggie pulled the car over to the side of the road and put it in park. "Just what the eating disorder wanted to hear?"

Cassie nodded, blinking back tears. "How can one little line make your head explode? All of a sudden I feel like I've gained fifty pounds."

Maggie handed Cassie a tissue. "Look, he had no idea it would trigger you; I'm sure he meant it as a compliment – inappropriate as it is."

Cassie shook her head. "He stared at me like I was a piece of meat. And he was *hitting* on me, too! What the hell is wrong with him?"

"What did he say?"

"He said I might be better for him than Julia, and when I told him not to screw things up with her he implied that she's not putting out for him. Then he told me to enjoy dinner because it looks good on me – and now I feel like I'll never want to eat pizza or calzone again."

"We'll deal with that last part in a minute," Maggie replied, "but do you think he might be wanting you back?"

Cassie sat for a moment and thought about it. "I'm not sure. I mean, he and Julia seem fine sometimes, but he's been flirting with another girl at rehearsal, and he's said a few things to me this past month that made me question if it was flirting. Today was obvious, though."

Maggie spoke with a gentle tone. "He might be seeing a healthier version of you right now – don't forget that last year you weren't in the best place when you dated."

"I guess that's an understatement," said Cassie reflectively. "We'd go out to dinner and I'd be petrified of the food – every time. I was always determined to eat as little as possible because I didn't want him seeing how fat I was."

"You do realize now that wasn't the case?"

"Yeah – I was in a bad place last year at this time – I was surprised he even wanted to date a girl like me."

"So why do you think he did?"

Cassie winced. "If I tell you, will you promise to keep it between us?" When Maggie nodded, she continued. "Natalie's the only other person I've told, but I let Mike….." Tears filled her eyes as she remembered.

Maggie spoke the words she was afraid to say. "Have sex with you?" She nodded, trying to answer through her sobs. "Only a few times……I….hated it…..I felt so….fat when he… touched me…..but he said everyone in Caldwell did it…..and I shouldn't be a prude."

Maggie held her hand and let her cry it out before continuing. "Cassie, did he ever force himself on you?"

"Oh, God, no…..not like that. I…..let him." Her voice regained some control as she spoke. "Look, I'm sure he would have liked it way more often than it happened, but other times when I said no, he stopped." She dried her tears and blew her nose. "The last time was a week after the show was over…..I was so messed up by then, knowing I was going inpatient as soon as there was room at the Phoenix. I told him I wouldn't be around over the summer, and he got all romantic, saying we should make the most of the night." Cassie cringed, remembering his hands touching her body and how painful the sex was. "I hated it that night….I just wanted it to be over. I didn't believe any of the stuff he said."

"What stuff?"

"Ya know, how I was beautiful and so much better than all the other girls. I just wanted to be invisible."

"But dating him must have served a purpose of some kind."

"That's what Natalie said, too. I think I was scared to death to be alone – even though my eating disorder screamed for me to isolate – and I did from almost everyone – I was afraid to be alone with nothing else."

"Like Mike was a way to appear normal and keep the eating disorder from taking over?"

"Something like that…..God, I thought I had worked through all this crap over the summer." She looked at Maggie with tear stained cheeks. "Will I ever be able to live like a normal human being? Or is this kind of crap gonna keep popping up over and over again?"

Maggie held her hand. "I *promise* you it will be easier over time, but Mike just triggered some major stuff, which takes a lot more time to work through, so be gentle with yourself. And thank you for trusting me enough to share all that."

"I know I can trust you."

"So," Maggie continued, "are you even up for seeing Tim tonight? I can text him to reschedule."

"Do you mind? I'm not sure I am." Maggie pulled her phone out, and as she listened to Maggie typing she closed her eyes and leaned her head against the headrest. *I wish I didn't feel so fat and out of control right now.*

When Maggie smiled and put her phone away, she sighed. "You

can drive me home if you want. I'm drained. I'll text Teagan and tell her we changed our plans."

Maggie turned the car around. "You may hate me in a minute, but there's no way I'm taking you home right now. We may have skipped our meeting with Tim, but I'm taking you straight to Gino's and we're gonna have dinner."

Cassie sat upright, anger flashing in her eyes. "That's the last place I wanna go right now!"

Maggie clenched the wheel as she drove. "And that's exactly why you have to. Otherwise you'll be letting your eating disorder win tonight – and that's too big a battle to lose, my friend. Trust me."

* * *

A FEW MINUTES later Cassie reluctantly followed Maggie into Gino's. As the smell of garlic and mozzarella greeted her she clenched her fists and felt her stomach knot up. *"No way am I gonna eat calzone,"* she resolved. *"I'll force myself to eat a little salad and then get out of here."*

Gino greeted both of them. "You here to meet your friends, right? They have a table ready in the middle."

Maggie smiled at the old man as she shook her head. "Do you mind if we grabbed a quiet booth near the back? We have some stuff to catch up on."

Gino nodded as the phone rang. "Pick any of them. The waitress will find you," he said before turning his attention to the customer on the phone.

Cassie spotted Teagan and Brian as they waved from across the room, and Maggie led the way to explain that they'd be grabbing their own table. Cassie tried to avoid eye contact as Teagan smiled from her seat.

Brian's eyes lit up as he swallowed his water. "Hey, we just put our order in – you sure you don't want to join us?"

Maggie chimed in before Cassie had to. "Hope you guys don't mind, but I'd like to have Cassie to myself tonight – a few things to talk over."

Cassie met Teagan's gaze and saw her expression change. *"Damn it, she knows."*

"No problem," Teagan replied with a questioning tone. "You okay?"

Cassie nodded, but didn't reply. She knew that Teagan could read her better than anyone, and right now she wanted to reach a different table before her expression revealed too much. She smiled weakly at her two friends and followed Maggie to a booth near the back window. She was glad Teagan's back was to her, as she suspected her food would be under scrutiny.

As she sank into her booth seat, Cassie exhaled slowly, feeling the tension in her body. "Look, I don't think I can manage dinner – I'm gonna order a salad."

Maggie stared at her and spoke firmly. "The hell you are. You're picking either a calzone or a couple slices of pizza – you can decide – and a side salad if you want. But we're not leaving here until you order and eat your dinner."

"You can't make me eat, "she spit out.

Maggie's voice was warm, but she didn't mince words. "As your coach, I need to be the bad guy right now. In reality that's Mike, but he's not here. You're in a crisis moment, and how you react in the next hour might determine whether you continue in recovery or head back to the Phoenix with a major relapse. I can't make that choice for you, but I'm gonna do everything in my power to keep you moving forward. He's not worth it, Cassie."

Cassie fought the tears as the anger shifted from Maggie to the real source. "How can I let him bother me like this? I'm so stupid."

"Hey, he's just an ass; I'm sure he has no idea of the impact of his words – and even if he did, I suspect he would have said them anyway. But that doesn't make *you* stupid."

"I sure *feel* stupid – *and* fat."

As the waitress approached with water, the knots in Cassie's stomach returned. She clenched her jaw and looked desperately toward Maggie for any sense of crumbling resolve, but instead found the same steady smile.

"You guys ready to order?" the waitress asked as she flipped her pad to the next page.

"Did you want to split a calzone, or would you rather have pizza?"

Cassie knew that any attempt to protest would draw even more attention to herself. "I think I'd like just one slice of pizza, please – and a small side salad with vinaigrette on the side."

Maggie handed the menus back to the waitress. "I'm in the mood for pizza as well, so why don't you bring us a whole pie with mushrooms, onions, and peppers, and then I'll take the leftovers home. Oh, and salad for me as well – same as hers."

"You got it. Anything else to drink?"

Cassie shook her head and glared at Maggie as the waitress headed back to the kitchen. "I don't like you right now." She ripped the straw sleeve open and jabbed the straw into her water.

"I've seen you pissed off and scared many times, and that's fine. We've got all evening to work through this."

Cassie cast a furtive glance toward Teagan and Brian's table where a huge calzone had been placed between them. She didn't have to hear them to know that cheerful banter was flying across the table as Brian cut through the crust and slid half of the calzone onto Teagan's plate waiting mid-air.

Maggie followed her gaze and caught Cassie's eye. "Kinda sucks that they can eat and enjoy the food, doesn't it?"

"Sometimes I wish I was more like her. She's comfortable with her body and absolutely loves her food. I seem to either hate it or I'm scared of it – or both."

"But is that true?" Maggie asked. "Think back to this past month, and I bet you can remember times when you enjoyed your meal and appreciated the tastes and textures."

Cassie leaned forward, plopping her elbows on the table while burying her face in her hands. She closed her eyes and tried to recover those moments in her mind. Memories of bacon and cinnamon rolls on Christmas morning, quiche and banana bread at Maggie's apartment, and countless croissant lunches and family dinners materialized in her thoughts. Her expression softened as Maggie continued. "Now think about how you ate all of those meals without letting your eating disorder take control."

When she opened her eyes she saw the soft steady gaze and exhaled.

"I hate it when you're right."

"Trust me, I only speak from experience. I know how quickly that voice can turn on you and start screaming—and it succeeds when we're most vulnerable. I'll do everything in my power to keep that from happening to you."

Cassie leaned back and crossed her arms, hugging herself as she nodded and met Maggie's gaze. "I have to wonder if I'll ever be where you are – or if I'll ever feel worthy enough for the kind of relationship you have with Tim."

"I promise you will – but you have to keep forging ahead through each battle."

As the waitress approached with their food, Cassie winced. "That's so much food. How will I ever eat two slices of that?"

"That's easy," Maggie said as she grabbed her knife. "One bite at a time."

$\mathcal{M}$aggie checked in with Cassie on a daily basis for the next couple of weeks, and was proud to see her continue to embrace recovery despite the incident with Mike and her busy rehearsal schedule. On this particular morning, however, a different topic was the highlight of the conversation after Valentine greetings and a chat about Tim.

"I know you'll be seeing Tim at *some* point today," Cassie teased. "Do you have the invitation for Gram's party to give to Carl?"

"In my purse," Maggie replied. "And I'll be heading over there in a few minutes for a quick breakfast before work. I'm sure he'll love getting it."

"I hope so. Gram wants him to come. I think she misses the daily crossword puzzles they did while he was there."

Maggie chuckled. "Carl still starts every day with his puzzle, and Ida's name comes up on a regular basis. He's been up to visit her a few times since he got back home, so I'm sure he'll be thrilled to come up for her birthday."

"Sounds good. I gotta leave for school. Have a nice day with that handsome fiancé of yours."

Maggie turned off her phone and admired her engagement ring. *"That won't be hard,"* she thought with a smile.

Within thirty minutes she was greeting Tim with a morning kiss as he opened the door to usher her into the house. Sharon had left for work, but Carl sat in the kitchen drinking coffee with his newspaper opened to the crossword puzzle. He smiled at Maggie as she followed Tim into the kitchen. "Morning, tomato girl. Hope you two aren't gonna be all lovey-dovey this morning. Too early for all that mushy stuff."

She grinned at him as Tim brought a mug of coffee to the table and gestured for her to sit. He placed the coffee in front of her and leaned down to kiss her before facing his grandad. "Never too early for love, Grandad – especially on your first Valentine's Day together. But we'll hold off on all the romance until later." He winked at Maggie. "Made your favorite omelet and homemade biscuits."

Carl slid the butter dish across the table. "You'll need this for those biscuits. I had three, and even Ruthie would have approved of them." As Tim brought a basket over he reached out his hand. "One more couldn't hurt…..a man's gotta eat, don't he?"

As Tim returned with two plates laden with omelets and breakfast potatoes, Maggie took a long whiff. "Hmm, this smell heavenly. You're spoiling me, Mr. Collins."

Tim passed the basket of biscuits to Maggie. "I love having people to cook for – especially the future *Mrs.* Collins."

Maggie blushed a bit as she took a bite into the warm biscuit. "Oh my God, I understand why your dad has eaten so many. They remind me of the ones at the seafood place in Brentwood."

Tim nodded as he took a bite of his omelet. "Hmm-mm. I found a recipe that comes close. Nothing like a little cheddar and garlic to start your day."

They chatted throughout their meal, occasionally responding to Carl's comments or requests for help with crossword puzzle clues. As Maggie finished her last bite, she leaned back in her chair and sighed. "Man, I could get used to meals like this."

Tim flashed her that dimpled smile as he stood up to take her plate. "Good to hear, because you know how much I love to cook."

"Let me help you with the dishes. If you're gonna do a lot of cooking then I guess I'll be washing a lot of dishes."

Tim placed both plates on the counter and turned around to gather Maggie in his arms. "They *do* have things called dishwashers, you know. I think I've even seen one in your apartment."

"Is that what that is?" she teased back, enjoying the hug. "What can I say? I've never minded washing dishes."

"Well, Grandad has offered to do them today, and we both have jobs. But I look forward to a romantic dinner at Gino's when you're done at the Manor."

"That reminds me," Maggie said, stepping back and heading to the table where she picked up her purse. She pulled out an envelope and held it out toward Carl.

"What's this? A Valentine?" he scowled, trying to hide his smile.

"I'm not sure," Maggie replied. "I'm only delivering this one." As Carl took it from her, she added, "But I can tell you it's from a lovely woman you know."

As soon as he opened the invitation his smile widened. "Someone's having a birthday later this week."

Tim walked up and peeked over his shoulder. "You got a special invite to celebrate with the family," he teased.

"Hey, she's just a friend, okay? But next Sunday, I'd like to walk up for a piece of cake if that's not too much trouble."

"We'd love to bring you up, Grandad. And I'm sure Ida will love having you there."

Maggie patted him on the shoulder. "So I take it I can give her a positive reply this morning?" As Carl nodded, she added, "Thanks for a wonderful breakfast – and the company of my two favorite men."

She wasn't sure whose smile was wider as she put her coat on. "Carl, I'll be back soon, and I'll let Ida know you'll be attending. And Mr. Collins, I'll see you tonight."

He walked her to the door and wrapped his arms around her,

gently planting cheddar garlic kisses on her lips before she left. "Looking forward to it, my love. You have yourself a beautiful day."

* * *

SEVERAL HOURS LATER, Maggie got a text from her sister. "Are you free for a quick visit? I'm out by the garden." Perplexed, she sent a quick reply and headed for the back door, wondering what would merit a visit at work. Once outside, the question was quickly answered, as Lucy stood hand in hand with Liz, with her left hand outstretched to reveal the sparkle of a diamond in the sunshine.

She wasn't sure who squealed louder as Maggie grabbed her sister for an excited embrace. "Oh, my God! Let me see it up close!" As she studied the simple gold band and gem, she kept talking. "Liz, I am so excited to have another sister. So tell me everything – how did it happen?"

Lucy, still beaming, chimed in. "This one here came to pick me up for lunch and asked if I wanted to head down the hall before leaving. When I gave her a confused look she said that she wanted to know who to talk to when the time came to apply for a marriage license – and then pulled out a ring."

Maggie laughed. "I hadn't thought of that – how easy it will be to take care of all those little details." She winked at Liz. "I guess dating someone who works at the town hall has its perks, huh?" Turning back to her sister, she continued. "Did you call Mom and Dad yet?"

"Yup – just before we texted you to come outside. Can you believe it? Both of the Richmond girls engaged?"

"I'm sure they were thrilled beyond words."

"Your dad said we should have a double wedding so we can save them some money," Liz replied. "We told them we'd be keeping it super simple, so it won't cost much at all."

Lucy grabbed Maggie's hand as a thought came to her. "What if we *did* have a double wedding? Sis, it might be perfect! We were hoping to ask Carl if we could be married out by his roses – they're so beautiful – and why not have you and his son do the same?"

Maggie's smile widened as the idea began to take shape. "I think it might be the perfect spot for both of us! Those rosebushes are what brought Tim and me together, and you guys helped to keep them alive while Carl was in rehab – and Liz, you work with Sharon. I think it might be an awesome idea!"

"What about the old curmudgeon? Do you think he'd want people in his garden?"

Lucy echoed her girlfriend's concerns. "When we were over there taking care of the roses last summer I was saying what a gorgeous place it would be for a wedding, and of course this one proposed the idea right after I said yes. But you're the one that knows the old guy best. Do you think he'd allow it? If not, we thought we'd look into renting the gazebo in the park."

"I have *another* idea!" Maggie exclaimed. "Timing might not be quite right, but what if we had the wedding in the garden and then all walked over to a little reception at the new community center? If it was ready, that would be perfect*!*"

Lucy almost jumped up and down, and Maggie could tell that Liz loved the idea as well. "How about I bring it up tonight when I have dinner with Tim? Obviously I need to find out how he feels about a double wedding first – but I can't imagine he wouldn't love the idea. Then I can ask him what he thinks about a garden wedding and if the community center is an option. I'm pretty sure it's supposed to open sometime this summer."

Liz grinned. "I swear, if this works out, your dad will go around telling everyone it was all his idea for suggesting a double wedding."

Maggie gave her a quick hug. "Well, it technically *was*, so we'll even give him the credit." She gave Lucy one more hug before stepping back. "I guess I better get back to work – but thanks for making this such a perfect Valentine's Day. I'm so happy for you guys."

"I suspect that handsome fiancé of yours will make your own Valentine celebration pretty damn special," Lucy replied. "And I'll be staying at *my* fiancée's place tonight in case you two want to continue your celebration after dinner." She gave her sister a wink as she grabbed Liz's hand. "Now back to work, sis. We're off to show Gino my ring."

Maggie headed back inside smiling at the thought of Gino and how he loved romance. This was one of his favorite days of the year, and having a newly engaged couple for lunch would be cause for cele-bration indeed. As she sat back down at her desk, she glanced at her ring and smiled again. *"And tonight you can welcome the second Richmond girl with a ring on her finger – and what a perfect spot to talk to Tim about getting married on the same day."*

CHAPTER 27

Cassie was eating her oatmeal the next morning when her dad came down. Philip was finishing his cereal and her mom was sitting next to her finishing up an order from one of her handbag parties from the night before. "Good morning, Dad," she said, noting his suit reserved for special occasions.

He poured his coffee and pulled out a chair across from her. "Sure hope it will be. Today's the big day."

"Big day for what?" Philip asked, drinking the last of his milk out of his bowl and wiping his mouth on his sleeve.

"Use your napkin, Philip," Eliana chimed in. "And today's your dad's big interview for the promotion he's been working so hard for." She reached out to pat her husband's hand as she turned toward him. "And you're going to be amazing."

Cassie watched him squeeze her hand in reply. "You look nice, Dad."

Frank sat up a little straighter and sipped his coffee. "Gotta dress to impress the big boss. But thank you."

Before Cassie could ask the question she'd been thinking for weeks, Philip beat her to it. He turned sideways in his chair and plopped his one arm on the table in front of him. "We're not gonna have to *move* again, are we? 'Cause Seth is my best friend now and I don't wanna have to leave. He said I could go with them to Vermont next summer, and I don't want anything to mess that up."

Cassie chuckled at her brother's reasoning but understood completely about not wanting to leave a new best friend. She held her breath as she waited for her father's reply.

"While there's never a guarantee, I don't think you'll have to worry, son. From what I've been hearing I'd have to travel more, but I can handle that if all of you can stay put. I think we all want to be in Caldwell."

Cassie relaxed a bit and sighed. "That's for sure. What time's your interview?"

"They want to take me out to lunch first, and then I interview at 2:00. I should head in soon to go over my notes one more time." He got up and gulped down the last of his coffee as his wife got up to give him a hug.

"Wish you'd eat a little something," Eliana said. "But good luck – I'll be thinking of you."

"I'll grab something when I get off the train, don't worry."

Cassie got up and approached her father as well. "Good luck. I know how much you want this." She gave him a quick hug to show her support.

"Thanks, sweetie," Frank replied, kissing her forehead. "Now if either of you want a ride to school you need to be ready in five minutes."

"On it!" Philip said, grabbing his bowl and spoon as he stood up. Cassie nodded. "As long as you're offering, I'll take you up on it. Neither Teagan nor Brian have a car today, and it's a cold day if the bus is running late." She retrieved her own dishes from the table and headed toward the sink.

Before she could turn the water on her mom gestured toward the door. "I'll take care of these. You go up and grab your books."

* * *

A FEW MINUTES later her dad dropped her off in front of school and waved as he drove off with Philip. She turned toward the front door, glad she had taken his offer as the chilly February breeze hit her face. *"Feels like snow,"* she thought. *"I hope it holds off till after rehearsal."*

Before heading into rehearsal she stopped at the restroom, and while washing her hands she was sure she heard sobbing coming from the back stall. She took a few steps closer. "You okay?" she whispered to the unknown person inside.

"I'm fine," came the sniffled reply—one that Cassie didn't recognize. With no further sound or movement from within, Cassie turned to leave, catching her reflection in the mirror. *"I might never like my body,"* she thought, *"but I'm beginning to like the rest of me a lot more."* Something caught her eye in the reflection, and she noted sneakers in the far stall with sparkles on them. *"I've seen those before, so I might know who's in there. I'll have to keep my eyes open. She might need to talk at some point."*

It wasn't long before she solved the mystery. During theater class, she found herself in a small group with both Julia and Sarah, the sophomore that she'd seen Mike flirting with. When she spotted the latter's sparkly sneakers, Cassie made eye contact with Sarah. She wasn't her bubbly self this morning, and her eyes were a little puffy. *"It had to be her,"* she surmised. *"So why was she in the bathroom crying before classes even started?"*

Julia was also quiet this morning, and Cassie noticed her clenching and releasing her fists several times during the group exercise. She wondered if Julia might have said something about Mike's flirting to Sarah as neither seemed to make eye contact with each other. *"I wish Teagan was in this group. She's so much better at reading people than I am,"* Cassie thought.

She had a chance to tell her best friend about it at lunch. "So what do you think might be going on?"

"Not sure," Teagan replied as she popped a grape into her mouth. "Your idea makes sense, but it could be unrelated. I guess we'll have to keep our eyes open at rehearsal. Mike has been super flirty with Sarah when Julia's not around."

"I feel so bad for Julia. She could do so much better than that jerk."

"Maybe she's starting to realize it herself. It would be better if she broke up with *him* rather than him dropping her. I guess time will tell. Speaking of which, is everything set for your Gram's party this weekend? Brian is super excited to be making her loukamades again."

Cassie nodded. "She adores those little Greek donuts – and she still talks about his baking classes at the Manor last summer."

"He loved them, too. And the residents are all looking forward to the party. Ida's become quite popular since she moved in. Kitty was joking with her this morning about whether her *boyfriend* was gonna be there."

"Better not let Old Man Pritchard hear that reference – might scare him from coming. But there *is* a little spark there, isn't there? I know how happy Gram is whenever he pops in to visit."

"Trust me," Teagan said, "any time there's a spark the residents pick up on it. Gossip doesn't end when you're old and in a nursing home. Heck, we even have residents who have occasional sleepovers."

Cassie wrinkled her nose. "Eww! I do *not* need that kind of image in my head, thank you very much!" She took the last bite of her croissant. "At least I know my Gram won't ever be one of them."

Grinning, Teagan closed up her lunch container. "I still remember the first time that Ida told me that she was asexual like I am. I guess it's why she became my favorite resident of all time. And I suspect she even told Carl about it at some point. They talked about a lot of stuff over those crossword puzzles."

Cassie noticed students leaving from the table closest to them. "I guess the bell is set to ring. And look at me, heading off to study hall with no lunch still left to finish."

"I'm so proud of you. You've worked so hard to get to where you are in recovery – even with some of the crap that you've had to deal with you keep choosing to move forward."

"That's true. Even though I may never like my body, it can at least be healthy. And I don't think about happiness as a number on the scale anymore, but being healthy enough to do the show, have real friends, and work at a job I love."

"Don't forget about dance, bestie. I can't *wait* to see you in that senior showcase."

Cassie's eyes got a little misty as she stood up. "Sometimes I'm afraid to even think about it – but this week after the cherub class Colleen is giving me a private lesson to let me hear the song she chose and work on the choreography for the first time."

"Any idea on the song?"

"Nope – but she said it was the perfect choice for me. I can't wait." As they headed off toward study hall, she tried to imagine what song would be that perfect choice. She was glad to have rehearsals to keep her busy until it was revealed.

* * *

SATURDAY MORNING the cherubs were super excited in dance class; they kept looking toward the stack of bright yellow bags on top of Colleen's desk.

"I can't *wait* to see my costume!" Tracey blurted out while practicing their routine. The other girls chimed in their agreement – except for Lydia, who smiled as she gazed over at the bags and caught Cassie's gaze.

"It's exciting getting your first costume, isn't it?"

Lydia nodded shyly, but her smile got a little bigger. "Are you gonna have one, too?"

Cassie squatted down to meet the little one's gaze. "When I'm out helping all of you I'll be wearing my leotard like I am now. But when I do my senior dance I'll have something special to wear, too. And I'm just as excited to see mine."

Lydia smiled wide and gave Cassie a hug. "I bet you'll look like a princess."

Cassie tapped Lydia on the nose with one finger. "How 'bout we finish up class so we can see *your* princess outfit, okay?"

Colleen gave her a smile from across the room as the other little girls lined up on their designated dots on the floor. Cassie smiled back as Lydia hurried over to her spot while Cassie moved off to the side

213

where she'd model their movements to guide them. As the music began, she smiled at the cherubs who had taught her so much. No competition. No pressure. Only the excitement of performing and the love of dance. Even her own eating disorder couldn't take that away from her today – and for that, her heart was full. And she could hardly wait to see her own "princess" outfit.

Maggie tried to stay away from the office on Sundays, but today she was happy to make an exception for Ida's birthday party. She and Tim walked up Lincoln Street past the park with Carl between them. The latter complained about the cold, but chose to walk rather than ride the short distance.

As they passed by the gazebo Tim gestured beyond to the community center building. "I'll have to take you over there this week Grandad – the inside is coming along now."

The old man squinted in the sun as he glanced over. "Outside looks better, that's for sure. McLean sure didn't care about the upkeep when he owned it."

Maggie guessed he was thinking about how things might have been different if Sean McLean had kept the property and put in the driving range he'd proposed. "And this year you won't have to worry about flying golf balls in your rosebushes."

"Thank God for that," Carl said, "although I wonder how many noisy kids will be running around instead."

"Grandad," Tim replied, "I can't promise there won't be kids outside once classes and camps start up, but I *can* promise I won't ever allow a golf camp, okay?"

"You better not." He turned to Maggie and winked. "It's bad enough I gotta put up with wedding shenanigans right outside my door."

Maggie reached out and squeezed his arm. "You can't fool me, Carl. You're gonna love every minute of that day and you know it. And I'm so happy that you agreed to it."

Carl shrugged, but he couldn't hide his smile. "Hey, it's gonna be his house someday. I guess I can't keep him from getting married in the backyard if that's what he wants."

"No better place in the world," Tim replied as they reached the back door of Caldwell Manor. "Now how about we head in to find out if the birthday girl is free in September? She'd love to be at her favorite social worker's wedding."

As soon as they entered the building Melvin greeted them from his regular post by the door. His eyes lit up when he saw Carl. "Look who came back! I knew you'd come!"

Maggie shook Melvin's hand. "He didn't want you alone with all those ladies."

Melvin pointed toward the library. "Everyone's in there. I guess they were waiting for you to arrive."

Tim patted Melvin on the back. "Why don't we all join them, Melvin? We don't want to hold up the festivities, do we?"

Melvin fell into step beside Carl as Tim dropped back and took Maggie's hand. "I think Melvin's happy to have his buddy back," he whispered.

Maggie agreed. "They hit it off when Carl was here."

As they headed into the library, Ida's face was beaming as Carl approached. He leaned down and gave her a little hug and kiss on the cheek. She grasped his hands and greeted him warmly. "So glad you could come. I miss our puzzle time." She looked past Carl to smile at Maggie. "Thanks for walking up with him – even on a Sunday."

Maggie gave Ida a hug. "I wouldn't have missed this for anything. And I promise I won't go anywhere near my office."

As Tim wished Ida a happy birthday Maggie turned her attention to Cassie, who was helping her mom and Teagan open the food containers that she recognized from Gino's. "Look at you – helping with a buffet table set up. Hi, Teagan. And Eliana – can I help with anything?"

The older woman shook her head. "We have everything all set. You can tell the others to come and grab a plate while the food's hot."

Cassie's brother Philip beat her to it. He jumped up from the chair that he'd been sitting in, his boredom replaced with energy in an instant. "Food's ready, everybody! Time to eat – *finally!*"

Maggie chuckled as she smiled at Cassie. "I'm not always that excited about my food, but it *is* Gino's, after all."

"I have to admit I'm a little more excited about this meal than the last time I ate Gino's food…but I'm sure grateful that you were there to make me eat that pizza."

Teagan came up and wrapped her arm around Cassie's shoulder as she addressed Maggie. "That makes two of us. If I'd known Mike was gonna be such a jerk that day I would have waited till you got there. He's so arrogant this year."

Maggie agreed as Cassie reached up to squeeze Teagan's hand. "I'm glad she has you and Brian at school." Looking around the room, she added, "Wasn't he coming today with dessert?"

"He's on his way," Cassie replied. "Told us to eat while the food was hot. And I have to admit, that eggplant parm is calling my name right now. Should we get in line?"

Maggie gestured toward the end of the line. "Best idea I've heard all day."

* * *

SEVERAL NIGHTS later she sat across the table from Tim at Gino's for a late dinner.

As she bit into her eggplant parm sub, Tim smiled. "Couldn't get enough of that at Ida's party, could you? Should we talk to Gino about catering our wedding so you can have more in the fall?"

Maggie had to pull on the stringy mozzarella to break it off from the rest of the sandwich, and after licking her finger and swallowing she answered. "Much as I love that idea, I think I'd have to go with fettucine alfredo instead – marinara sauce would ruin a wedding gown. So how's your cheesesteak?"

Tim had taken his first bite and hesitated before answering. "Hmm," he mumbled, reaching for his napkin. "Wonderful. I'm glad the meeting ended early – I was starving."

"Everything is moving along. And Jim was a great choice as your contractor."

"No doubt. He's been one of the best I've ever worked with. Unless something unexpected happens, we're on track to open this summer – at least in some capacity."

Maggie took a sip of water. "Are you sure you still want the wedding over Labor Day weekend? Won't life be insanely crazy for you then?"

"Honey, life will always be crazy with one thing or another. We may not go on a real honeymoon right away, but marrying you out in the rose garden is too perfect to give up."

"Aren't you forgetting that we're heading up to Gloucester for the rest of that weekend? Sounds like a honeymoon to me."

He flashed that dimpled smile that she loved. "I can hardly wait."

Maggie took another bite of her sandwich, enjoying the gooey cheese. As she glanced around the restaurant a certain table caught her eye.

"What are you smiling about?" Tim asked.

She gestured with her eyes toward the other side of the room. "Amanda apparently figured out you weren't gonna change your mind."

Tim followed her gaze and laughed. "Well, what do you know? I thought she and Jim were a little chatty during the meeting."

"They seem more than a little chatty right now," Maggie teased, watching Jim offer the attractive blonde a bite of garlic bread with his fingers and having them licked in return. "Please tell me she didn't lick your fingers when you had dinner that night."

"Hey, by the time I realized that she was hitting on me I was halfway through dinner and trying to figure out how to escape if Rich didn't show up soon." He reached over and took Maggie's hand. "What can I say? I waited a long time for the right woman, and there won't ever be another." With a twinkle in her eyes, Maggie lifted his hand, kissed it gently, and licked his fingers.

CHAPTER 29

With the show still a month away Cassie was amazed at how strong the cast was. She was finishing her solo number and dance as rehearsal ended, and Brian, Teagan, and Beth had stayed to watch. Beth flew up onto the stage first to hug her. "My God, that was so incredible! I have to fly outta here 'cause my dad's outside waiting, but I couldn't leave in the middle of your number. See you guys tomorrow!"

Brian chuckled as Beth departed. "Man, that kid's got more energy that I'll ever have!" As he joined Teagan in a group hug, he grinned. "Cassie, you're killing it as Irene."

Teagan agreed. "I got chills, girl…..your voice is so much stronger than it was last year."

Cassie thanked them both as she started to gather the props she had used. "You mean when I was trying hard not to faint? Trust me, I can feel the difference – and I like this version of Cassie way more than last year's model."

Brian offered to help. "Want me to carry those for ya?"

She shook her head. "Thanks, but they're super light. You guys can go on ahead – I'll meet you outside as soon as I put these away."

Cassie gathered her hat and hat boxes and carried them backstage.

She placed them on the prop table, and as she turned to leave she was startled by movement as Mike emerged from the shadows to her right. "Jeez, Mike! You scared the crap out of me!"

"Sorry 'bout that," he murmured, stepping in close. "I was back here listening to you sing and just had to stick around to tell you how amazing you sounded."

Cassie felt butterflies in her stomach, but it was an uneasy feeling – not the romantic ones from the previous year. "Well, thanks," she stammered.

Before she could leave, Mike reached out and wrapped his arm around her waist and stepped in close. As he leaned in Cassie could feel his warm breath on her cheek. "I really miss you," he whispered huskily, "and can't stop thinking about you lately."

As his lips found hers her entire body tensed up and she pushed him back with an angry glare. "What about Julia?' she hissed. "Aren't you two still together?"

Mike ran his finger over her lips as he gazed into her eyes. "Only 'cause I'm trying to let her down easy. I want you back, Cassie – and you know I get what I want." He once again leaned in to continue the kiss, but this time Cassie stepped back. "You should go," she said icily. "I'm not interested, okay?"

Instead of backing up, Mike came forward again, this time pinning her against the prop table as his lips found hers again. He kissed her hard as he pressed against her, wrapping one hand around her head and the other on her breast. "I can get you interested again," he grunted, reaching down to pull up her skirt.

Cassie's heart raced as she wondered if anyone would hear her if she screamed. In desperation she used all of her strength to shove Mike backwards. "You are an *ass*," she spit out. "Don't you *ever* touch me again – or I'll call the cops, ya hear?"

Mike shook his head and laughed. "You wouldn't dare. And if you tried, I'd quit the show, and then you'd screw it up for everyone and piss a whole lot of people off. So don't even think about it, or next time I won't be so nice." As he turned to go, he glared back at her. "I think I liked you better when you were thin and needy – at least you were open to a little affection back then. Now you're just a waste of my time."

Cassie watched him leave, unable to move, her legs shaking beneath her. The tears came as fear overwhelmed her, and she sank to the floor sobbing uncontrollably. *"See where all this recovery gets you?"* The eating disorder lashed out from deep within her brain as she wrapped her arms around herself and tried to disappear. *"No one wants a fat girl like you – Mike just made that clear. You're worthless."*

It was Teagan that found her. "Cassie? You back here?" When she spotted her, she rushed to her side. "What happened? My God, you're trembling," she said gently as she knelt down and wrapped her arms around her best friend.

Cassie clung to her, her body shaking as the aching sobs took over. Unable to speak, she held on to Teagan as her friend stroked her hair and let her cry. Eventually Cassie raised her head from her friend's wet shoulder and accepted the tissue packet that Teagan had retrieved from her pocket. She tried to choke the words out. "Mike…..he grabbed me……tried to……."

Teagan's eyes sparked with anger. "Did he hurt you?"

Cassie shook her head as she wiped her eyes. "He…tried to…I was able to push him away."

Before Teagan could answer, Brian arrived, and he knew immediately that something wasn't right. "What's going on?" When Cassie buried her face in Teagan's neck, he knelt down and reached out to offer support, but Teagan shook her head slightly to let him know to keep his distance. "Wait for us out there," she whispered, glancing toward the door.

Brian nodded and he slowly stood back up. "It's gonna be okay, kiddo," he whispered gently to Cassie. "Take all the time you need."

Cassie waited until she heard the backstage door close. "Thank God you came looking for me.…I don't think I could have fought him off if he'd kept— "

"Shh…." Teagan said, putting her finger to Cassie's lips. "I wish I'd come sooner. But then I might have hit him on the head with some-thing heavy and knocked him out." Glancing at the prop table, she shook her head. "Then again, I'm not sure a hat box would have done much damage."

Cassie actually smiled a bit. "Might be therapeutic to smash a hat box over his head and around his neck."

"Why waste a gorgeous prop on that bastard? Do you think you're ready to get up off the floor? We can sit somewhere for awhile if you need to."

Cassie nodded as she reached for the prop table to steady herself. "I think so. And I hate to leave Brian out there waiting. You guys can drop me off at home."

Teagan helped Cassie to stand up before meeting her gaze. "He'll wait. And I think you should come home with me. You shouldn't be alone right now."

Cassie looked down, almost afraid to let Teagan see how scared she still was. "Maybe you're right," she whispered. "Just don't tell Brian anything, okay?"

Teagan lifted Cassie's chin with one hand to make direct eye contact again. "I won't right now – but you're gonna have to talk about this. With Natalie or Maggie first – but you can't pretend this didn't happen."

Cassie's lower lip trembled. "But he said he'd quit the show and then I'd ruin it for everyone and they'd all hate me."

Teagan's anger flared. "You are *not* gonna let him get away with this by trying to manipulate you. He *attacked* you, for God's sake."

Cassie began to shake again. "Can we go home? I just wanna get out of here."

Teagan's expression softened. "Of course we can – come on, I'll help you."

"And Brian?"

"He'll understand if I tell him we'll talk later – trust me, he's simply concerned."

Cassie let Teagan guide her out into the hallway where Brian sat on the floor with an open textbook. He saw Cassie's furtive glance up the hallway as he stood up and wondered why she seemed so nervous.

"You okay, kiddo?" he asked gently, wondering if she had fainted like last year.

Cassie nodded but avoided eye contact. Teagan spoke up for her. "She's not up for talking yet. Do you think you could drive us both back to my house? She's gonna hang out with me for a bit."

"Sure, Teags." He tried to sound reassuring to Cassie. "I moved the car while I was waiting. You ready?"

Cassie didn't reply as Teagan opened the door and scanned the area before turning toward her. "There's no one outside – and Brian's car is right out front." She didn't remember darting toward the car, scrambling into the back seat, or locking the door. She tried to avoid Brian's concerned look in the rear view mirror as he glanced back at her while driving. All she could do was to close her eyes and try to block out the memories of Mike's hands on her backstage – which only brought more painful images of Mike's hands on her last year. She prayed for anything to fill that void, but even her eating disorder remained insidiously silent for the moment.

* * *

THE NEXT DAY Cassie headed in to school late with Teagan by her side and Maggie driving. It had been an emotional evening with Maggie's arrival and a video chat with her counselor Natalie, and then a phone call with her mother for permission to stay over with Teagan until morning. After much discussion, Cassie had agreed to report the assault to school officials. As they pulled into the visitor lot, the lead knot in her stomach kept her frozen to her seat in the car. She peered out the windows as fear overtook her, scanning the parking lot for Mike's car.

"I'm not sure I can do this," she croaked, crossing her arms in front of her and rocking a bit.

Maggie opened her door and squatted down beside her. "Cassie, this is gonna be one of the hardest things you've ever had to do, but think about all the battles you've fought this past year and won."

"Those were different.....they were just inside my head."

Teagan joined Maggie from Cassie's other side. "They're not gonna let anything happen to you. That's the law – they have to protect you."

"How? How can they promise that? He's always around ……and what about the show?"

Maggie pleaded with her. "Cassie, we went over all of this last night with Natalie. Those aren't *your* problems to worry about.….you're the *victim,* and they have to keep you safe."

Cassie's lips trembled. "Everyone in the show is gonna be pissed at me. Just like he said."

"That's crap," Teagan answered. "The cast loves you – and most will agree he's a jerk."

"What about Julia?" Cassie whispered. "She's gonna hate me for sure."

"I'll talk to her. And if she's mad for a bit, then we'll work through that. But she needs to learn what kind of an ass she's dating, doesn't she?"

With all of her arguments being countered, Cassie slumped back in her seat and sighed. "I'm so scared."

Maggie reached in and took her hand. "It's okay to be scared. It's *normal.* But if you don't face this fear head on, I can guarantee that your eating disorder will use it against you. Do you want to let Mike be the weapon that beats you down after all the victories you've had so far in recovery?"

Cassie straightened up and took a deep breath and exhaled. "No. Not him." She took one more look around the parking lot and met Maggie's expectant gaze. "Okay. Let's do this. Before I change my mind." With her friends on either side, she fought the thoughts screaming inside her head and headed for the guidance office.

* * *

WITH CASSIE'S PERMISSION, Natalie had called and spoken with Mrs. Kearns, the guidance counselor who was the appointed Title IX coordinator for the school. She greeted Cassie with a warm smile as she escorted all of them into the office and invited them to sit down.

Cassie sat between Maggie and Teagan, across the desk from where Mrs. Kearns had forms already filled in and a pad and pen ready. She glanced around the office to make sure there were no windows where people could look in; she found none, but did notice a sign on the wall that gave her strength. It was a simple sign: "Believe in yourself." She took a deep breath and tried to quiet the eating disorder voices that had broken their silence. *"You're so stupid to be here....Mike's gonna hurt you next time...no one's gonna believe you...Mike's right, you're worthless... you should shut up and leave now..."* Clenching her fists in her lap, she swallowed hard and smiled weakly at the woman seated before her. *"I'm not going to listen to you,"* she told her eating disorder. *"I trust Maggie and Natalie and Teagan way more than I trust you – because they've proven themselves to be credible and I don't trust anything you're saying to me."*

An hour later, she wiped the tears from her eyes as Maggie and Teagan held her hands. Mrs. Kearns had been extremely gentle and supportive throughout the interview, and after recording all the pertinent information, she asked if Cassie would allow Mr. Calabreschi to join them to address the immediate issue of Mike's presence in the cast. "I won't reveal any more than I have to," Mrs. Kearns had explained, "but if this account is true then we need to address some safety issues for you in terms of theater—and since the show is getting close, that needs to be dealt with immediately." Cassie remembered how caring Mr.C. had been the previous year when she had fainted, and she believed that she could trust him as she nodded.

When Mr.C. arrived, he looked at Cassie and Teagan and sighed. "If this involves one or both of you then you have my full support."

As he sat down next to Maggie, Mrs. Kearns gave Cassie a reassuring smile before turning toward him. "Cassie's given me permission to fill you in on why she's here. She also knows that I'll be notifying the student that a complaint has been filed against him. Usually I inform them first, but because of theater rehearsals, I wanted to tell you right away."

Mr. C. leaned forward. "If there's a viable complaint toward someone in my cast then I appreciate all you can tell me. I have a zero tolerance policy for bullying and hurtful behavior in my productions." Looking toward Cassie, he added, "You might remember me spelling that out at the first rehearsal."

Cassie swallowed hard to try and clear her dry throat as Mrs. Kearns continued. "Cassie was here to report a sexual assault by one of her cast mates that took place backstage yesterday afternoon."

She watched his face first harden with anger. "One of *my* cast? Damn it! I left right after rehearsal yesterday for a meeting, but there were only a few students left and they were all preparing to leave." His expression softened as he continued. "Cassie, I am so sorry. This is my fault."

Cassie shook her head. "No, Mr. C. – don't blame yourself. You had no way of knowing that he… was backstage…and Teagan and Brian thought I'd be right out after putting my props away." Her voice got shakier as memories came flooding back.

Mr. C. responded in a calm and quiet voice despite the clenched jaw. "Cassie, I do need to know who this was."

As Cassie's eyes filled with tears, she nodded toward Mrs. Kearns to speak. "The student involved is Mike Blanchett. We'll be notifying him this afternoon that a complaint has been filed."

Mr. C's body tensed up and he sat quietly for a moment with a tight lip. Cassie almost held her breath waiting for his reply. *"What if he doesn't believe me?"* she thought.

Instead, Mr. C. turned toward her and responded almost in a whisper. "You say this happened backstage?"

She nodded. "Right by the prop table."

He gave a reassuring smile. "It's gonna be okay, Cassie." He turned his attention back to the guidance counselor. "The theater department has security cameras set up backstage to protect the set pieces and props we rent out each year. I hate myself for leaving early yesterday, but at least I turned them on as I left."

He looked back to Cassie. "If Mike attacked you by the props table, the video will verify your story within the first few minutes of footage."

Mrs. Kearns put her pen down and leaned forward in her chair.

"How long would it take for you to obtain that footage, Mr. Calabreschi?"

"I could have it back here in about ten minutes."

"If you wouldn't mind going now, having the footage would be helpful. Cassie, would you and your friends mind waiting a little bit longer? I know this has been a stressful time, but it would help to expedite the process moving forward."

Cassie nodded and Mr. C. stood up to leave. "Hang tight, Cassie – I won't be long." Teagan reached over to squeeze her hand. "We're not going anywhere, either, don't you worry."

Cassie looked up at the clock. "I don't want you to have to miss your afternoon classes on my account."

"Teagan will be fine," Maggie said. "We both figured this might take a while. Do you have any questions for Mrs. Kearns while we're waiting?"

Cassie bit her lip as she thought for a moment. "Will everyone in school know it was me who filed the complaint?"

The guidance counselor tried to give a reassuring smile, but Cassie could see the strain. "In the best of circumstances, we try to protect both of your names until the investigation is over. However, this is a small school, and I can't guarantee that details won't come out. You're probably well aware of how quickly news travels sometimes."

Cassie wondering what to say. Maggie spoke up on her account. "Cassie didn't mention it in the earlier questions, but Mike did threaten her if she said anything. He said he wouldn't be so nice next time."

Mrs. Kearns made a quick note on her pad. "We'll add that to your account, and hope to resolve this issue as quickly as we can. Are there any other people that might be able to share information on Mike's behavior toward Cassie – or any other girls, for that matter? It's common practice for both you and Mike to be able to give us a list of witnesses of people who might shed more light on the case."

Cassie spoke first. "He's dating Julia Jackson right now – although I'm not sure how solid their relationship is at the moment."

Mrs. Kearns wrote her name down as Teagan spoke up. "What

about the sophomore we've seen Mike flirting with? Sarah somebody?"

"Peabody – Sarah Peabody," Cassie confirmed. "She's in theater class and in the ensemble in the show."

Mrs. Kearns folded her hands in front of her. "When you say 'he was flirting with her', can you be more specific?"

"At the first rehearsal, he was sitting next to Julia and she was standing a couple of people away. He was looking at…."

"Her breasts," Teagan finished. "She had on a snug top and he was openly staring at her breasts. Later in rehearsal they made eye contact several times, and he was talking to her off stage while Julia went to the bathroom. They've continued flirting in numerous rehearsals."

By the time she had finished writing down the information Mr. C. returned with a flash drive in his hand. "Here's the footage – if you open the drive the files are arranged by date, and yesterday's should be the first one."

Cassie's body started to tremble as Mrs. Kearns took the flash drive. As she made eye contact, she stopped what she was doing. "Cassie, I understand this footage might be troubling for you. We can turn the monitor so that only Mr. C. and I have access – or you can wait out in the waiting area if you'd prefer."

"I don't want to be out there – people are coming in and out." She faced Mrs. Kearns again. "If there's any audio, can you turn the sound down?" When the guidance counselor nodded, she took a deep breath. "Go ahead. Put it on."

Maggie squeezed her hand as Mr. C. pointed at the computer. "That file right there."

Cassie watched their faces as the churning in her stomach got worse. She saw Mr. C's brow tighten up as Mrs. Kearns shook her head slightly. "May I copy this file to my computer?"

Mr. C. nodded. "Only if you promise to show it to the bastard."

Cassie saw Teagan's slight grin. *So they did see it…..and they do believe me.*

Maggie had also come to the same conclusion. "Can you tell us how things will proceed at this point?"

Mrs. Kearns again folded her hands in front of her. "The video footage will help to expedite the situation. This afternoon I'll bring Mike in and inform him that you've filed a complaint; I'll also have to read the basic information you've provided in terms of how the incident occurred."

"Won't he just deny it?" Cassie blurted out.

"I almost hope he does," Mr. C. replied. "It will be far more satisfying to show him the video after he gives his own version of what happened."

"What about the show? Won't everyone hate me if we have to cancel it?"

"Cassie, dear, to quote an old phrase, 'the show must go on'. Mike's role will be recast over the weekend, and on Monday I'll inform the cast of the change. Happens in theater all the time."

Cassie's stomach continued to churn. "Will everyone know it was my fault? I don't want them all hating me." *"Especially Julia,"* she thought. *"Please don't let Julia hate me."*

Mr. C. leaned forward and met Cassie's gaze. "I wish I could assure you that no one will find out, but experience tells me your peers will talk. It's not your fault, but some people will make judgements – but I think most people will stand behind you for stepping forward." He leaned back and continued. "Your name won't come up at Monday's cast meeting, but you know me -- I tell it like it is. I *will* explain that Mike has been suspended for an incident I'm not at liberty to discuss, and consequently, his role has been recast. I'll then introduce his replacement and start rehearsal."

"How long will he be suspended?" Teagan asked.

Mrs. Kearns closed her folder. "That isn't determined until the entire case is resolved – however, because of the desire to ensure Cassie's safety, and the status of the rehearsals for the show, I'm sure a minimal suspension will be ten days."

Cassie's eyes got wide as her body tensed up. "That's....all? Then he'll be back?"

"With the video footage, I'm estimating it will be closer to thirty days – which I believe should take you right up until show weekend."

"And he won't be allowed on school grounds for the show – I can assure you of that." Mr. C. was obviously concerned for her safety. She wondered if he'd ever been in this situation in earlier years.

"Unless any of you have further comments or questions, that's all I have for today," Mrs. Kearns said. "Cassie, I know when I spoke with your counselor Natalie this morning she said you had no plans to file any reports with the police. If this has changed at all, that will slow down the process at this end in that we will have to follow police procedure in terms of gathering information and conducting interviews. Have you thought any more about your decision?"

Cassie hesitated before answering. "I don't wanna go through all that if I don't have to. I just want him to leave me alone."

Mrs. Kearns nodded. "I can assure you those instructions will be clearly spelled out to Mike. In addition, he'll be informed that additional charges might be filed if he *does* try to retaliate in any way. You can also file for a restraining order if you still feel unsafe. If it helps at all, from what I know of Mike, my gut tells me he'll try to keep a low profile through the rest of the year--especially since he's applied to colleges for next year."

Maggie smirked. "I guess most schools would frown on that kind of behavior." She smiled at Cassie. "You're more than welcome to stay at my place this weekend if you'd like."

Cassie took a deep breath and exhaled. "Can I go now?"

Mrs. Kearns nodded, and Mr. C. got up and patted Cassie's shoulder. "I wish every girl was as brave as you are. Don't ever doubt that. Now go home and try to rest, okay?"

*"He thinks I'm brave? "*she thought as they left. *"Please let me feel that, too."*

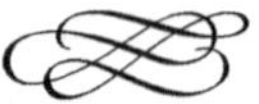

CHAPTER 30

Maggie was taking a banana bread out of the oven when Cassie emerged from the bedroom. "Morning. I'm glad you finally got to sleep. You'll find a clean towel and a new toothbrush next to the sink if you want to grab a shower. I'm gonna scramble some eggs while the banana bread cools off, so take your time."

Cassie mumbled something that sounded like "thank you" and disappeared into the bathroom as Maggie's phone indicated a text from Teagan. *"How is she this morning?"*

Maggie sent a quick reply: *"Just woke up, so at least she got some sleep. Feel free to call or visit later. We're having breakfast soon."* As she cracked the eggs Teagan replied with a heart emoji and a short message: *"Will do – give her a hug from me."*

Cassie was more awake when she rejoined Maggie. "Thanks for lending me an outfit for the day," she said. "Fits pretty well, and the fleece is so soft." She came into the kitchen and accepted the cup of coffee that Maggie handed her. "Hmm....I needed this. Thanks."

Maggie slid a plate with eggs and banana bread across the counter. "You need this, too. Do you wanna sit in here or on the couch?"

"In there, I think. That way Tramp can have his head scratched now and then."

The beagle did indeed curl up next to Cassie as they settled on the couch. Maggie smiled as Tramp rested his head and looked up at Cassie with big brown eyes, gently thumping his tail. "I think you're one of his favorite people. He seeks you out every time you're here."

Cassie smiled a bit as she massaged Tramp's head between his ears. "He might sense those who need some extra assurance – that would certainly explain his attraction to me."

"Well, he's certainly learned that over the years with all of *my* mental health issues, so that's possible." She picked up her coffee to make a toast. "To your very own emotional support dog while you're here." As she picked up her fork, she grinned. "Of course, it also might be you're more likely to give him a bite of something now and then."

Cassie almost laughed. "I'm hungrier than I thought I'd be. Last night I felt like my stomach would never stop churning."

"What time did you fall sleep?"

"Not sure. After midnight, I think. Funny how the voices in your head are so much louder when it's dark and quiet. Thanks for letting me stay here, by the way. I would have been a wreck at home."

"I'm glad you at least talked to your mom last night. I know that wasn't easy."

"Nothing about this has been easy. Last night I was lying there waiting for my phone to ring again – he was so pissed off after his meeting. His text last night scared me."

Maggie took a sip of coffee. "I'm sure *he* was scared when he got called in and had the charges read – especially with Mr. C. there, too. And texting you right after the meeting was probably the stupidest thing he could do. That's gonna lengthen his suspension."

Cassie shuddered. "I bet he's still fuming." She had an overwhelming urge to put her plate down. Her voice dropped to a whisper as the doubts crept in. "I'm still not sure I did the right thing."

Maggie reached over and patted her shoulder. "You *absolutely* did the right thing. Those doubts are your eating disorder trying to sneak in through the back door. And don't even think about putting your plate down yet – I saw that look." She picked up a piece of banana bread and held it up. "To quote something you said to *me* not too long ago, here's to recovery." She took a bite as she gestured toward Cassie's plate. "Now eat something. You'll thank me later."

* * *

AFTER FINISHING breakfast and getting the kitchen cleaned up, Maggie turned to Cassie and took the dish towel from her. "Thanks for helping…and I'll leave the bread out with a little foil on it in case you want another piece at some point. Lucy and I have been known to sliver our way through an entire loaf in a day." As she hung the towel up, she continued. "I didn't know if you'd be up for yoga today, so I texted Colleen. I didn't go into details, but told her you'd had a rough day yesterday and might not be there today."

Cassie eyes widened as she reached for her phone. "Crap! I'm supposed to help with the little kids."

Maggie held up her hand. "She also said not to worry about the cherubs class and that you can practice for the showcase next week. And that she'd be praying for you."

"I hate letting her down – even the cherubs will be mad at me."

"Like hell they will – they adore you. Next week they'll be all over you telling you how glad they are that you're feeling better."

"I guess so…" Cassie's body tensed up a bit. "I wonder if Julia's heard yet. She'll hate me."

Maggie stepped in and placed her hand on Cassie's shoulder. "Julia will be upset, but if she's mad at you then she's misdirecting her anger from where it needs to be. Besides, didn't you say they were having some troubles between them?"

"It's hard to tell since Julia's so quiet anyway, but there's something going on. I hope she doesn't hate me – I really like her."

"She won't – trust me. You might have done her a favor by showing her what kind of jerk she's dating. Give her time and she'll come around. She has to process all this, too."

Cassie shrugged. "I guess you're right. I'm glad I don't have to face

234

her yet – though I'm a little bummed that I'll miss being at the studio later for my lesson. Then again, I'm not sure I'd be able to focus on the showcase right now anyway."

"Hmmm…." Maggie paused for a moment as she mulled over something. "I have an idea – and only if you're up for it – but I might be able to give you a different spot to run through your dance if you wanted to." Seeing Cassie's questioning look, she continued. "Tim's been wanting to show me the latest work on the community center, and I know they got the floors done during the last couple of weeks. If you're up for a walk we could take Tramp over to see how things are shaping up."

"But that'd mean walking through the park…..and anyone might be there."

"Hey, aside from the Christmas celebration, have you ever seen Mike in the park? Do you think he'd be there on a Saturday morning?"

"I suppose you're right. He's not into nature – especially on a weekend."

"So is that a yes on the walk?"

"I….guess so."

"Look, for awhile those fears are gonna jump out of nowhere, and that's a normal reaction after being assaulted. You can't erase those fears, but you can *face* them. And each time you do, you're gonna be more empowered. It's not that different from standing up to your eating disorder – and look how much stronger you've gotten doing that this past year."

Cassie agreed. "I'm glad you invited me here for the weekend. It's like having a prolonged therapy session before having to go back to school." She exhaled slowly. "I don't know how I'm gonna get through Monday."

"You can discuss it with Natalie on your video chat later today. For now, let me text Tim and find out if he's over there or if we need to stop by the house for the key, okay?"

Within minutes, they were strolling through the park enjoying the warmth of the morning sun. Tramp was excited by the hints of spring and stopped often to sniff the ground, occasionally barking at a squirrel who scurried by. Maggie noticed that Cassie seemed more relaxed as they got closer to the community center, and as they cut through the little pathway behind the gazebo, the morning sun's rays lit up the façade of the renovated building.

"Wow, it so different with all the new windows," Cassie said. "And so much brighter."

Maggie nodded. "With all the overgrowth cleaned out and the new roof and windows, the place looks awesome. Can't wait to see inside. Tim said the floors are all in and they're starting to paint and work on the kitchen and gaming room." She paused a moment to admire the outside improvements. "Tim's put his heart and soul into this project."

"It shows. You must be so proud of him. And you were the inspiration behind it."

"Well, I might have mentioned the need, but I think Carl and Sharon were the driving force behind his efforts. Transforming this place has given him a true home here in Caldwell. His family is reunited, and the town has embraced him and his ideas. It's been so satisfying to watch."

"Don't sell yourself short, lady. I think you might be part of that whole inspiration equation, don't ya think?"

Maggie grinned as they reached the front door. "Maybe a bit. Shall we check out the inside?" She led the way through a small lobby area into the main space.

Cassie was drawn to the sunlight dancing on the walls and the stage directly in front of her at the other end. "Wow. This is gorgeous."

Maggie gestured toward the room and stage. "Feel free to check it out. I'm gonna go find Tim."

Almost on cue, a familiar face peeked out of one of the smaller rooms off to one side. "I thought I heard voices," he said with a grin. "Let me wipe my hands off and I'll be out to say hello."

Maggie could tell he was painting from his work clothes. "I thought that was on tomorrow's agenda with the whole committee here to help."

"I figured I could at least start – there's still plenty more to do. Hi, Cassie. What do you think?"

Cassie continued studying the windows. "It's beautiful. And I love all the light."

"Yeah, it gets a little toasty in here when the morning sun shines through. I suspect we'll have to consider that with any matinee performances down the road with some shades. So how do like the stage?"

Cassie had crossed halfway to the stage before he'd found them, and now she took a few more steps forward. "It's bigger than I thought it would be. But I'd never seen the inside before."

"Would you like the grand tour?"

Cassie looked at the stage one more time, but then nodded as she turned to see Maggie give Tim a quick kiss.

Maggie smiled back at Cassie. "You can check out the stage afterwards while Tim fills me in regarding tomorrow's plans. Come on, let's start with the kitchen. No appliances or anything yet, but cabinets are in."

* * *

MAGGIE WAS AMAZED at the amount of work that had been completed since her last visit. As they toured the kitchen and the three smaller rooms she joined Cassie in numerous compliments. The last room they stopped in was where Tim had started painting, and Maggie smiled at the pale blue wall that was half done. "I guess I can add painting to your list of talents, Mr. Collins," she teased as she admired his work.

Cassie nodded. "It's a lovely color. When the afternoon sun comes through I bet it will look like the sky."

Maggie gave Tim a knowing look and brought up a subject that had been postponed. "I bet it would look better with a few accents on the wall – a couple of birds in flight, or simple clouds?"

She watched Cassie's imagination come alive as she perused the walls. "I like the idea of the birds – and a simple border with vines or ivy."

Tim used the moment to introduce his idea. "I don't suppose you'd be interested in doing some of the artwork?"

"Tim's been wanting to talk to you for awhile," Maggie chimed in. "He's seen a lot of your work and would love to hire you to do some accent painting here."

Cassie's interest grew. "Hire me? Like a job?"

Tim nodded. "I know right now the show's taking up all your time, and afterwards you'll be back at Brooke's, but a lot of the job could wait until the end of the school year. I'm hoping you'll think about it - - I talked to Brooke and she thinks the two of you could add some awesome last touches before we open. Not only in all the rooms inside, but outside as well. There's a big bare wall out back that's perfect for a mural."

Cassie's eyes widened. "A mural? On a whole wall?"

Maggie smiled. "Come on, I'll show it to you." She led Cassie out the back door where only a small window was located above the space inside where the stage was. "This whole spot needs something. Tim had asked for ideas at an early meeting and a mural was proposed – and he thought of Brooke, who suggested asking you to help."

Cassie surveyed the wall and her creative urges began to flow.

"Look, I know you need time to think about it," Maggie said, "but it might be a productive way to fill the early part of your summer with something that you love, and some distractions in the coming months might keep your mind on track."

Cassie enjoyed the warmth of the sun on her. "I don't need to think about it. I can't imagine any better way to spend my summer than with a paintbrush in my hand. As long as it fits with my work schedule, and...." Her voice trailed off as she scanned the property. "As long as I wasn't alone out here..."

Maggie gave her a hug. "You'd never be alone – and I can promise that we'll keep you safe any time you're in this building." She looked at the wall and smiled. "I had a feeling you'd say yes. Let's head back inside and I'll tell Tim while you check out the stage. Art might be your newest passion, but that stage is a perfect place for your true passion to come out and play from time to time. Now get in there and dance."

Cassie didn't need any further encouragement, and Maggie watched her ascend the few steps to be the first one to dance on the new floor. *"Hopefully she'll find a place for dance in her life again,"* she thought as she headed off to meet Tim. *"Nothing makes her more alive – not even her art."* She peeked back once more before entering the side room and smiled as Cassie began to move.

CHAPTER 31

Cassie got through the weekend with phone calls from both Mrs. Kearns and Mr. C. to keep her informed. With Maggie on speaker phone, she shared that Mike had texted with an angry message on Friday after being suspended, and Mrs. Kearns told her to text her if any other retaliatory messages came through.

Maggie had driven her home Sunday afternoon and stayed for a family video chat with Natalie and her parents. Cassie remembered her dad's reaction, watching his face darken with a quiet fury at Mike's actions, and then enfolding her with a protective hug as he fought back tears. Her mom cried enough tears for both of them as she held Cassie and rocked back and forth. "I'm so sorry, baby…..it's going to be okay…"

She had begged her dad to put the phone down when he started to call the police, and after more talking all agreed that a school investigation would be enough for the time being. Natalie had even explained that a criminal complaint would slow the process down, and possibly allow Mike to return to school sooner, as court proceedings might take weeks or months to resolve.

"I just want him to leave me alone," Cassie pleaded.

She had a visit from Teagan Sunday evening as they made plans for the following day's return to school.

"I talked to Brian and explained things as simply as I could," she admitted. "I hope you're not mad, but he was so concerned. He sends his love and prayers."

"I'm not looking forward to the cast meeting tomorrow. I feel like everyone will be staring at me."

"Mr. C. assured you that he wouldn't reveal any names, remember?" Teagan reached out and took her hand. "Look, I know word will get out, because Caldwell's a small town, but people will believe you – and anyone who doesn't is almost as guilty as Mike is."

Cassie bit her lip nervously. "I'm sure some of his friends will think I deserved it. That's what my eating disorder started screaming at me last night."

Teagan leaned in until Cassie met her gaze. "Well then, we'll treat them the same way we treat your eating disorder – by telling them to shut up and go to hell, because it's nothing but a destructive lie." She wrapped her arm around her friend and rubbed her back. "You doing okay?"

"It comes in waves. One minute I'll be fine and ready to stand up and face him, and the next I'm scared to death and feel like a worthless piece of meat." She tried to smile. "I guess it's not that different than all the other battles with my eating disorder."

"But it *is* different," Teagan pointed out. "This time the battle's with an external force, and not the voices in your head. Direct your anger away from you to where it belongs."

"I guess. Now can you tell that to my eating disorder?" Tapping the side of her head, she added, "It's been like a tag team event in here for most of the day. I'm not sure if I'll sleep tonight."

Teagan gave her a hug. "Don't forget all the other times that you've stood up to your eating disorder in the past year and prevailed. You are *so* much braver than you think you are, Cassie Durand."

"That's what Mr. C. said, too. I guess I'll have to trust you guys, because I feel like a big quivering blob right now – and tomorrow will be even worse."

"Yeah, but tomorrow you won't be alone. Brian and I will be on either side of you, and we'll help you through it, okay?"

Cassie nodded, lacking the confidence she wished for. The sound of an incoming message on Teagan's phone startled her, reminding her again of Mike's resentful text.

"It's Brian," Teagan assured. "And I do have *one* bit of news. He got a text from Lou on Friday night, and Mr. C. has given him the role of Horace. He apparently didn't give any reason for Mike's departure, but said he'd explain it to the cast on Monday. So I guess I'll be flirting with Brian's boyfriend now – that'll be different."

"So he *is* gone," Cassie whispered. "I hope he doesn't show up."

"Hey, Brian and I would beat you to him, and there might not be much left for you after we're finished with him."

Cassie almost chuckled. "Thanks, bestie. I don't know what I'd do without you."

"Honey, you'll never have to find out. I promise. Now I'm gonna head home and you're gonna try to manage a little sleep. I'll text you from school in the morning if I hear anything, and then meet you after lunch when your mom drops you off, okay?"

Cassie tried to quell the churning in her stomach. *"Now if I can just keep ignoring the eating disorder, I might manage a little rest before then."* Later on it took several hours lying in the dark before sleep greeted her, and she woke up Monday morning wondering how she'd fight both the voices in her head and faces waiting for her at school.

* * *

Cassie had a counseling session with Natalie Monday morning before heading to school for her afternoon classes. She was relieved to find Teagan and Brian waiting outside the main door when she arrived; they all had study hall together and she was grateful for their presence.

She welcomed Teagan's arms around her while noticing that Brian didn't join in the "group" hug they often shared. Instead, he gave her a reassuring smile. "How ya doin', kiddo?"

"Okay, I guess," she stammered. "And thanks for respecting the boundary – it's not personal."

Brian nodded as Teagan stepped back. "How was your counseling session this morning?"

Cassie scanned the outside of the school for Mike's car. "It was hard to concentrate – my mind was wondering what was going on at school."

Teagan noticed her apprehension and took her arm. "He's not here," she reassured, "and we can fill you in on some stuff during study hall, okay?" When Cassie nodded, she continued, "Are you ready to go in?"

"No," Cassie sighed, "but standing out here isn't going to change that, so let's do it."

Brian held the door open. "We've got your back, don't worry."

As they walked down the hall, Cassie tried to keep her eyes on the floor when she could. She flinched a bit whenever she made eye contact with someone passing her in the hall. *"They all know what happened,"* her eating disorder teased, *"and they're all mad at you for screwing things up for Mike – you're just worthless and fat."*

By the time they found a quiet table in the corner of study hall Cassie was almost convinced that every person was judging her. She caught Teagan's concerned face. "So if I'm the victim," she asked, "why do I feel like they all hate me for what happened?"

"Sounds like your eating disorder voices are alive and well again, huh?"

"I *know* it's my brain lying to me, but right now it's all I'm hearing."

Brian leaned in. "If we answer whatever questions you have about this morning will that help? I can tell you that Mr. C. didn't say anything in theater class, but did make sure to announce a quick mandatory meeting for everyone in the show right before rehearsal. I heard a little chatter in the next class that Mike had been suspended, but the guys were discussing either plagiarism or cheating on a test as the likely reason – so I don't think word has gotten out yet."

Cassie bit her lower lip as she met Teagan's gaze. "What about Julia? How was she?"

"She was quieter than normal, but that doesn't mean that she's heard anything. I think we'll have to keep an eye on her later on. She's not in your math or art classes, so you won't see her until then. I didn't hear anything at the theater table during lunch – not even from Kyleigh, and she has a tendency to talk if there's something going on. Julia had a French Club meeting so she wasn't there. Anything else you wanna know?"

Cassie shook her head. "I guess we have to wait. I hope my stomach can handle it; it's churning right now."

Teagan agreed. "Mine is too, if that's any help. I wish the meeting was over and done with. How about I pick you up right outside the art room when you're done and we can walk over to the auditorium together?" When Cassie nodded, she asked, "So do you want me to fill you in on English and Psychology classes? I have a couple of hand outs and you can copy my notes if you'd like."

Cassie reached into her bag and pulled out her binder. "Might as well. Maybe it'll keep my brain from exploding in the meantime."

* * *

WHEN THE BELL rang after art class, Cassie took a deep breath as the stage manager Terry approached and spoke almost in a whisper. "Mr. C. told me what happened, and you can be sure I'll keep it confidential. He thought you might have a little trouble going backstage, so I'll be there to meet you on every exit and entrance until you can feel safe. Thought I'd grab you now so I don't have to talk in front of anyone over there." She smiled warmly. "Everything's gonna be okay – although I'm sure you're a little on edge right now, aren't you?"

Cassie blinked back her tears, determined not to cry, trying to swallow the lump in her throat. "I'll be glad when rehearsal's over. And....thanks – for being close by."

As Terry headed out the door she passed Teagan heading in. Cassie met her with a determined smile on her face, even though the voices in her head continued to taunt and tease. "Ready or not, let's do this," she mumbled.

They met Brian and walked down the hall to the auditorium. "Let's sit toward the back," Brian suggested. "You'll be able to watch everyone else instead of imagining their eyes on you."

Cassie thanked him as the three of them filed in behind most of the others. She automatically scanned the group for Mike, even though she knew he wouldn't be there. Her eyes next sought out Julia, who was sitting with Kyleigh and chatting quietly. She couldn't tell if she knew anything or not. *"They're all gonna know now,"* her eating disorder chided, *"Mr. C. is all set to tell them what you did."* Cassie clenched her fists and blinked back tears. *"I am not going to listen to you,"* she silently told the voice. *"This is hard enough without all the lies that you're piling on."* As Mr. C. faced the group, she wished she could hide.

The cast quieted down quickly when they saw the serious look on their director's face. "I wanna thank you all for getting here promptly," he started, "and hopefully this will be short and sweet so we can start rehearsal. I don't know what kind of chatter has been going around, but I wanted a cast meeting to give it to you straight. At the same time, I can't give you all the information, so I expect you to take what I have to say and then move on. Is that clear?"

Cassie was sure everyone could hear her heart racing as the hush in the room was overpowering. "You might have noticed Mike Blanchett's absence today," Mr. C. continued. "I became aware late last week of an incident that he was involved in that I can't talk about. At this time he's been suspended from school, so his part in the show has been recast as of Saturday. Lou Donovan will be taking over Mike's role of Horace, and Rich Martin will now play the head waiter."

Cassie almost expected everyone to turn around and stare at her, but all eyes remained on their director. "I'm not at liberty to share anything more than that right now," Mr. C. continued, "and rather than wasting time speculating, I need all of you to pull together to make the changes as smoothly as we can. The show is only a month away. If anyone has anything they really need to talk to me about, you can find me after rehearsal. We all okay?" Seeing no objections, he clapped his hands together. "Good – I know we can make this show the best yet……so let's get into places, shall we?"

Cassie exhaled softly, hearing soft whispers as various cast mates got up and headed toward the stage. She saw Kyleigh take Julia's arm and say something to her, but she wasn't sure if she'd known already. *"Maybe I can get through this after all,"* she thought as she followed Teagan up on to the stage to get into place.

Even though it was the opposite side of the stage, her heart raced when she reached the curtains. She grabbed Teagan's arm, but then caught Terry's reassuring smile waiting just offstage. Despite the churning stomach inside, she focused on that smile and gave thanks for the steady support that waited in the shadows.

* * *

IT WASN'T until rehearsal was over and Cassie was heading backstage to the prop table that she froze entirely. She stood with hat boxes in hand, unable to move her legs toward the spot where Mike had been waiting. Her eyes widened in panic as she saw movement in the shadows, but before the silent scream could reach her mouth she realized it was Terry coming to meet her.

The stage manager saw the terror on her face and quickened her step to reach her. "I'm so sorry….I was putting something away. I should have waited until you had left for the day." She held out her hand and added, "I'll be right beside you – or I can take them and put them away if you're not up for it."

Cassie licked her dry lips and swallowed hard. "No, I have to do it. The show's only a month away and I can't freak out every time I need to put props away."

"I'll be with you every step of the way, okay?"

Cassie nodded, and willing her feet to move forward, she stepped into the shadows to face the prop table head on. Memories of the attack flooded through her, and tears filled her eyes as Terry supported her. "You can do this," she whispered. "Don't let him win."

Cassie dropped the hat boxes on the table and turned to bolt back onstage, but as she stepped forward something else made her freeze.

Mr. C. was alone on stage, and Sarah Peabody was approaching him cautiously. Cassie watched as the director turned to face her only a few feet away.

"Sarah, are you okay?" he asked, noticing the anxious look on the sophomore's face.

Cassie watched Sarah glance back toward the empty auditorium. "I just wanted to know...." she stammered, "how did you find out what Mike did? He told me not to tell anyone or I'd get in trouble."

As Sarah's tears began and Mr. C.'s face froze in shock, Cassie fought the urge to scream and instead walked calmly toward the sophomore. Sarah's face told her all she needed to know as Cassie met her gaze and whispered, "Did he attack you, too?"

Sarah nodded, breaking down entirely as Cassie embraced her with more understanding than anyone else could provide. They clung to each other and shared their tears while Cassie stroked her hair and Mr. C. quietly cursed and threw his folder onto the floor.

Cassie stepped back and gently wiped Sarah's tears away. "Mr. C. wasn't talking about you," Cassie explained. "He attacked me, too."

Mr. C. had to wipe his own tears before he could speak. "Sarah, I am so sorry – for both of you. I wish he was here right now so I could...." He took a deep breath to control his anger before continuing. "This never should have happened...." he choked out as the reality sank in.

Cassie found an inner strength she didn't know she had. "Could you please see if Mrs. Kearns is in her office? I think my friend Sarah would appreciate me going with her to have a little talk." As Sarah's eyes widened with anxiety, she gave her shoulders a reassuring squeeze. "Trust me, I'll help you through it. You don't have to be afraid anymore, okay?"

As Sarah sniffled, Mr. C. agreed. "Cassie's right. I'll call ahead and tell her you're coming, and she can walk you down." He addressed Cassie. "Are you sure *you're* okay to go back so soon?"

Cassie stood up a little straighter. "This may sound weird, but

Friday I thought there must be something wrong with *me* – now I know that it's something wrong with *him*." She hugged Sarah with one arm. "And I'll be damned if I let anyone else have to go through what we did."

Cassie walked past Teagan and Brian, who stood with shocked expressions on their faces as their friend guided the still sobbing sophomore down the hall. Somehow her own fears had been replaced with a determined protectiveness toward Sarah – and a now burning desire to make sure the one responsible paid for what he had done.

CHAPTER 32

Maggie was returning home after walking Tramp when Cassie texted. *"Any chance you're free for a quick visit from me and Teagan? We're leaving school now. Major developments today."* Maggie texted back and told them to stop by; she'd been wondering all day how going back to school and rehearsal had gone.

Lucy was working late, but she'd put chili in the slow cooker before leaving that morning. Maggie took a long whiff as she took off her coat and hung it up. *"That smells heavenly – and there's plenty if the girls want to stay."* She checked to make sure there was enough salad to offer, and took out a container with homemade corn muffins Lucy had made the day before.

By the time her doorbell rang, Maggie had changed into jeans and a sweatshirt. She gave them both a hug as they entered, and Tramp greeted Cassie with tail wagging and dancing around her feet. Maggie smiled at Teagan. "Can you tell she's one of his favorite people?"

Cassie had squatted down to receive kisses from Tramp and was now patting his belly. "How can anyone resist showering this guy with love and attention?"

Teagan had only been to Maggie's apartment a few times, but she knew Tramp from occasional "take your pet to work" days at the Manor. "He does have a way of winning people over. Even Gladys, who says she hates dogs, always seems to smile when Tramp visits."

Maggie hung their coats up in the closet. "Are you guys hungry? I have a pot of chili all ready if you want dinner."

Cassie glanced at Teagan as she stood up. "I think I'd love that… not sure what you're schedule is like for the night."

Teagan grinned. "I could smell it when we walked in – I'll text my mom to check in, but if you're sure you have enough, I'd *love* some chili."

Maggie continued as they followed her into the kitchen. "Lucy made corn muffins last night, and there's plenty of salad as well. I thought we could serve ourselves and eat in the living room." She handed a bowl to each of them. "Cassie has her favorite spot on the floor where her buddy can be close by."

Minutes later, they were curled up with steaming bowls of chili in front of them. Maggie held it up to feel the steam against her face as the bowl warmed her hands. "Hmm….one of my favorites." She looked over at Cassie who was nibbling on her corn muffin. "So….how did rehearsal go? Been thinking about you all day."

"It ended up being quite the day. Rehearsal wasn't too bad; no one stared at me or anything, and Mr. C. announced the cast change and a few basic details and then told everyone to focus on working together. He also had the stage manager – a girl named Terry -- meet me back-stage on every exit so I wasn't alone. There was only one time at the end of the day when I had to return my props when I almost freaked out—"

"Exactly when Mike attacked you, though," Maggie said. "No wonder it made you uneasy. Are you okay?"

Cassie glanced over at Teagan for a nod of support. "I was shaky for a minute or two, but something else put things into much clearer perspective." Noting Maggie's perplexed look, she continued. "As I was coming back on stage, another girl from the cast was talking to Mr. C. – and she asked how he'd found out about Mike attacking *her*."

Maggie almost choked on her chili. "Wait! You mean he attacked someone *else*?" As Teagan nodded, she put her bowl down. "What the hell is *wrong* with him?"

"When Sarah realized Mr. C was talking about *me* she broke down."

"She's the girl we told Mrs. Kearns about on Friday—the one Mike was flirting with at rehearsals," Teagan added. "Cassie remembered finding her in the bathroom one morning before school, crying in one of the stalls. The girl had said she was fine, so Cassie left."

"I recognized the sneakers when I got to theater class," Cassie chimed in, "but I had no idea she was crying because of Mike. Turns out he offered her a ride home from rehearsal one afternoon." Her voice dropped to a whisper. "I was the lucky one; she wasn't able to stop him."

"He…raped her?"

Cassie wiped tears from her eyes. "She told Mrs. Kearns rape wasn't the right word, but sat there rocking back and forth as she cried….she kept telling him to stop, but he held her down and told her it was gonna be the best she ever felt." Cassie almost spit the words out. "Afterwards he told her to keep quiet about it or she'd be sorry. She's only a friggin' sophomore, for God's sake."

"That poor girl."

"She's been terrified at school – Mike still flirts with her and asks if she needs another ride home. She said he sat right behind her at rehearsal one day and kissed the back of her neck and whispered that he could make this ride even better than the last one."

"What an *ass*," Maggie said. "Wait a minute – if she told all this to Mrs. Kearns—"

"Today was different," Cassie answered for her. "She called both the police and her parents. Mike's gonna be charged with rape this time."

Maggie sat in silence for a moment. "Wow. Isn't he eighteen now?"

Cassie nodded. "And Sarah's only fifteen. He might go to jail for this."

"Are you okay? This is a whole lot more to take in after what you faced yourself."

"That's what I told her when she called me for a ride," Teagan chimed in. "When she walked past me with Sarah I knew something else was going on, but never expected this. I think she's still in a little bit of shock."

Maggie reached out to rub Cassie's back. "I'm sure you are – have you thought about calling Natalie again?"

"I will tomorrow. Right now all I can think about is how to help Sarah through this. When the police arrived I had to tell my story all over again, and they'd like me to press charges as well. I told them I needed to talk to my parents first."

"Your dad will go ballistic," Teagan said. "He'll certainly support you pressing charges since he wanted to when Mike first attacked you. But….can you handle it?"

"What if I don't, and then they don't believe Sarah? I'd hate myself if he got away with this because I was too afraid to say anything."

Maggie smiled. "You're incredibly brave--especially since Mike told you to keep quiet."

Cassie's eyes flashed with anger. "Yeah, well he told her the same thing – and she's being way braver than I was last week And wait till you hear the *worst* part. He raped her on Valentine's Day! I found Sarah crying in the bathroom the day after, and Julia was also upset that morning. Turns out Mike had told Julia they'd have to reschedule their date at Gino's 'cause he had stuff he needed to do. Can you friggin' believe that? He cancelled his plans with his girlfriend on Valentine's Day so he could drive this poor sophomore home to rape her? What kind of animal is he?"

Maggie shuddered. "One who belongs in jail. I'm so proud of you for standing up for Sarah after all you've been through yourself. I hope you can handle the times when something triggers memories of your own assault. I'd hate it if you relapsed because of that jerk."

Cassie met her gaze with resolve. "My eating disorder will always find things to say about it, but I'm stronger now. When Mike attacked *me,* my eating disorder used it against me. But attacking Sarah proves the problem isn't me, but *him.* Somehow the eating disorder crap in my head is easier to ignore with something way more important to focus on."

Maggie smiled. *"That's* the voice of recovery talking. Now shut up and eat some chili."

CHAPTER 33

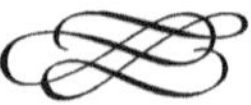

The next day both Cassie and Sarah filed charges with the police and Mike was arrested. Even though his father posted bail, he was suspended from school for a minimum of thirty days and was not allowed to have any contact with either of the girls. As Mrs. Kearns had predicted, gossip spread quickly around the school as to who had filed charges. Surprisingly, Cassie found that most students and teachers had been supportive, and several other girls had stopped her to share similar experiences with other boys and thanked them for their bravery. There were a few students who supported Mike and told her that she was ruining his life for a stupid little incident.

There was one reaction, however, that meant more than all the others – and that came from Julia. As Cassie arrived for yoga that Saturday, Julia was in the waiting room. Cassie could tell that she'd been avoiding her the past few days, and wondered if Julia would even talk to her during class. Her heart raced as Julia took a step toward her and reluctantly made eye contact.

"Look," Julia began, "I admit I've been avoiding you the past few days, but I needed some time to process everything." She was almost shaking as she continued. "I want to tell you that I believe both you and Sarah – and I'm sorry for what you guys must be going through right now."

Cassie opened her arms and Julia stepped in to her embrace. She almost sobbed as Cassie hugged her. "He's been such a jerk the past month, but I had no idea what he was capable of."

"Did her ever—"

Julia shook her head. "But he's been pressuring me for over a month to stop being such a prude. On Valentine's Day we went for a little walk at lunch time and..." She looked down at the floor and whispered, "He said he was looking forward to our date at Gino's and 'dessert' later on." She had tears in her eyes when she looked back up. "He gave me a romantic kiss and told me it was the perfect night to finally show him how much I loved him – and then he grabbed my breast and my ass and told me it would be awesome."

"Oh, Julia...."

"I think the only reason he cancelled that night was because I told him again I had no intention of having sex with him.....but I had no idea he'd take Sarah home later or I would have said something. I am *so* sorry if I contributed to any of—"

"Holy crap, Julia! Don't you dare let him make you feel guilty about anything!" She lifted Julia's chin with one hand to make direct eye contact. "I mean that. He's a manipulative bastard who doesn't respect any boundaries. I'm glad that dinner never happened."

Julia nodded. "Me, too. I've wondered this week if it was just a matter a time before he crossed that line with me, or if he was only dating me – the prude – to keep his image squeaky clean. Either way, I feel used."

"But he *did* cross that line with you – I'm assuming you didn't give him permission to grab you at that point."

Julia again looked down at the floor. "I've let him touch my breasts a couple of times when we were making out after a date, but any time he tried to lift my shirt or move his hand lower I'd tell him to stop."

"And he did?"

Julia nodded. "He always told me I was teasing him – and that I better start acting like all the other girls that knew how to keep him happy. That always made me think of you and wonder..."

Cassie fumed inside, remembering Mike telling her almost the same thing while she'd dated him the previous year. "Let me guess....then he told you that if you *really* loved him you'd let him show you how wonderful he could make you feel." Julia was surprised, but nodded. "He's a bastard. He told Sarah the same thing the whole time he was raping her. And Julia..." Cassie's voice got shaky as she continued. "I'm ashamed to admit that his lies worked on me last year. I hated every minute, but I was so sick at that point that I felt I deserved it. He kind of validated every single thing my eating disorder was screaming at me."

"I'm so sorry. I never would have started dating him if I'd known any of this."

"Don't beat yourself up over it. I suspect there may be others who heard the same lines – if not from him then from someone else."

Julia took a deep breath. "That's what I've been thinking about the past few days. And I'm even surer after talking today. If you and Sarah need me to testify during Mike's trial, I'm willing to do that."

As the little bell rang over the door to signal Maggie and Brooke's arrival, Cassie gave Julia another long hug. "It's gonna be okay," she whispered in Julia's ear. "And thanks so much for confiding in me." Julia smiled weakly before leaving them. Cassie greeted both of the older ladies and gave Maggie a quick hug. "I'll fill you in later – but we're good." With that, she headed into the studio herself, grateful that the tension between her and Julia was gone, but concerned about how many other girls might be out there, too afraid to share their stories.

* * *

After an hour of yoga to center herself again, Cassie's heart leapt when the first cherub came charging in to welcome her back. Little Tracey flung her arms around her for a hug. "I'm glad you're better!" With sparkling eyes, she started right in. "Can I tell ya something?

Last week we only goofed up *three* times – and we had to do it without you, so that's pretty good, right?"

Cassie loved how they made her laugh. "That's awesome! You guys won't even need me for the spring showcase."

Lydia had snuck in and heard her, and her eyes got wide as she shook her head. "I don't think that's a good idea," she whispered.

Cassie smiled. "Don't worry – I was only kidding. But I heard you guys did a super job last week. I can't wait to see what you worked on."

"I'm glad you're back," Lydia said as she adjusted her tights. "I like being able to watch you when I'm not sure of the next move."

Tracey had run off to greet the other arriving cherubs as Cassie smiled at Lydia. "But inside, you really *can* do it on your own. We're all just a little braver when there's someone next to us, huh?"

Lydia smiled and nodded, tugging on her tights one more time as she turned to greet her friends. Cassie stood up and questioned the expression on Colleen's face. "What's that look for?"

"I'm amazed at how well you interact with them. Her confidence has grown so much since you started as my assistant. You're helping them to believe in themselves – that's a sign of a great teacher."

"Thanks," Cassie said. "Sometimes I think they teach me way more."

Now that's the sign of an even *better* teacher. Why don't you line them up and we'll show you what we went over last week. Then I'm gonna sit back and let you take over for the rest of the class on your own." She smirked a bit and added, "After all, inside you *can* do it all by yourself." With a full heart, Cassie did exactly that.

* * *

BY THE TIME her private lesson was over, Cassie was feeling better than she had all week. Dancing through her solo for the spring show-case helped her forget everything for an hour – her assault, the upcoming show, the trial that awaited, and even her eating disorder. When she broke her final pose both she and Colleen had tears.

The older woman smiled as she took a tissue out of her pocket. "I think that was the best you've ever danced." She touched her heart. "I felt it right here."

Cassie nodded. "It was like the dance just filled me up completely – there wasn't room for anything else inside. It was like magic."

"I think you're gonna be okay to have dance back in your life. You've connected it to your soul again – and gotten it out of your head. I don't think your eating disorder is strong enough to steal it back at this point."

"From your mouth to God's ears," Cassie said. "I hope you're right – and that it's not simply the perfect song choice."

"Well, I *did* choose it with you in mind. But you're the one that's brought it to life. I guess there *can* be miracles-- if you believe."

* * *

SEVERAL WEEKS LATER, Cassie experienced another miracle coming to life as she stood backstage in the dark without fear. It was opening night for "Hello, Dolly", and she waited during Teagan's opening scene. As Teagan's monologue had the audience laughing out loud, she took a deep breath to center herself and give thanks. Her eating disorder still tried to tell her she was gonna screw it all up and forget her lines or freak out backstage, but she had relied on the support of those currently on stage to help her ignore the destructive voices and learn to believe in her talent and inner strength.

Earlier in the week she had panicked the first time she had to dash off stage in the dark to the spot where Mike had attacked her, but her friends had been there to support her. Every rehearsal during tech week gave her more strength to manage each scene change, and now she stood in full costume beside Brian and Beth. Brian would head out for scene two, and she and Beth for scene three – but for the moment, they offered vocal support to the chorus onstage until Teagan's first solo began. Then they stood hand in hand, silently beaming as their best friend proved to every person in the auditorium that she was the perfect Dolly Levi.

CHAPTER 34

$\mathcal{M}$aggie was back in her happy place, kneeling in the dirt with seedlings in her hand. The morning sun promised a gorgeous spring day as the community garden bustled with activity. She leaned back on her calves and stretched her back out as she watched Sharon and Liz preparing their new plot for the season.

"I don't know about you guys," she heard Colleen say, "but I think yoga is easier on the body than the first day back here. God, my back is stiff."

Barb laughed as she stood up to grab another flat of seedlings from her cart. "It's the knees for me," she groaned. "Maybe next year we'll add a section of raised beds for the older folks." She scanned the various plots – some planted, some still waiting for their first visitors, and most alive with banter and gossip as community gardeners gathered once more.

Brooke was finishing a row of kale seedlings. "I can't believe we're almost full this year. And the idea to allow split plots was genius."

Maggie agreed. "I think Tim is worried there won't be any left to offer gardening classes when the community center opens."

Barb chuckled. "Tell him not to worry. We always have a few folks who decide by early June that tending a garden is too much work. I think we'll be able to find four or five plots to keep open for them."

"Are they still on track for a grand opening in August?" Colleen asked.

"That's the plan," Maggie said. "Tim will be interviewing for a director and assistant director early in May, and other staff in June. They'll offer a variety of mini classes and camps for August, and then settle in to regular fall programs in September."

"Aren't you forgetting the main event?" Colleen teased.

Brooke laughed as she stood up to stretch. "Yeah, I vaguely remember something about a wedding on Labor Day weekend?"

Maggie couldn't hide the smile. "Well technically it's not an official community center event – just the first catered reception, that's all." She gazed over at the line of rose bushes at Carl's house next door and sighed. "I still can't believe we're lucky enough to be married right over there."

Barb followed her gaze. "The old man will be in his glory that day. I guess we all better start praying now for perfect weather, huh?"

Colleen smiled as a newcomer approached the garden. "Morning, Cassie! I heard you might be stopping by."

Tramp sat up at his post and started thumping his tail on the ground. Maggie laughed. "He sure gets excited whenever you show up." As Cassie bent down to give her a hug, she leaned in and whispered. "How are you doing?"

"Okay," Cassie replied at a normal volume. And you don't have to whisper – Brooke and Colleen are well aware of what's happening, and I guess that means I can trust....Barb, is it?" she asked, looking toward the older woman. "I'm not sure if we've ever met, but I've heard nothing but amazing things about your bed & breakfast."

Barb pulled off her gardening glove as she walked over to shake Cassie's hand. "Nice to finally meet you. I've heard lots about you from these ladies – and I've seen how amazing you are on stage and singing here at Christmas time."

Brooke nodded. "The show was awesome this year – although I must admit I'm glad to have Cassie back at the store again. She's working her butt off with a whole new display for Mother's Day. And I suspect some of her gardening items will be popping up here within the next week or two."

Cassie blushed as she admired the gardens. "This place is amazing – I've never grown anything on my own before, but I'm looking forward to learning a bit this year."

Maggie gestured toward her basket. "I packed an extra pair of gloves and another trowel in there. And you might want to grab the other kneeling pad, too."

Colleen laughed. "Trust me, your knees will thank her when you're done. And you better keep those knees in great shape for another week!" She grinned at the other ladies. "This one's been helping with my cherub class this year and they can't wait to have her beside them as they dance in their first recital….and then they'll get to watch her dance in her last recital."

"I bet you're getting super excited, aren't you?" Maggie asked as Cassie knelt down beside her.

"Hmm-mm. Almost as excited to dance with them as I am for my solo."

"I can't wait." Maggie replied, "I'll be your biggest fan—outside your family at least."

Cassie shrugged as she put on the gardening gloves. "Most of them, anyway. I found out this week that my dad's not gonna be there. His first business trip is the same weekend."

"He got the promotion?"

"Yeah…..and I'm trying not to let it bug me, but it does. At least a little bit."

"I'm not surprised. Your senior showcase is a big deal – especially after fighting so hard to dance again. I'm sorry he won't be there."

"Thanks. So is he. He almost cried when he told me he'd be away until Sunday. I don't think he was expecting a business trip this soon. At least my mom can video it."

"And you're okay?"

Cassie nodded. "Sad, but I'll be okay. He really wanted this promo-tion, and that helps."

"You two have grown a lot closer since your family session with Natalie."

"Finding the compromise made a huge difference. He's softened in his expectations, and I'm more open. We're in a really good place right now." Gesturing down toward the greenery in front of her, Cassie changed the subject. "So are you gonna show me what to do here?"

Maggie picked up her trowel. "You're gonna dig a small hole like this..."

Before Cassie reached for the extra trowel her phone buzzed. "It's the District Attorney's office calling; I better take it."

Maggie stopped planting as Cassie answered the phone, holding up her hand to the other ladies to keep the volume down; instead, all four women stopped talking as Cassie spoke quietly. Maggie waited until she hung up and put the phone back in her pocket. "I take it that was about Mike?"

"He's accepted a plea deal from the D.A."

"So he's pleading guilty then?"

"To a lesser charge. He won't have to register as a sex offender, but he's still looking at some jail time." Her voice trembled a bit. "Anywhere from six months to a few years, depending on the judge."

"You okay?"

"I think it'll hit more as it sinks in. I'll have to call Sarah later to see how she's doing."

Brooke spoke as the other ladies stepped in closer. "He was facing major jail time if a jury convicted him – and it was a pretty strong case."

"Pisses me off," snorted Barb. "Any case where a guy gets off easier with a plea deal almost encourages the next guy to keep the cycle of assault going."

Cassie agreed. "It'll be up to the judge now."

Maggie jabbed her trowel into the dirt. "I'm glad we live in a state with such strict laws — it's so much worse in other places around the country. I hope he faces a tough female who gives him the stiffest sentence recommended."

Colleen knelt down next to Cassie, placing an arm around her shoulder. "You must be somewhat relieved to know that it's over. A trial would have dragged on forever."

"That's true," Cassie replied. "At least I won't have to worry about running in to him around town.....well, at least not after his sentencing." She pulled her gardening gloves back on and picked up her trowel. "For now, I think I wanna release some tension and dig like Maggie's doing."

Colleen stood back up. "Ah....you're about to get your first session of garden therapy."

Maggie pointed to a spot in front of Cassie and grinned. "Nothing like it in the world. Start here and follow my lead..."

* * *

LATER THAT MORNING Maggie picked up the last seedling to plant. "This is the last of the spinach and we're done."

Another voice spoke up as Tramp's tail began thumping again. "I do seem to have a habit of finding you in the garden with spinach in your hand."

Maggie beamed at the dimpled smile. "Sounds like a positive habit – spinach is good for you." She handed the last seedling to Cassie for planting as she got up to greet her fiancé.

"So are you," Tim murmured as he wrapped his arms around her and kissed her. "You ladies have been busy."

Maggie nodded as the others greeted Tim. "How are things going over there?" she asked, gesturing toward the community center.

"Another productive morning. I have five lined up for director interviews and another three for assistant. And the outdoor sign is coming this week. That reminds me," he said, turning toward Brooke and Cassie. "I'll need your sketches for the mural by the end of the month along with a list of what paint you'll need. I'll run it by the committee, but they've given their okay to just about anything you come up with." Looking down toward the other end of the garden, he held up his hand to block the sunlight and squinted. "Is that my mom with Liz?"

"They're sharing a plot this year. Your mom's always grown flowers, but she wants to learn veggies now. I'll walk down with you to say hi if you want. We're done here aside from watering." Turning toward Cassie, she smiled. "Thanks for all the help today, and call me anytime in the next few days if you need to talk, okay?"

"I will, believe me."

"And you're still planning to come for Carl's birthday party Friday?"

"It's all Gram talked about this week. We wouldn't miss it. I can meet you at the Manor to help bring her over to Gino's."

"We'll finalize plans on Tuesday. Until then, you know where to find me if you need me." After saying goodbye to the other ladies, Maggie picked up her basket and Tim untied Tramp. As they strolled hand in hand down to chat with his mom and Liz, she glanced one more time toward Carl's house and the rose garden out back. She couldn't wait until the end of summer when she'd move in with all of them and officially become part of the family she'd come to cherish.

* * *

AT THE END of the week, she joined in the family tradition of eating Gino's food on Friday nights – this time celebrating in person for Carl's upcoming birthday the following week. Gino had left his position by the door to come and greet his old friend. He patted Carl's shoulder and smiled at everyone else. "Now this makes Gino happy – it's been too long since you sat here on a Friday night. And look at you – surrounded by family once again. Life is good, no?"

Carl smiled up at his old friend, not even trying to hide it behind a usual scowl. "Better than I ever thought it would be."

Tim raised his glass. "Let's drink to Grandad on his birthday."

Carl gazed around the table before picking up his own glass. "To family," he croaked out as his eyes got misty. He then winked at Ida who sat beside him. "And to friends who have become like family."

Gino clapped his hands. "Happy birthday, you old curmudgeon! And Buon Appetito!"

Maggie caught Carl's eye as she drank her wine. She smiled as he gave her a wink before turning his attention to Ida. Tim was responding to his mom on the other side of him, and Maggie turned her attention to Cassie seated between her and Ida.

Cassie hadn't yet picked up her fork and was staring down at her plate. "You okay?"

Cassie scanned the room nervously. "I'm not sure. All of a sudden I'm really anxious. What if he were to walk in here tonight? I'm not sure I could handle that." Without even thinking, she reached up and pushed her plate away from her just an inch or two, and then sat back.

"That's why you wanted that seat, isn't it?" Maggie asked. "So you could see the door."

Cassie nervously grasped her hands in her lap. "It's a public place – and he loves Gino's pizza. He might be really mad now that he's looking at definite jail time."

Before Maggie could reply, Ida reached over to take her granddaughter's hand. "Cassandra, he can't hurt you here – not when you surrounded by those that love you." She leaned over and kissed Cassie's cheek. "You're stronger than both of them."

Cassie looked at her perplexed. "Both?"

"Both. Mike..." She glanced down at Cassie's plate. "*And* your eating disorder."

Cassie sat quietly for a moment and then pulled her plate back toward her and picked up her fork. Maggie smiled as their eyes met and held up her own fork. "To recovery," she whispered, "and all the wonderful miracles it brings back into our lives." Cassie's nod was all the response her heart needed.

CHAPTER 35

Cassie was sitting on the floor trying to keep her cherubs from talking too loud as she tried to ignore the butterflies in her stomach. The little ones pointed to older dancers as they adjusted their buns or laced up pointe shoes. They'd whisper to each other and giggle as their excitement bubbled over.

She smiled at Lydia, whose eyes widened every time a new sparkly costume passed her by. "Nervous?" she whispered.

Lydia nodded back. "My tummy doesn't feel so good."

Cassie reached over and patted her hand. "That's just the magic butterflies waiting to dance. I feel them, too."

"You do?"

"Hmm-mm. Almost every dancer does before a recital. But once you're out there on stage, you take a deep breath and let it out slowly. That lets all the magic out to help you dance the best you can. Pretty cool, huh?"

The little girl looked back down at her tummy and smiled weakly.

Cassie glanced across the room and caught Julia's eye. A silent nod of support and love passed between them before Kyleigh stepped in front of Julia to wave excitedly toward Cassie. "Break a leeeeg!" she mouthed in an exaggerated stage whisper. Cassie waved back and smiled. She watched the two of them gather with others in their first performance group and felt a twinge of envy. She'd miss out on the craziness of costumes flying between various dance numbers together. *"But I won't have to listen to my eating disorder telling me how fat I am compared to all of them, either,"* she thought. *"And I still get to change into one special outfit"* she thought as she eyed the royal blue costume waiting for her solo showcase.

Tracey interrupted as she tugged on Cassie's arm. "Look! Miss Colleen's bringing you flowers."

Cassie stood up as all the cherubs buzzed with excitement. "They're beautiful!" she said as Colleen handed them to her. "You didn't have to do that."

"Trust me. The bouquet from me comes later on – these were dropped off at the stage door. I think you'll like them more than any flowers I could give you."

As Cassie sat back down all the cherubs leaned in to sniff the multi-colored roses as Cassie opened the card. "Who's it from?" Tracey asked.

There were two messages written on the card. The first one was clearly written, probably by a florist taking a phone order: *"So sorry I can't be there, but I know you'll be amazing."* Cassie's eyes filled with tears because it had been crossed out and replaced with a much shorter message – this one written in familiar handwriting: *"I'm here. Love you."* She reached down and lovingly stroked one of the rose petals as she smiled at her cherubs through her tears. "They're from my dad."

THE CHERUBS HAD DANCED ALMOST PERFECTLY, and Cassie's heart swelled with pride as they exited the stage chattering with excitement. She had to wave her arms almost frantically to grab their attention and put her fingers to her lips. With round eyes they all tip-toed down the hall to the backstage room before once again bursting out with excited chatter.

Cassie gave them all hugs as Julia approached in her solo costume.

She stood up in time to grab Julia's arm and hug her tightly. "You look phenomenal, "she whispered in her ear. "Thanks," Julia replied, dressed for her ballet solo in a silver tutu. Her eyes gestured toward the costume rack. "Now take that leotard off and change into your own," she whispered before heading out the door.

Cassie smiled as Colleen approached with two other dancers. "We're here to take the cherubs out to meet their folks at the stage door. They'll be able to watch the rest of the show." She leaned in closer. "And stay out of everyone's hair back here."

After getting lots of hugs for luck, she waved to the last cherub and turned her attention to the costume she'd been waiting to put on all year. After missing last year's recital she had spent months wondering if she'd ever be able to dance again, and now here she was pulling the royal blue outfit up over her thighs and sliding her arms into the sleeves. As she met her own reflection in the mirror to check her bun, she smiled at how the fabric flowed past her hips. She might not ever totally love her body, but she could appreciate that it was healthy as she made her way down the hallway to take her place on stage for her final senior performance. *"There really are miracles,"* she thought, and with a heart overflowing, she took a deep breath, exhaling slowly to let all the magic out as the music began.

* * *

TWO DAYS LATER, Cassie sat nervously in the car as Maggie and Teagan chatted about how wonderful her dance had been. "I thought Ida was going to jump out of her wheelchair when you finished," Teagan blurted out. "And I *still* start bawling when I remember that hug from your dad when you came out afterwards. He was so damn proud of you."

Cassie eyes got misty at the memory. After fighting through the disappointment of his business trip keeping him out of town, to the resolved determination to do her best despite his absence, she'd been overwhelmed when her solo ended and she could hear his voice cheering out past the stage lights. He'd worked late into the night and caught an earlier flight home, driving straight to the auditorium just before the recital started.

She caught Maggie's eyes glancing her way. "You nervous?"

"To quote one of my cherubs," she replied, "my tummy doesn't feel too good. Are you sure I'm ready for this?"

Maggie pulled into the parking lot of the Phoenix Center. "Trust me – you've never been so ready."

As they mounted the front steps Cassie froze. Teagan wrapped her arm around her shoulder and pointed toward the stained glass phoenix in front of them. "A year ago this week you walked through this door for the first time…and what a big hot mess you were."

Cassie couldn't help but grin as Teagan continued. "You worked your butt off while you were here, struggling through the denial of how sick you were until you embraced the help that was in front of you."

Maggie had come up on Cassie's other side. "And we've both watched you since that day when you came back through this door ready to face the world again."

"I was so scared that day," she whispered.

Teagan squeezed her arm. "But look at you now, all these months later. You're just like that phoenix – letting your deepest pain help you grow into your highest self."

"I have a long way to go still, but I couldn't have made it this far without you guys."

Maggie nodded. "It wasn't only us – it was your whole recovery family. Your folks, your Gram, Natalie, and all your friends -- we were all there to support you every step of the way. But *you* were the one who did the work – don't ever forget that."

Cassie stood up a little straighter and took a deep breath. "I guess I'm as ready as I'll ever be – let's do it." She reached out and touched the phoenix for luck, and then bravely opened the door to once again visit the Phoenix Center – this time as their guest speaker. A few minutes later she stood before about a dozen females of all ages – some alone, and some with family or friends. She took a deep breath and got a reassuring smile from Teagan.

Looking around the room, she recognized the fear and denial that some of the residents held on to, and saw sparks of hope in the faces of others. Smiling, she greeted them all. "Hi. My name is Cassie, and a year ago I was sitting right where you are today. As a recovering anorexic, I'm here to share my own journey, and to assure you that recovery is possible. I encourage you to embrace the help here. You'll be given the tools you need to fight your eating disorder, and trust me, you'll use those tools every day when you leave. You'll find the people who will support you along the way—parents, siblings, or maybe friends. Whoever they are, they'll become a family to cherish. And along the way you'll discover that miracles really *can* happen – but first, you gotta believe."

Return one last time for the fourth and final book of the Caldwell Series. *A Place to Belong* will be released in December of 2021.

Join Teagan as she and her friends Cassie and Brian navigate their first year of college. Throughout the challenges of classes, new friends, and work, they rely on each other for love and support as they find a place to belong.

But first, there's a special wedding celebration for the Richmond sisters that brings all of your favorite Caldwell characters together. Be sure to join in!

LOOKING AHEAD.....

A lot of older women loved their time in Caldwell, and my next series will be written with you in mind. Set in the coastal town of Gloucester, MA, you'll meet a group of friends who are dealing with all that life brings in middle age — ailing parents, empty nests, divorce or losing a spouse, dating, and bodies that don't move as well. Through it all, it's friendship that helps them to cope and keep laughing! Who knows? There might even be a few familiar faces...

Special thanks to the following...

To Noel Sellon for creating the beautiful book covers.

To Sarah Neville for the gorgeous detailed map of Caldwell.

To those who helped with beta reading and editing — especially Cheryl and Jill.

To the talented authors in my weekly writers' cafe, as well as the members of Greater Lehigh Valley Writers group — your input and camaraderie push me to improve my craft.

To Cheryl, Maria, Patti, Randi, and Jackie — you pray for me, listen while I vent, make me laugh when I need to, and know when the best medicine is a night of food and drink together. I love you all so much!

Finally, to Bob, Beth, and Rebecca — for being the family that I cherish each and every day!

———————————————————————————

If you or anyone you know is struggling with anorexia or other eating disorders, know that there is lots of support available. Please contact the National Eating Disorders for help in your recovery.

National Eating Disorders: (800)-931-2237

https://www.nationaleatingdisorders.org/help-support/contact-helpline

ABOUT THE AUTHOR

Laurel Wenson's love of reading and writing began in her childhood home of Concord, Massachusetts, a place rich with the literary history of Thoreau, Emerson, Alcott, and Hawthorne. After 15 years of teaching English and theater in the homeschool community, she retired in 2016 to rekindle that love of writing.

Her love of small town life has served as an inspiration for the Caldwell series, which began with *A Promise to Keep* in July of 2020 and *A Heart to Heal* in December of 2020. The fourth and final book of the series will be out in December 2021.

Laurel lives in Bethlehem, PA with her husband, two daughters, and a frisky feline. She is a member of the Greater Lehigh Valley Writers Group and an avid participant in National Novel Writing Month.

Follow her on social media or visit her website at: laurelwenson.com